Her wedding day...

She'd thought the ceremony would be in a church—in spring. She'd have flowers to carry, and afterward she and her new husband would take a short wedding journey.

None of her dreams had included a stark ceremony in a small, four-room house. As for the groom...he bore little resemblance to her vague imaginings. Matt wasn't a fair-haired, blue-eyed knight on a white steed. But Matt *was* real and vibrant, a man unlike any other she'd known.

And she loved him...

Dallas Schulze loves books, old movies, her husband and her cat, not necessarily in that order. She's a sucker for a happy ending whose writing has given her an outlet for her imagination and hopes that readers have half as much fun with her books as she does! Dallas has more hobbies than there is space to list them, but is currently working on a doll collection.

TEMPTATION'S PRICE

Dallas Schulze

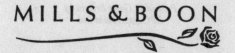

MILLS & BOON

MILLS & BOON, the Rose Device and LEGACY OF LOVE are trademarks of the publisher.
Harlequin Mills & Boon Limited,
Eton House, 18-24 Paradise Road, Richmond, Surrey TW9 1SR

© Dallas Schulze 1992

ISBN 0 263 79529 2

Set in Times Roman 10 on 12 pt.
04-9603-74126 C

Printed in Great Britain by
BPC Paperbacks Ltd

Chapter One

September 1860

The Kiowa were north of their accustomed range. A raiding party of braves, they had precious little to show for their efforts. Until they ran across the small wagon train.

It was late in the season for a group of immigrants to have just crossed South Pass. California was still more than half the journey away and the worst of it lay ahead—deserts and mountains that would try the endurance of both animal and human.

Their scout had already warned them that they stood little chance of making it through the Sierra Nevada before snowfall. Vivid in everyone's mind was the fourteen-year-old tragedy of the Donner-Reed party. No one wanted to be trapped in the mountains with winter coming on.

On the other hand, no one wanted to spend the winter in Fort Bridger, eking out scant supplies. Nor was there much more enthusiasm for traveling farther south to Great Salt Lake City and spending the winter dependent on the generosity of Brigham Young's people.

A decision had to be reached. Tonight, when they reached Little Sandy Creek, the men planned to hold a meeting and make it.

The Kiowa had no interest in the immigrants' problems. The ten wagons and the stock with them meant they wouldn't return to the village empty-handed. There were horses, oxen if they cared to drive them south, and the wagons were sure to hold goods worth taking.

Though they had yet to realize it, the Miller train had far more pressing problems than which trail to take at the Little Sandy.

Dawn was only a shadow of gray to the east. The land lay still and quiet. Somewhere to the west, a coyote howled, a lonely call that was answered from a greater distance, like echoes in a canyon.

Liberty Ann Ballard lifted her skirt to keep the hem from brushing across the dew-moistened grass. Behind her, the wagon train was beginning to stir. Soon the smell of coffee boiling and bacon frying would drift on the still air.

She should be there, helping Mrs. Miller prepare breakfast, making ready for the day's travel. She stifled a surge of guilt and continued on. She'd be back in plenty of time to help with breakfast. And they were to linger in camp this morning. One of the wagons needed repairs so they'd not be leaving as early as was their usual custom. She'd just steal a few minutes alone to watch the sunrise and then she'd hurry back and do her chores.

Glancing over her shoulder, she could see the wagons, their tops gleaming white against the darkness. They looked out of place in this wild country. They looked like what they were, visitors on the land, not really a part of it.

She turned away from the wagons and hurried on. At first, she'd felt as out of place as the wagons looked. But more and more, she was starting to see the beauty in the land, to view it as something more than a distance to be traveled as quickly as possible, a passageway to California and nothing more.

Looking back again, she saw that the wagons were out of sight. Up ahead was a stream, its banks lined with willow and cottonwood. There she'd wait and watch the sun come up, savoring the stillness of the land before she returned to the bustle of the wagon train.

If she was lucky, no one would even know she'd been gone.

Matt Prescott had just swung into the saddle when he saw the slender figure hurrying away from the camp. His fingers tightened on the reins, making the big roan shift nervously. He stroked his hand over the gelding's neck, soothing him. His eyes were adjusted to the gloom, making it easy to follow the girl's progress as she darted through the damp grass.

He caught the gleam of pale hair as she turned to look back at the camp. Liberty Ballard. No one else on the train had hair the color of moonlight. In all his life, he'd never seen hair like hers. It made a man want to feel it sifting through his fingers, to see it spread across cool linens.

He wasn't likely to get a chance to see either of those things, of course. Liberty Ballard was not the sort of girl who'd let a man run his fingers through her hair unless there was a wedding ring on her finger, which was just as it should be but it didn't stop a man from wondering.

She disappeared from sight as the land sloped down toward the stream. Matt had planned on going hunting today. Part of his job as scout was providing fresh meat for the train. He tightened his fingers on the reins and nudged the big roan with his heel. Before he went looking for game, he was going to see what Miss Ballard was up to.

He'd signed on as a scout for the Miller train at Fort Kearny. Guiding pilgrims across the prairie was a task little to his liking, but their first guide, Zeke McLeary, was a friend and when Zeke broke his leg and couldn't continue, Matt had agreed to take the Miller train west.

The train had left St. Joseph later in the season than they'd any business doing and they hadn't been able to make up for the time since. He'd told them when

they left Fort Laramie that they couldn't hope to make
it through to California before snowfall.

But Joe Miller had a head harder than granite and
he insisted they could get through with a little persis-
tence. Well, it was going to take more than persis-
tence. It would take their oxen growing wings to fly
them over the mountains. They sure as hell couldn't
make it through them. But if they insisted on trying to
make California, Matt Prescott supposed he was
damn fool enough to try to get them through.

But there would be time enough to worry about that
later. Right now, he wanted to know where Liberty
Ballard was sneaking off to.

There was a large flat rock planted firmly by the
edge of the stream. Liberty had seen it in the twilight
the day before when she and some of the other women
had come to get water. Benjamin Devers and Ethan
Lawrence had scrambled up and sat atop it with their
legs swinging over the water, and Liberty had envied
them the freedom that came of being only eight.

At eighteen, she was, of course, past the age where
she could clamber over any rock that caught her fancy.
Most of the time, the benefits of having put up her
hair and let down her skirts outweighed the restric-
tions that went along with moving from child to adult.
But there was something about that rock that made
her wish she was eight years old again.

The horizon was pale gray by the time she reached
the stream. Liberty paused, closing her eyes for a moment, the better to take in the silence. It seemed as if
the whole world was holding its breath, waiting for sun

to come up and spill light over the plains and mountains.

Liberty opened her eyes and studied the rock a moment before stepping toward it. A quick glance over her shoulder to make sure she was still alone and she lifted her skirts to expose slim ankles clad in brown cotton stockings. The side of the rock was rough, offering plenty of hand- and toeholds. A quick, if undignified, scramble and she was atop.

Grinning with delight, she moved to the side of the rock and sat down. Feet swinging, she looked at the world from her new perspective. Though the rock was not more than six feet from base to top, it was high enough to make everything look different.

Looking east, she could see the first sliver of light edging the horizon. It must surely be full light back home, she thought. Pennsylvania's green valleys and hills seemed an incalculable distance away. Between here and there lay miles of prairie—the Great American Desert, some called it. Liberty had walked most of those miles, finding walking preferable to the swaying of the wagon.

Looking east, she felt a twinge of homesickness. She'd spent all of her eighteen years in Pennsylvania and might have spent the rest of her life there if her parents hadn't died last year. First Papa had been killed when his wagon overturned, and then Mama had taken a chill and died just after Christmas.

Liberty had been left alone, dependent on the generosity of family friends, a position she found difficult to tolerate. No matter that she'd made it a point to do all she could to earn her keep, it still sat poorly to be beholden to the charity of others.

Which was why, when her mother's brother—and Liberty's only surviving relative—had written to ask her to join him and his wife on their ranch in Idaho Territory, she'd said yes without hesitation. The Millers had agreed to let her travel west with them in return for her help with the children and the household tasks.

She'd been frightened by the thought of leaving behind all that was familiar. But there was little left for her in Pennsylvania. And she was young enough to be excited by the thought of seeing new sights. Not even all the weary weeks of travel had been able to beat that thrill from her. Sitting on the big rock, looking back the way they'd come, she felt no regrets.

"It isn't smart, coming out here alone like this."

Liberty had been so absorbed in her thoughts that she hadn't realized she was no longer alone until Matt spoke. The quiet voice startled a small cry from her and she jerked around to face him so suddenly that, for a moment, she was in danger of sliding from her perch on the rock.

"Mr. Prescott!" She regained her balance almost immediately.

"Miss Ballard." Matt touched the brim of his hat. He sat his horse a few feet away, his dark eyes watching her.

"You startled me." She pressed one hand to her chest as if to still the too rapid beat of her heart.

"I'd have startled you a great deal more if I'd been a Sioux brave, ma'am. That hair of yours would look mighty nice hanging from a lance. Color like that's prized.''

Liberty lifted her hand to touch her hair, feeling her scalp prickle.

''I haven't seen any Indians,'' she said.

''The ones you see aren't the ones you have to worry about. It's the ones you *don't* see that cause problems.''

''Are there hostile Indians around here?'' she asked, glancing about uneasily. The light had increased while she sat contemplating, but only enough to make the shadows seem thick and ominous. The little stream that had looked so peaceful and inviting a moment ago was suddenly full of potential hiding places.

''Ma'am, most any Indian has the potential to be a hostile Indian.'' Matt pushed his hat back on his head. ''It just doesn't pay to go assuming that, because there's been no trouble, there *won't* be trouble.''

''I'm not that far from camp,'' Liberty said.

''Far enough that a scream wouldn't be heard. If you got a chance to scream,'' he added bluntly.

''You certainly do know how to spoil a sunrise, Mr. Prescott,'' Liberty said tartly. If she'd been standing on the ground, she would have turned and stalked back to camp. But there was no way to make a dignified descent from her current perch, and she wasn't going to scramble down off the rock and scuttle back to camp like a naughty child.

''You came out to watch the sun come up?'' Matt glanced east.

''I suppose you think it was very foolish of me,'' she said, lifting her chin.

"I'm not sure a sunrise is worth risking your scalp over, ma'am."

"I didn't realize I *was* risking my scalp. We've had no trouble thus far."

"True enough. But out here, it pays to stay a little wary. A person tends to live a good bit longer that way."

"I'll try to keep that in mind, Mr. Prescott." She'd pulled back from the edge of the rock in the first moments after his appearance. Now she drew her knees up under her full skirt and looped her arms around them.

It was the first time she'd been alone with the scout, and she found herself oddly reluctant to end the moment. She'd seen him often enough and everyone on the train knew who he was, of course, but he'd rarely exchanged more than a few words with anyone but Mr. Miller.

He'd kept to himself, though he was polite enough when spoken to. There was a certain reserve about him that she'd secretly thought rather romantic. In his soft buckskins, his tobacco-brown hair brushing his shoulders and a thick dark mustache framing his mouth, he looked the very picture of a man born to action and adventure.

Coming from a small Pennsylvania town where the most adventurous thing any of the boys of her acquaintance was likely to do was try to steal an apple from old Mr. Whipplebee's orchard, Liberty had allowed her imagination free rein in speculating about the quiet scout.

"Have you lived long in the west, Mr. Prescott?"

Matt had been studying the area around them, marking in his mind the places that offered shelter enough to conceal a man. There were too many of them for his liking, but the fact that they weren't dead yet indicated that they were alone. At Liberty's question, his eyes shifted back to her face.

"Long enough to learn a little caution, Miss Ballard."

She really was a beauty, he thought. She'd left off her bonnet, and that pale hair of hers gleamed in the weak light. Her skin looked as soft as a rose petal, despite the hard weeks of travel that lay behind them. But it was her eyes that lingered in a man's mind more than they had any right to. Wide set and surrounded by thick dark lashes, they were green, like deep woodland pools that invited a man closer.

"Have you been to California, Mr. Prescott?"

"A time or two," he admitted.

"Is it as beautiful as they say?"

"Parts of it."

"Maybe someday I'll see it," she said, just a hint of wistfulness in her voice. "I'm to stay with my uncle, who owns the Rocking S ranch near Fort Bridger, you know. So I won't be going on with the rest of the train."

"If the rest of them have any sense, they won't be going on until spring," Matt said shortly.

"Do you think we're foolish to come west?"

"No, ma'am. Folks like this are the ones who'll settle this country."

"Not people like you, Mr. Prescott?" Liberty had forgotten all about the sunrise. There would be other sunrises, but this was no doubt the only opportunity she'd have to talk to a man like Matt Prescott.

"People like me aren't the sort who settle a country. We open it up a bit, soften some of the rough edges, maybe. But we aren't the ones who'll build churches and schools. People like these folks are the ones who'll build something lasting."

"I'd never have imagined you were such a philosopher, Mr. Prescott." She smiled and tilted her head to look at him, as if seeing him for the first time. "You sound like you've given it a good deal of thought."

"And I'd never have imagined you were so adventurous, Miss Ballard." He nodded to her perch on the rock, his smile white beneath the dark mustache.

"Looks like we're both full of surprises this morning," Liberty said, her smile widening.

"Looks like." Matt reached in his pocket and pulled out the makings of a smoke. It wasn't often he had the chance to talk to a girl as pretty as Liberty Ballard. He relaxed back into the saddle, as he rolled the tobacco into the paper with one hand.

"Do you have a family, Mr. Prescott?"

"No. Cholera took my folks, ten years back." He flicked his thumb over the head of a match and held the flame to his cigarette. It was a habit he'd picked up from the Mexicans in Santa Fe.

"So you're all alone?"

"Not right at this moment," he said, giving her a slow smile.

"No wife?"

"Nope. Never really thought of myself as the marrying kind."

"Don't you like women, Mr. Prescott?" Liberty looked at him from under her lashes and Matt's fingers tightened on the cigarette. He wondered if she was even aware of the invitation in her eyes. He forced his hand to relax and lifted the cigarette to his mouth, drawing in a lungful of smoke.

Liberty reminded him of a young filly in the springtime. She was old enough to be testing her feminine wiles and young enough not to know how dangerous such testing could be. In her blue calico dress with its white collar and cuffs, she looked as inviting as a fresh-cut rose. But roses had thorns to punish anyone foolish enough to pick them, and Joe Miller's shotgun was a mighty big thorn. Still, Matt could tell she wasn't looking for anything more than a little innocent flirtation.

"I like women well enough," he said at last.

"But you never met one you wanted to marry?"

"Maybe I did meet such a woman and she wouldn't have me." His grin made it clear that there was no old heartbreak behind the words.

"I'd pictured you as the sort of man who generally gets what he wants."

"Had you now? Perhaps she was a very stubborn woman."

Looking at him, Liberty was inclined to think such a woman would have to be not only stubborn but made of stone. Just talking to him made her heart beat a little faster.

"Or maybe she just wasn't the right woman," Matt continued. "Maybe I was waiting for a girl with hair the color of new corn silk and eyes like polished jade and a mouth as soft as anything in creation.''

Liberty felt her heart stop as his eyes lingered on her mouth. Her lips parted, her breath coming too quickly. What would it feel like if Mike Prescott kissed her? She'd only been kissed once when Billy Joe Sauderton had caught her behind his father's barn and given her a peck on the lips. She'd promptly boxed his ears for him.

She didn't think Matt Prescott's kiss would feel anything like Billy Joe's hasty effort. Would his mustache tickle?

Matt had thought his words would startle her, make her realize that she was playing with fire. He'd expected her to poker up, her soft mouth going all prim and proper. What he hadn't expected was the sudden awareness in her eyes, the curiosity in the way her gaze dropped to his mouth. He could read her thoughts as clearly as if she'd spoken them aloud.

Perched on the rock the way she was, he'd have only to walk the roan a little closer and he'd be able to reach out and catch her around the waist. He could draw her down in front of him on the saddle and see if her mouth could possibly be as soft as it looked.

The roan shifted suddenly, his ears pricking forward as if he heard something he didn't like. Matt flicked the remains of the cigarette into the stream, his hand dropping to the butt of his pistol in one smooth movement. His eyes scanned the area around them, seeking the source of the horse's unease.

''What is—''

A sharp gesture cut off Liberty's question. Matt loosened the thong on his pistol. The roan was mustang bred and as good a trail horse as a man could ask for. A man who spent a lot of time in the wilderness learned to depend on his mount's more acute senses. If the roan thought there was something out there, Matt was willing to trust his judgment.

"Get off that rock," he ordered quietly.

After a quick look at his face, Liberty obeyed, sliding awkwardly off the side of the rock and then staying pressed against it. It suddenly seemed very foolish indeed to have wandered so far from camp. How far had she come? A mile? Perhaps a mile and a half? As the scout had said, too far for anyone to hear a scream.

There was a quick rustling in the brush across the stream and Matt's gun was suddenly in his hand, though Liberty hadn't seen him move to draw it. His fingers tightened on the reins, backing the roan until the shoulder of the big rock half shielded them. It was scant protection but the best to be had.

The rustling stopped and then started again. A moment passed with Liberty hardly daring to breathe and then the tall grass on the opposite side of the stream parted abruptly.

And out came a large raccoon.

He paused on seeing them, rising on his back feet to get a better look. His masked face swung back and forth, his nose twitching as he tested the air to see what sort of creatures he was dealing with. Apparently satisfied that they were harmless, he moved down the bank to the stream, his rolling gait giving him the look of a furry sailor not long off a ship.

"I guess my scalp's safe," Liberty said, her voice holding a shaky edge of relief.

"For now, anyway."

Relaxing in the saddle, Matt slipped his gun back in the holster. He turned the roan to face Liberty. "I'd better get you back to camp. The Millers are bound to wonder where you are."

It had become full light while they talked. There was no possibility that her absence wouldn't have been noted. She'd missed her morning chores, and no doubt, missed breakfast as well.

"Mrs. Miller must be worried to death," she said, guilt stricken. The Millers had treated her as one of their own, never making her feel like hired help.

"She'll forgive you soon enough once she sees you're safe," Matt said easily. He pulled one foot out of the stirrup and reached his hand down to her. "You'll get back a good deal faster if I take you back."

Liberty hesitated. It surely wasn't proper for a lady to ride double with a man. Mrs. Miller would scold her for being unladylike. But she could ask the scout to let her down just out of sight of the camp.

She put her hand in his, feeling his fingers close over hers, hard and strong, callused from work.

"Put your foot on mine and I'll swing you up behind me."

Hesitantly, she set her foot on his boot and then gasped, startled, as he swung her up onto the back of the horse. It was the first time in her life that she'd been astride a horse. Back home, she'd ridden side-saddle. The new position felt strange and awkward. She clutched at Matt's waist, her fingers digging into the soft buckskin of his shirt.

"You set?" he asked over his shoulder.

"Yes." Her answer was more sure than she felt, and when he nudged the roan into motion, her grip tightened and she pressed herself against his back.

It only took a moment for her to settle into the rhythm of the horse's gait and gain some confidence that she wasn't going to tumble off. Her hold on Matt grew a little easier.

But once she was assured of her physical safety, Liberty became aware of the intimacy of her position. Only inches separated her from Matt. She could see the way his shoulders filled the buckskin shirt, feel the ripple of muscles under her hands. If she leaned forward the smallest amount, her breasts would be pressed against that broad back.

She stiffened her spine ramrod straight, her cheeks flooding with color. What was the matter with her? How could she even think such a thing? There must be something wrong with her. First, she'd wondered what it would feel like to have Matt kiss her, and now, here she was, actually thinking about...she wasn't sure just what it was she was thinking about but she knew she had no business doing so.

It was just that she'd never in her life met a man like Matt Prescott. There was a toughness in him the like of which she'd never seen. He was like the land around them. Hard and rugged, and yet just as there was a beauty to the land, there was a gentleness in him that drew her.

But gentleness or no, she'd no business thinking the sort of thoughts she'd been thinking.

Even before he nudged the roan into a walk, Matt was regretting the impulse that had led him to draw Liberty up behind him. From the instant he'd felt her slender hand in his, he'd known it was a foolish move.

With that moonlight-colored hair and those wide green eyes, she'd already figured in his thoughts more than he'd any wish for a woman to do. She wasn't like the women he'd known in saloons and dance halls. Those women expected no more of a man than he chose to give. Liberty Ballard was the sort of woman who went with tidy little houses and neatly fenced yards.

It was easy enough to keep that in mind when he only saw her at a distance, walking alongside the wagon or helping with the chores. But with her arms wrapped around his waist and her body hardly more than a deep breath away from his, it wasn't quite so easy to remember all the reasons he couldn't pull her down in the tall grass and find out if her lips were really as soft as they looked.

Matt had grown to manhood in the wilderness. From boyhood on, he'd known that to stay alert was to stay alive. It took only a moment's inattention to spell the difference between life and death. It wasn't only the threat of Indians. The land itself offered more dangers than any man, white or red, ever could.

Rattlesnakes, rock slides, flash floods, even something as simple as a carelessly placed foot leading to a
broken leg—any one of them could lead to a man dying younger than he'd had any intention of doing.

That Matt had stayed alive was proof that he'd
learned that hard lesson very well. But every man
makes mistakes.

With Liberty mounted behind him, her arms around
his waist and the soft scent of her filling his head, Matt
momentarily forgot that one vital lesson. The roan
suddenly balked, his ears twitching. The horse's
abrupt move made Liberty tighten her arms around
Matt, and her breasts brushed against his back.
Distracted, Matt nudged the roan forward, rather than
paying attention to his warning behavior.

It was a nearly fatal mistake.

They came up over a shallow slope and the wagon
train lay before them. But it wasn't the peaceful scene
it should have been.

The Kiowa had hit hard and fast, catching the train
just as people were waking. Most had died without a
chance to get off a shot. The few who'd reached their
weapons had been cut down instantly.

When Matt and Liberty came over the rise, the
braves had nearly finished ransacking the wagons. The
first curl of smoke was rising from the canvas tops.
Bodies lay sprawled among the wagons that were supposed to take their owners to better lives.

"God!" The word was as much a prayer as a curse.

Matt's reaction was instantaneous. His hands
tightened on the reins, drawing the roan back hard
enough to make the big horse nearly sit on his

haunches. He'd heard men boast that their horses could turn on a dime and give a nickel's change. That day, the roan returned a good nine cents, spinning hard and fast. Matt's heels connected with the horse's ribs and he stretched out in a dead run.

If they were blessed with more luck than a man had any right to expect, maybe the Kiowa hadn't seen them. But a glance over his shoulder told Matt that luck wasn't with them today. Topping out over the rise behind them were three horses, their riders bent low over their necks.

hunches. He'd heard men boast that their horses
could turn on a dime and give a nickel's change. That
day, the roan returned a good nine cents, spinning
hard and fast. Matt's boots connected with the horse's
ribs and he stretched out in a dead run.

If they were blank, it meant no more than a man had
any right to expect. Maybe the Kiowa hadn't seen
them. But it wasn't. Just the same, old Matt that
luck wasn't the same. Over the rise, over the rise
behind them were three horses, their riders bent low
over their necks.

Chapter Two

The roan was a good running horse. Ordinarily, Matt
would have bet his life on his ability to outrun just
about anything short of a pronghorn. But not when he
was carrying double.

Glancing over his shoulder, Matt could see the
Kiowa were gaining. Ahead was a place where rocks
thrust upward from the grass. Matt had camped in
those rocks a few years ago and he knew that if they
could reach them, they might be able to hold off the
Kiowa, at least as long as his ammunition held out. It
was a thin chance, but it was the only one they had.

But they had to reach the rocks far enough ahead of
their pursuers to have time to dismount and reach their
shelter. And the Indian ponies were eating up the distance between them.

Gripping the reins in his left hand, Matt drew his
gun with his right. Twisting in the saddle, he caught a
glimpse of Liberty's frozen features out of the corner
of his eye. But there was no time to think of her, no
reassurance he could offer.

He snapped off three quick shots. He had no expectation of hitting the Kiowa. But the scattering of shots might slow them and every second gained could mean their survival. The Indians returned their fire and Matt bent low over the roan's neck, feeling Liberty press herself close against his back.

Looking ahead, he felt the bitter taste of defeat rise in his throat. They weren't going to make it. The rocks were in front of them, not more than a hundred yards away. But the Kiowa would be on them before they reached shelter. He could feel the roan laboring, the strain of carrying two riders slowing him.

Feeling Liberty's arms clutching at his waist, Matt knew that if he had the chance, he'd kill her himself before letting her fall into the Indians' hands. This was a raiding party. They were too far out of their accustomed range for it to be anything else. They wouldn't be taking prisoners back to the village. But they might take time to amuse themselves on her before they slit her throat.

The rocks were only a few yards ahead but that was too far. A glance behind showed their pursuers nearly on top of them. Matt made a quick decision. He drew back on the reins to slow the roan. Grabbing Liberty's arm with bruising strength, he swung her off the back of the horse.

"Run for the rocks," he snapped, turning the roan even as he spoke. With a bloodcurdling yell, he slapped his heels to the horse's sides and sent him charging directly toward their pursuers. There was no time to take a defensive position. They'd be cut down long before they reached shelter. Which left him with only one choice. He had to take the battle to the foe. Perhaps the element of surprise would tip the balance in his favor.

Liberty stared after Matt, momentarily incapable of movement. She felt dazed, her mind spinning. Terrible images were locked inside—burning wagons, sprawled bodies. But there was no time to deal with that now. The rocks, Matt had said. She was to get to the rocks. Turning, she stumbled toward the jumble of boulders, wondering what she was to do when she reached them.

Looking over her shoulder, she saw that Matt had ridden right into the middle of the warriors. One was down and unmoving in the long grass, his pony running for the horizon. Matt and a second warrior were grappling together, their horses pressed side to side as they fought.

But the third Indian was riding toward her. Terrified, Liberty ran faster, struggling to keep her long skirts out of the way. Glancing back, she saw he was practically on top of her, his face a savage mask. In that moment, he seemed more demon than human. He was holding a rifle by the barrel, the stock poised to club her down.

Acting on instinct, Liberty swerved abruptly. The sudden movement caught the brave by surprise. The blow he'd intended for her whistled through thin air, the momentum of it throwing him off balance just as his pony stumbled over a hidden rock. He tumbled from its back.

He was on his feet instantly, his dark eyes glittering with fury as he lunged after Liberty, who was running toward the rocks, though she couldn't imagine what safety they could offer her now.

She cried out as a hard hand closed over her shoulder, spinning her around. His other hand caught her across the face in an open-palmed slap that sent her to her knees, her head spinning dizzily.

She was going to die. The realization brought with it a bone-deep chill. Hard on its heels came a frantic rage. This man had been among those who'd ravaged the wagon train, who'd killed the Millers. And now he was going to kill her. She knew, with cold certainty, that she was about to die. But she wasn't going to make it easy for her killer.

The brave had his hand in her hair, his tomahawk drawn back for a killing blow. With a cry that mixed anger and despair, Liberty lunged forward. Her head caught him squarely in the stomach. Off balance, he stumbled back. The hand that was still tangled in her hair pulled Liberty with him as he fell to the ground.

She struggled wildly, raining blows on his head and shoulders. She tried to kick but her legs were hampered by the fullness of skirt and petticoats. There was no real question of the outcome of the struggle. She could only postpone the inevitable. But it wasn't in her to quit.

She had no expectation of help. For all she knew, Matt was already dead or wounded. Her right hand flailed out and her knuckles brushed against a rock. The Kiowa's fingers were around her throat, choking her into submission. Liberty had heard enough stories of what happened to women captured by the Indians to know she'd rather be dead.

Blackness was clouding the edge of her vision. Her lungs felt as if they were about to burst. She knew she was about to lose consciousness. Her groping fingers closed over the rock. With her last ounce of strength, she brought up her hand, slamming the rock against the brave's head as hard as she could.

His hold loosened and Liberty drew in a gasping breath. But the blow had enraged him more than it had caused physical harm. She saw the glitter in his eyes, his lips drawn back from his teeth in a fierce grin and knew she was about to die. There was no strength left in her. She could only lie there as he drew back his arm to strike. She wanted to close her eyes but she didn't even have the strength left for that. She was helpless to do anything but watch death coming at her.

The tomahawk started to descend and she offered up a garbled prayer.

A long arm suddenly appeared over the brave's shoulder, a razor-edged knife clenched in a broad fist. Liberty saw realization flash across her attacker's face and then the knife slashed across his throat.

She couldn't move, couldn't think. Her mind was frozen with horror. As if from somewhere outside herself, she saw Matt roll the Kiowa's body away. She felt him take hold of her arms and draw her to her feet. She could see his mouth moving but she couldn't hear the words.

The stickiness of blood was on her face, in her hair. Staring down at herself, she could see blood staining the blue of her dress. Her white cuffs were spotted scarlet and she knew her collar must be the same. She held her hands out away from her sides, not wanting to touch herself.

From somewhere far away, she could hear someone screaming, the sound holding little sanity. It wasn't until she felt the sharp sting of Matt's hand against her cheek that she realized the screams were hers. She broke off on a gulp.

"Are you hurt?" When she didn't answer, Matt grabbed her by the shoulders, giving her a quick hard shake, forcing her eyes to meet his. "Answer me, Liberty. Are you hurt?"

She drew a shuddering breath and shook her head. Seeing awareness returning to her eyes, Matt felt relief wash over him. For a moment, there'd been nothing but emptiness looking back at him and he'd wondered if he'd rescued only a shell.

"We have to move away from here," he told her, speaking slowly. "The others might come after us." He felt the shiver that went through her, saw the fear come up in her eyes. But there was no time to offer reassurance, even if he'd had any to give.

In the distance were the foothills of the Wind River Mountains. If they could reach those, they'd have shelter, a place to hide, if necessary. He didn't think it likely that the Kiowa would follow them very far. They were in enemy territory themselves. They'd already lost three braves trying to capture two people who had little to offer in the way of material goods. Chances were they'd decide to cut their losses and head south with what they'd taken from the wagon train.

The Indian ponies had scattered, but the roan stood not far away. He shied a little as Matt approached, uneasy at the scent of blood. But Matt spoke to him, reminding him of the long miles they'd traveled together, his voice low and soothing.

When he led the horse up to Liberty, he saw that she hadn't moved. She stood just where he'd left her, her hands held out from her sides, her face ghostly pale beneath the blood that streaked it. The dead Kiowa lay practically at her feet but she kept her eyes averted from the body.

She turned docilely enough when Matt touched her shoulder but he didn't think she was really aware of him. His face grim, he lifted her into the saddle and then swung up behind her. She'd had a hell of a shock. But the only thing he could do for her now was to try to see that she stayed alive.

He nudged the roan into a fast walk, heading toward the foothills, which were too far away for comfort. If he'd been alone, he'd have been riding hell for leather, figuring to put as much distance as possible between him and the remaining Indians. But if he tried to do that now, all he'd do was kill a damn good horse.

So he set the roan's head toward the foothills and kept a sharp watch back the way they'd come, hoping to see nothing but empty prairie.

It was midafternoon when they entered the trees. The land had been gradually climbing as it sloped up toward the mountains. Once in the shelter of the pines, Matt stopped the roan and turned to look back over their trail. There had been no sign of pursuit and the grasslands below were still empty. Just as Matt had expected, the Indians had decided that the chase would not be worth the price he might extract.

He didn't relax. They might have left one danger behind, but there were plenty more to take its place. This morning, he'd let himself be distracted by a pretty face and the softness of a woman's arms. That moment had nearly cost them both their lives. If he hadn't been so busy thinking about the shape of her mouth and the pale silkiness of her hair, he would have paid more heed to his horse's uneasiness and wouldn't have simply ridden up on the massacre like a raw pilgrim.

It wouldn't have saved any of the people with the wagon train, but if they'd been able to slip away without being seen, Liberty wouldn't have had to endure the fight that followed.

She lay back against his chest like a tired child. She hadn't spoken since seeing the ravaged wagon train. Worried, Matt looked down at her, wishing he could see her eyes. He didn't try to break the silence. There was nothing he could say to ease her pain.

She felt so slender and fragile in his arms. Remembering the emptiness in her eyes after he'd pulled the Kiowa brave from her, Matt felt cold fear. He'd heard of people who never recovered from a shock like the one she'd had this day.

If he hadn't been holding her so close that he could feel her heart beating, he might have thought he was carrying a dead woman. She didn't react when he lifted his hand and put it against her cheek. She was colder than the temperature warranted. Shock, no doubt. They needed to find shelter, somewhere he could build a fire, heat some water. They needed rest and so did the roan.

The trees thinned out into a small clearing with a narrow stream bubbling through it. Halting the horse, Matt swung off his back.

"We'll stop here for a bit," he told Liberty. He reached up to lift her down. "Water the horse and let him rest. I know of a cave a couple of hours from here. We should be able to make it before dark. We'll stop there for the night."

"I need to wash." It was the first thing she'd said all day. Matt doubted she'd heard a thing he'd said.

"I hadn't planned on taking that kind of time here," he said slowly, staring at her bent head. Her hair had come loose from its pins during the struggle with the Indian. Matted with blood, it swung forward to conceal her face.

"Please. I need to wash." Her voice held a tight edge that told him just how fragile her control was. She stood in front of him, her slim body unnaturally rigid, her hands held out from her sides as if she couldn't bear to touch herself. She didn't look at him but focused on some point beyond his shoulder.

Blood turned her face into a ghastly mask and stained her hair. Her dress was even worse than he remembered, the blue turned to purple where blood soaked it. He understood her need to wash the stains away but he'd prefer to put more distance behind them before they stopped for any length of time.

"Please," she whispered, her voice trembling. Matt was not proof against the vulnerability in that one word.

"All right." Going to the roan, he opened a saddlebag and took out a thin bar of soap. "Take this and go upstream. Wash away the worst of it. But don't get your clothes wet. Or your hair. It's too cold for that. And don't take any longer than you have to. I want to reach the cave before dark."

Matt watched her walk away, the bar of soap clenched in her fist as if it were a weapon. He turned back to his horse and loosened the cinch before leading the animal to water. Unsaddling him and rubbing him down would have to wait until they stopped for the night.

While the roan drank, Matt looked up at the patches of sky visible through the trees. Another hour or two and it would be dark. He wanted to get them settled in for the night before then. The nights were cold now. The cave he remembered was deep. He'd be able to build a fire far enough back from the mouth to prevent it from shining like a beacon for miles.

Warmth, rest and food. That was what all three of them needed now. There was food in his saddlebags. Not much, but enough to last a day or two. He drew the mustang back from the stream and ground-hitched him in a patch of grass.

He lowered himself to the ground, bracing his back against a convenient tree. He winced as the movement tugged at a shallow knife wound that crossed his abdomen. He'd barely been aware of the injury until now, more concerned with putting distance between them and the scene of the massacre. A quick glance showed him that the Kiowa's knife had skated across his ribs, leaving a wound that was little more than a scratch. When they stopped for the night, he'd heat some water and clean it.

Just as soon as Liberty returned from washing up, they'd be on their way. A fire, a hot meal and a few hours' sleep was the best thing for both of them. Morning would be soon enough to worry about where they were to go from here.

His eyes on the stream, Matt frowned, wondering how long it was going to take her to get cleaned up. They shouldn't have stopped even as long as they already had. Rising, he stared upstream. She'd been gone a long time. How long could it take to wash her hands and face? Had she even heard him say not to get her hair and clothes wet?

Liberty had heard Matt's instructions but the words held little meaning. The only important thing was that she had to get clean. She had to get rid of the sticky feel of blood on her skin and in her hair.

A few yards upstream, there was a place where several boulders thrust into the water, forcing the stream to slow and widen. In a daze, Liberty stopped near the half-formed pool. She set down the precious soap on a rock. She sat on the bank and unlaced her shoes, setting them neatly to the side, her socks draped over them before she stood up again.

Without a moment's hesitation, she picked up the soap and waded out into the stream. Her skirts grew heavy with water, clinging to her legs, making it difficult to walk. She hardly noticed the discomfort. When the water reached her thighs, she sank to her knees.

It never crossed her mind that there was anything odd about her actions. She had to be clean.

She ducked her head under the surface, running the fingers of one hand through her hair, feeling the cleansing water run through it, rinsing away the stickiness.

She focused her thoughts carefully on washing away every trace of blood from her skin and hair. She wouldn't think of anything else—not of the Millers lying murdered next to the wagon that had been taking them toward the dream of a new life; not of Sally Devers, who'd been heavy with child, her sixth. She refused to think of Mr. Miller, who'd insisted that they'd make it through to California before winter, despite the warnings they were given at Fort Laramie.

No one was going to have to make the decision of whether or not the train should spend the winter at Fort Bridger and continue in the spring. There would be no more arguments about whether it might be better to take the cutoff for Oregon, after all.

They were all dead. And their dreams had died with them.

Liberty squeezed her eyes shut, forcing down the pain. She wasn't going to think about it now. She wasn't going to think about anything at all. All that mattered was getting clean.

She rubbed the soap over her face and neck and then down across her breasts. She repeated the motion again and again, rubbing the fabric of her dress. The water bubbled past her, carrying away all traces of red. But she still felt the horrid stickiness, still saw the stain of the Kiowa's blood on her flesh. It was as if it were more than his blood. She felt as if she bore the stain of all the people who'd died with the wagon train.

Her side hurt, a sharp, gnawing pain that demanded attention. But she ignored it. She had to get the feel of blood off her skin. If she could just get clean, everything would be all right again.

The soap disappeared beneath the repeated rubbings. Liberty scooped up a handful of sand from the streambed and rubbed it methodically over her face and neck. She had to get clean.

Matt found her there, on her knees in the stream. He stepped out of the trees and stopped, the sight of her jolting him with the force of a blow.

She knelt in the stream, the water rippling just below her shoulders, her hair floating behind her like a silken banner.

She seemed unaware that she was no longer alone. Or perhaps she didn't care. As he watched, she bent and scooped up another handful of sand and began rubbing it over her chest, crushing it against the wet fabric of her dress. The skin of her face and throat was already flushed and angry looking where she'd been rubbing.

With an oath, Matt strode forward. After pausing just long enough to pull off his boots, he waded into the water. Liberty was oblivious to his approach, continuing her methodical rubbing even when his hands closed over her shoulders, dragging her to her feet. Matt grabbed her hand, pulling it away from her body and forcing her fingers down until the sand washed away in the current.

"Liberty!" He spoke her name quietly, his hand coming up under her chin to lift her face to his.

"I have to get clean."

"You are clean."

"No. I can still feel it on me. All the blood. I have to get it off."

"It's gone, Liberty. You washed it all away." But she didn't seem to hear him.

"Mama will be upset. I got blood on my blue calico. It's my second-best dress. I have to get it clean."

"Liberty, stop it!" He gave her a sharp shake.

"Mama will be angry," she repeated, her voice soft as a child's, her eyes looking beyond him to something that wasn't there. "I have to get it clean."

Matt felt a fear greater than any he'd felt when facing the Kiowa. Physical danger he understood. He'd lived with it all his life. But this was something new. New and frightening. Liberty had retreated from the terrible reality of what she'd seen. She'd pulled back somewhere inside her mind, hiding from the things she'd seen.

Staring at her smooth features, Matt tried to decide the best course. He could just leave her in this state and hope she came out of it on her own. There might be a doctor at one of the forts who could help her, if she didn't. But they were a long way from both Bridger and Laramie.

"I have to get clean," she murmured again, pulling against his restraining hands. "Mama will be upset."

Matt made his decision.

"Your mother has been dead a long time, Liberty. And the Millers are dead, too. We're the only ones left." The words were gentle but implacable. He felt the impact of them strike her.

"No." Her wide eyes met his and he saw a kind of plea in them. He hardened his heart against it. They had a long way to go before they reached safety. If he had to carry her along like a helpless child, it was going to narrow their already slim chances.

"They're all dead. You've got to be strong."

Liberty sucked in a shallow breath, feeling his words sink into her mind, dragging her back from the safe little room she'd been trying to lock herself inside. She didn't want to hear him, didn't want to believe him.

"Liberty." Matt's voice pulled her back to a reality she didn't want to face. She stared up at him, seeing the pity in his golden-brown eyes.

"No." The word was little more than a breath.

"Yes."

She shuddered as if the word was an actual, physical blow, her eyes closing. Pain lodged in her chest, tight and hard, somehow connecting with the sharper pain in her side.

"Oh God." The words were thick with pain. When she opened her eyes, they were dark with loss but they remained dry. Matt brushed her wet hair back from her face, almost wishing she'd cry. Tears could be a healing force. But at least she no longer had that frightening blank look.

"It gets easier with time," he said, knowing the words offered scant comfort. But they were all he had to give.

Bending, he put one hand behind her knees and scooped her up against his chest. Water ran off her, soaking his shirt. He waded out of the stream. Her sopping skirts wrapped around his legs, making walking difficult.

She lay against him, her eyes closed, her face white with grief. The stream had its origin high in the mountains above them and the water had been cold. He had to get her out of her wet things, had to get her warm and dry as soon as possible. She'd be lucky if she didn't catch pneumonia.

His face grim, Matt carried her through the trees to where the roan waited. There was a buffalo coat tied to the back of the saddle. He'd spent too many years in snow country not to be prepared. Though it was early in the season, blizzards were not unheard of, especially in the mountains. One year he'd seen it snow in July.

The coat would serve to keep her warm until they reached the cave where he could build a fire and make some coffee. She was young and healthy. With luck, she wouldn't catch a chill.

"You've got to get out of these wet clothes." He set her down and reached for the buttons that marched neatly down the front of her dress.

"I can do it." She pushed his hands away. Her eyes were a muddy green and her skin was still too pale, but she was in the here and now.

When Matt turned back with the coat, Liberty had only managed to unfasten the first few buttons. Her fingers were shaking too much to manage the rest of them, whether with cold or shock, he couldn't be sure.

He brushed her hands aside and began opening the buttons with quick, impatient movements.

"This is not the time to be worrying about modesty," he told her brusquely when she murmured a protest.

He stripped the dress off her shoulders, fighting the wet fabric that clung to her skin. If it hadn't been the only garment she had, he might have been tempted to cut it from her. The sun was dropping rapidly and the temperature with it. He wanted to reach the cave before dark. They needed the warmth of a fire and something hot to drink.

The dress yielded at last, dropping to the ground around Liberty's feet with a sodden thump. The tapes on her petticoats resisted his fingers. Growling his impatience, Matt drew his knife and slashed through them. He pushed the water-laden layers of fabric down over her hips.

Since that first halfhearted murmur, Liberty had offered not a word of protest. She might have been a statue if it hadn't been for the shivering that grew worse with every passing moment.

Somewhere in the back of his mind, Matt was aware of the delicate curves of her. The thin chemise and pantalets would have offered scant modesty when dry. Wet, they were little more than a tantalizing veil drawn over peach-tinted flesh. Cold had drawn her nipples into taut peaks, their darker color clearly visible beneath the wet cotton. At another time and place, he might have bent to taste those dark buds.

But here and now, his awareness of her as a woman

was a distant thing, hardly noticed amid the need to care for her health.

He put his hands on her waist, planning to lift her away from the heap of wet clothing at her feet. But the moment his palms pressed against her, she cried out in obvious pain, her face losing what little color it had held.

Startled, Matt jerked his hands away, only to grab for her shoulders as she swayed. He caught her against his side as her knees buckled. Supporting her without effort, he stared at his left hand, at the crimson stain that marked his palm.

The right side of her chemise was similarly marked. He pulled up the garment, exposing her bare skin and the long ugly gouge that scored her side. Obviously, they hadn't been as lucky as he'd thought in their encounter with the Kiowa.

Matt's hand, covered with her blood, clenched slowly into a fist. He lifted his head and looked around the empty clearing. They were miles from decent shelter and more than a hundred miles from the nearest settlement. He had only what food was in his saddlebags, one horse and an injured girl on his hands.

And he wouldn't have taken even money on their chances at this moment.

Chapter Three

It seemed to Liberty as if she'd spent half her life on the back of the roan, seeing the world framed between his ears. Perhaps it was because the world she'd known had disappeared forever since this morning when Matt offered to give her a ride back to camp. Life could never be the same again. Everything had changed, even more than it had the day they left Pennsylvania.

She closed her eyes to try to shut out the thought of so many people dead. Good people, people with hopes and dreams now unfulfilled. And the children. God, the children. She opened her eyes and deliberately focused on the pain in her side. It hurt less than the pain in her heart.

Matt had examined the injury, seeming relieved by what he found. One of the Kiowa's bullets had grazed her side, leaving a long, shallow wound. The morning's events had left her in shock, shutting her off from the pain she would ordinarily have felt from the injury. It was unfortunate that, once the shock wore off, the pain was still there, eager to make its presence known.

Matt had bound the wound with a strip torn from her petticoat and told her not to worry. But Liberty had seen the concern in his eyes and knew he was worried about infection. She couldn't help but remember Bill Pettygrove, who'd cut himself while repairing a wagon axle not far out of Fort Kearny. The wound had putrefied, and Sam Larson, who was the closest thing they'd had to a doctor, had amputated Bill's arm. He'd died two days later.

Liberty knew Matt was remembering the same thing. A strong, healthy man, dead and buried on the prairie because of a cut no worse than the wound in her side.

After binding the wound, Matt had wrapped her in the buffalo coat and then fetched her shoes from where she'd left them by the stream. When he returned, he lifted her into the saddle and mounted behind her.

The roan was tired and the pace he set was slow. Liberty was grateful. Even that much movement made her side hurt more, a dull ache that nagged like a sore tooth. She wanted nothing more than to put her head on a soft pillow and sleep until all the pain was gone. Maybe when she woke up, she'd find that all of this was nothing more than a nightmare.

But she knew that wasn't going to happen. The events of the day were real, and if she slept a hundred years, nothing would have changed. She and Matt were the only survivors from the wagon train.

If she hadn't wanted to see the sunrise this morning, she would be lying back there with the rest of them. If Matt hadn't followed her, she might have stumbled into the massacre or been left alone on the prairie, which would have meant death as surely as if she'd been with the train.

Matt. She could feel the width of his chest against her back, the strength of his arms holding her. He'd saved her life. If the roan hadn't been carrying double, Liberty was sure he could have outrun the Indian ponies. She'd heard Mr. Miller talking about the scout's horse being one of the fastest he'd seen in a long time.

Slowed by the extra weight his horse was carrying, Matt had been forced to turn and fight. He could have been killed. And if he'd died, she would have died. She didn't have to close her eyes to remember the Kiowa's savage face over hers, the tomahawk drawn back for a killing blow.

The memory sent a convulsive shiver through her. Matt's arms tightened in response.

"We're almost there," he told her, his breath brushing against her ear.

"I'm all right."

She wasn't all right. She didn't think she'd ever feel all right again. Twenty-four hours earlier, she'd been wondering if there were any young men on her uncle's ranch, daydreaming about meeting a special man who'd make her heart beat faster. Those dreams seemed a thousand years ago.

"There." She followed the direction of Matt's pointing finger, narrowing her eyes to see through the gloom. As the sun set behind the mountains, it had grown increasingly difficult to see, especially with the trees crowding close around them.

At first, all Liberty saw was what seemed to be a bulge in the side of the mountain. But as they drew closer, she could make out the dark outline of a cave mouth. This was what Matt had been looking for.

He drew the roan to a halt a few yards away from the cave and swung down. Liberty clutched the saddle horn with both hands, watching as he approached the cave, studying the ground for any tracks that would indicate that it was home to a grizzly or a cougar. After a few minutes, he returned to the horse.

"Looks clear," he said, taking hold of the bridle. He led the mustang up to the mouth of the cave and then reached up to lift Liberty down.

Careful to avoid her injured side, he put his palms against her rib cage, lifting her easily from the saddle. Loss of blood and long hours in the saddle had left her legs unsteady. She stumbled and would have fallen if she hadn't caught hold of Matt's arm.

"I'm sorry," she said, trying to stiffen her weak knees. Whether or not Matt heard her apology, she couldn't be sure. With one smooth movement, he lifted her against his chest.

Even through the heavy buffalo coat, Liberty could feel the strength of his arms around her. He carried her as easily as if she'd been a child, seeming not to notice her weight. If the day's events had drained his strength, she could see no evidence of it.

"Stay here while I get a fire going." He set her down on a fallen log next to the cave entrance.

"I can help."

"Just stay put," he ordered.

He disappeared into the cave before she could offer a protest. Liberty stared after him, feeling a stir of annoyance at his brusque tone. But it faded immediately. To tell the truth, she wasn't at all sure her legs would hold her for more than a step or two. He could probably prepare a campsite more quickly alone than he could with her inexperienced help. If his tone had been a little abrupt, well, no doubt he was as tired as she was.

She reached up and thrust her fingers through the heavy mass of her hair. It was still damp underneath. It had been foolishness to wash it as she had, but she couldn't regret it. She didn't think her sanity would have survived another minute with the sticky feel of blood on her skin and in her hair.

She hugged the thick coat closer around herself, aware of her near nakedness beneath it. Matt had allowed her to retain her chemise and pantalets, but only because the cotton was thin enough to dry quickly. Her dress and petticoats had been wrung out with a ruthless force that had left them hopelessly wrinkled and tied to the back of the saddle. She wore her shoes and socks.

When Matt had fetched her out of the stream and then stripped her sopping clothes from her, she'd been dazed, hardly conscious of what was happening. Thoughts of modesty had been far from her mind. Now, it occurred to her that Matt Prescott had seen her more nearly naked than any man had since she was a little girl. And she had the uneasy feeling that he planned on tending her wound as soon as they were settled into their camp.

Sliding one hand under the coat, Liberty lightly pressed her fingers over her side. Reluctantly, she admitted that it would be awkward for her to clean and bandage the injury. She'd have to twist her torso to get to it, which would undoubtedly break it open again.

Sighing, she let her hand drop away. She might as well resign herself to Matt's ministrations. Picturing the strong set of his jaw, she suspected he was perfectly capable of applying physical force if she was so foolish as to argue with him about it.

"All clear."

She'd been absorbed in her thoughts and hadn't heard Matt's approach. At the sound of his voice, she jumped and then bit her lip against a gasp of pain as the movement jarred her side.

"There's a fire laid ready," he continued. "I'll get you settled and then take care of the horse. Once I've got some water boiled, I'll take a look at your side."

"I can walk," Liberty said firmly, putting her hand out to stop him when he moved to pick her up. "Take care of the horse. He's earned it."

"That he has, but I'll see you settled first."

Briefly, Liberty considered refusing the hand he held out to help her. Pride demanded that she rise on her own. Common sense suggested that she not be foolish. In truth, she was grateful for the easy strength with which he pulled her to her feet.

It was only a few yards to the cave but it felt like miles. She'd walked most of the way from St. Joseph—nearly seven hundred miles—but she didn't think the entire journey had been as difficult as the few steps required to reach the cave's mouth.

Matt stayed next to her, ready to catch her when she fell, which seemed likely. *Stubborn little fool.* He felt both irritation and admiration. Damned if she wasn't too stubborn for her own good. Any fool could see she was no more steady than a newborn calf. He should just pick her up and carry her. And so he would at the first sign that she was going to fall.

Sheer pride and stubbornness were all that were keeping her on her feet. But pride and stubbornness were things he understood. He had more than a goodly share of both himself.

Firelight flickered on the walls of the cave, softening the harsh edges of the rock. Unfortunately, the unsteady light failed to reveal the shallow ridge in the floor before Liberty's foot connected with it. The small bump was all that was necessary to upset her already shaky balance.

Matt caught her even as the startled gasp left her. He swept her off her feet as easily as if she were a child, lifting her against his chest. Even in his hurry, he was careful to avoid putting pressure on her injured side, cradling her in his arms with a gentleness at odds with the scowl on his face.

"Little fool," he said gruffly, carrying her the few feet to the fire.

"Thank you," she said, the tartness showing even though her voice was weak.

She saw one corner of his mouth kick up as if in appreciation, but he didn't respond to her sarcasm.

Which was just as well, she admitted. At the moment, she was far from ready for a battle of wits.

"I'm going to bring in the horse," he said as he settled her on a drift of leaves and pine needles. "Do you think you can stay put?"

"I'll stay put." She could make the promise without hesitation. What little strength she'd had had been used up in the short walk. Unless it were a matter of life and death, she didn't plan on moving. Even then, she wasn't sure she could stir a muscle.

Matt led the roan into the mouth of the cave and stripped the saddle from his back. He rubbed the big horse down with a handful of dry grass, while water was heating in a battered pan over the fire. By the time the horse was cared for, the water was bubbling.

Liberty had been watching Matt work through drowsy eyes. But she came fully awake when he crouched next to the fire and lifted the pan from the coals. She was still wrapped in the buffalo coat and her fingers drew the front protectively tighter.

"That wound needs to be properly cleaned," Matt said. He picked up her petticoat and drew his knife from its sheath.

"I can take care of it." She watched him cut her second-best petticoat into neat strips. No, it was her best petticoat now. It was the only one she owned. In fact, all she owned in the world now was the clothes she'd donned this morning. And Matt was busy cutting up her petticoat.

"You can't reach the wound," Matt told her. He slid the knife back into its sheath. "If you're worried about your modesty, don't be. I'm too damned tired to care what you look like," he said bluntly.

Liberty felt herself flush. It wasn't a matter of whether or not he cared what she looked like. It was a matter of propriety. She'd never in her life allowed a man to see her in her undergarments. And she'd expected that to remain true until the day she married. Even then, it was a bit daunting to think about standing before a man with so little to protect her modesty.

"It's nothing to be ashamed of," he said more gently. "If we were in town, you'd let a doctor take a look at you, wouldn't you?"

"Yes." She didn't need him to tell her she was being foolish. This day had surely taken them past the point of worrying about details like modesty. After all, he'd already seen her wearing nothing but her chemise and pantalets, and they'd been wet at the time, no doubt leaving little to the imagination.

"Out here, I'm the only doctor you've got," Matt continued. He dropped a square of white cotton into the scalding water. "We're just going to have to make do. Now, I'm going to help you get that coat off and then I'll see what I can do with that wound."

His tone left no room for argument. Liberty guessed that if she didn't give in gracefully, he was capable of holding her down and tending her injury, anyway.

Using a folded piece of fabric to protect his hand, he carried the pot over to where she sat and crouched beside her.

He reached for the coat. Her fingers tightened over the thick fur and her eyes lifted to meet his. What she saw was understanding and determination in equal measure. But it wasn't the knowledge that he would probably force her if he had to that made her loosen her grip on the coat. It was the tiredness around his eyes, the deep lines that bracketed his thick mustache.

Even in the soft firelight, he looked exhausted. It struck her suddenly that this day had been as hard on him as it had been on her. Worse in some ways since he'd been burdened with the responsibility for her.

She kept her gaze focused somewhere near his collarbone as he eased the coat off her shoulders and then drew it away completely. Despite the fire, the cave was chilly, and Liberty shivered as the cool air touched her bare arms and shoulders.

Matt had wrapped a strip of petticoat around her waist to hold the makeshift bandage in place and now he reached around her to unwind it. The movement brought him so close that she felt the brush of his hair against her shoulder. She closed her eyes, trying not to think of the intimacy of their situation.

She was being foolish, she told herself. There was certainly nothing wrong with what he was doing. He was right. If he'd been a doctor, she wouldn't have felt this uneasiness. But he wasn't a doctor and no amount of imagination could turn him into one.

Color flooded her face as she felt his hands on the bare skin of her waist. She had to bite her lip to keep from protesting.

"Doesn't look too bad," he said, after inspecting the wound. "The bullet just grazed you. If infection doesn't set in, you should be good as new in a couple of days. You're lucky."

"Yes." She sucked in a quick breath as he cleaned the wound.

"Done," he said a few minutes later.

"Thank you." Liberty quickly tugged her chemise down, covering the bandage. She reached for the buffalo coat again as Matt stood up, but the movement was not completed.

"You're hurt!" For the first time, she noticed the tear in the soft buckskin shirt as well as the dried blood that stained it.

"It's nothing." Matt bent to pick up the pan of water, intending to throw it outside but Liberty grabbed hold of his arm.

"Let me look." Matt would have protested—it was nothing more than a scratch—but he realized that, for the first time since the massacre, Liberty was focused on something besides the tragedy. If letting her tend an injury that didn't need tending would help her to forget, he'd put up with it.

He knelt on the hard floor in front of her. Taking hold of the bottom of his shirt, he drew it up and over his head. Despite her concern for his injury, Liberty drew back a little, her eyes wide and startled. It was the first time in her life she'd ever been so close to a man's bare chest. She'd seen her father once or twice without his shirt, but her father's pale skin and narrow shoulders were nothing like the body in front of her.

Matt's chest was broad and tanned and liberally dusted with curling black hair. Muscles rippled as he tossed the torn shirt in the direction of the saddlebags, which he'd placed against one wall of the cave.

It must be the blood she'd lost that made her feel light-headed. She wished suddenly that she hadn't noticed that he was injured. Or that she'd believed him when he said it was nothing.

He'd cared for her, she reminded herself sternly. *The least she could do was to return the favor.* She blinked and focused her eyes on the long scratch that skated across his rib cage.

"It's hardly worth noticing," Matt said somewhere over her head.

"It should be cleaned," she said, her tone brisk. "Even a small cut can be dangerous."

"I've had cuts worse than that on my eyeball."

"Really?" Startled, her head jerked up, her eyes meeting his. The laughter in his made her realize how foolish she'd sounded.

"It's not nice to make fun of someone who's trying to help you, Mr. Prescott." Her words were stern but her eyes smiled.

"Sorry, ma'am," he said meekly. Her mouth was tucked up all prim and proper, and he had the sudden urge to kiss it until her lips softened beneath his.

She dipped a clean piece of cloth in the warm water and began washing the dried blood from his skin. Matt felt his stomach muscles tighten, not in reaction to the water but in reaction to the feel of her hand on his body.

The firelight cast a reddish glow over her skin and hair. Her hair, dry now, lay in a thick silver-gold sheet down her back, falling almost to her hips. In her concern for him, she'd apparently forgotten all about her own scanty attire. The modest white cotton chemise and pantalets were more alluring than if she'd been wearing black lace and satin. He wished suddenly that she'd put the coat back on.

He looked away from her, trying to focus his thoughts on other things. Like what had to be done to ensure their survival. They'd made it this far but they'd had a good share of luck. He couldn't count on that luck holding.

Her skin was milky white, and he knew now that it was every bit as soft as it looked. He could see the sway of her breasts beneath the thin cotton and he curled his fingers into his palms to resist the urge to reach out and touch them.

Gritting his teeth together, he forced himself to look away again. He knew what was happening. He'd nearly died today. He'd killed three men to save this woman. And some primitive part of him wanted to claim her as his reward. Having faced death, his body was anxious to reaffirm life. He probably would have felt the same desire for any woman in reach.

But looking at the gentle curve of Liberty's cheek, feeling the soft touch of her hands as she cleansed the knife wound, Matt couldn't quite convince himself of the truth of that.

"There. That should be better." Liberty tilted back her head to give him a shy smile, and Matt had all he could do to keep from burying his hands in her hair and drawing her mouth up to his.

"Much better," he said, his voice husky. He cleared his throat, focusing on the innocence in her eyes, reminding himself that this was not some dance-hall girl he'd rescued. This was an innocent, *virginal* girl.

Exactly the sort of girl he'd been avoiding for the past fifteen years. This was the sort of girl a man married, not the sort he bedded when the urge took him.

"Thank you." He stood up suddenly. "You'd better wrap up in that coat again. I don't want you catching a chill."

Liberty flushed at his abrupt tone and reached for the heavy coat. Funny how she'd forgotten her lack of attire until now. Obviously, Matt hadn't done the same. He probably thought her completely lacking in propriety.

There was little conversation between them after that. Matt heated fresh water in the pot and shaved some jerky into it to make a simple broth. He had a tin cup in his saddlebags, even more battered than the pan, but it was functional. They shared the broth and the cup.

By the time the scanty meal was finished, Liberty's eyelids were drooping and she offered no argument when Matt suggested that she try and get some sleep. He'd supplemented her bed with several pine boughs broken off the trees nearby. Still wrapped in the buffalo coat, she lay down, and the sharp, fresh scent of pine floated up around her.

Liberty was sure she wouldn't be able to sleep. There was too much to worry about, too many dark images waiting to jump out as soon as she closed her eyes. But exhaustion won out. She slept almost immediately.

Matt sat near the fire, though not directly in its light. He'd checked, and the way the cave curved into the mountain made it impossible to see the fire from outside, but habit kept him back from the flames, just as habit kept him from looking directly into the fire. A man who stared into a fire was blind for an instant when he looked away. Only an instant, but often enough that was all the time there was between being alive and being dead.

The roan stood between them and the mouth of the cave. He'd run wild before Matt caught and broke him and his senses were sharper than any man's. He'd let them know if they had visitors—human or animal. Indians weren't the only thing they had to worry about. There were wolves and grizzlies in the area. But most animals would avoid the scent of man if they could.

Behind him, Liberty stirred, whimpering softly in her sleep. Matt set his fingers on her shoulder. The whimpering stopped but he left his hand where it was. If the truth be told, he wasn't adverse to a little bit of human contact at the moment, himself.

They were a long way from any chance of help. And they couldn't expect anyone to come after them. Even if someone stumbled across the wagon train and took word of the massacre to one of the forts, it would be assumed that he and Liberty had died along with everyone else.

No, he couldn't count on help coming from either Bridger or Laramie. His hand tightened on Liberty's shoulder for a moment and then dropped away. If he'd been alone, he wouldn't have worried. He'd hunted and trapped his way through most of the west over the past fifteen years.

But with an inexperienced girl and only one horse between them, it was a different story. Not to mention that the winter he'd warned the immigrants about was not far away. The air was still warm during the day, but there had been frost on the grass the past two mornings and there was a crispness in the air that spoke of colder weather to come.

He shook his head and got up. He tossed a blanket over the mound of pine boughs he'd brought in earlier. There'd be time enough to worry in the morning. One thing there was always plenty of time for and that was worry.

He unbuckled his gun belt and set it where he'd be able to reach it at a moment's notice. He tugged off his boots and then stretched out on the thin bed. It wasn't a feather tick but he'd slept in worse places in his time.

Tilting his hat over his eyes, he settled in to get what sleep he could.

Chapter Four

The first thing Liberty was aware of when she woke
was the scent of roasting meat. Her eyes weren't even
open yet when her stomach let it be known that too
much time had passed since her last solid meal. Still,
she resisted waking up.

If she'd hoped for a merciful period of forgetful-
ness where she didn't remember what had happened
the previous day, she was disappointed. All the memories were there, vivid and intact, the moment she
woke. She pulled the buffalo coat tighter around her
shoulders, her dark brows coming together over her
nose as she tried to push away the thought of all the
people on the wagon train and all the dreams they'd
never fulfill.

The memories didn't go away and neither did the
hunger that gnawed insistently at her belly. It seemed
crassly insensitive that she should be so hungry when
all those people were dead, but the smell of food
couldn't be ignored. Groaning, she sat up and pushed
the hair out of her eyes.

"I thought the smell of food might wake you. It was that or firing a shot next to your ear." Matt grinned at her from across the fire.

Liberty blinked at him, thinking he looked much too wide-awake for such an early hour of the morning. It surely couldn't be much past dawn.

"It's closer to dinner than breakfast but if your stomach is as empty as mine, I'd guess you won't have much trouble eating for two meals at one sitting."

"Dinner?" She narrowed her eyes at the wedge of sunlight just visible past his shoulder. It did look too bright for early morning. "I never sleep so late," she said, as if saying it would make the clock turn back to her accustomed hour of rising.

"Sleep was the best thing for you. I hope you like rabbit."

"Rabbit?" She lowered her gaze to the fire and found the source of the smell that had awakened her. He'd arranged some green wood to form a spit and was roasting a rabbit over the fire. The smell made her mouth water but she still felt a twinge of guilt. Was it completely insensitive to be thinking about food at a time like this?

"Going hungry isn't going to bring any of them back to life," Matt said bluntly, reading her thoughts in the clear green of her eyes.

"I know." She sighed unhappily. "It just doesn't seem fair."

"Lots of things in life aren't fair. Only a fool thinks that's going to change." He pressed a finger against the meat. "This is just about done. If you've anything you want to tend to before we eat, do it now."

Liberty was glad he didn't look at her as he spoke. At least he didn't see the color come up in her face.

When she returned to the cave a few minutes later, Matt had removed the rabbit from the spit and disjointed it. A crude plate made of bark lay in front of her bed, several pieces of browned meat in the center of it.

Liberty seated herself on the pine boughs, curling her knees to one side and tucking the coat securely around them. Her dress lay draped across a rock only a few feet away. It was probably dry by now, if incredibly wrinkled. Briefly, she'd considered putting it on before she ate, but her hunger discouraged that idea.

Liberty hesitated only a moment before following Matt's example and picking up the rabbit with her fingers. Biting into the succulent meat, she was sure that she'd never tasted anything so delicious.

They ate without speaking. There was plenty to discuss, decisions to be made. But for the moment, it was enough to savor the food.

"That was wonderful," she said, sighing as she unashamedly licked the last of the juices from her fingers.

"Hunger tends to whet the appetite." Matt picked up the knife he'd used to cut up the rabbit and wiped it against the leg of his pants before sliding it back into its sheath. "How is your wound?"

"Fine," she said hastily, afraid that he might insist on looking at it himself. "I'd hardly even know it was there."

Matt's brows rose, making it clear that he doubted the accuracy of her claim. In truth, her side throbbed annoyingly, but to her relief, he didn't pursue the question.

"Probably best to leave it undisturbed for now. I'll take a look at it when I get back."

"Get back?" Liberty's head jerked up, her questioning eyes fastening on his face. "Where are you going?"

"I'm going back to the wagon train."

"You mean in case there were other survivors?"

"I mean in case the Indians left any supplies."

"But some of the others might still be alive," she insisted, reluctant to let go of that hope.

"Not likely," he said bluntly. "We're only alive because we were away from the train."

"Someone else might have been away."

"Maybe." But his tone made it clear that he wasn't holding out any hope. "We're going to need food. We'll hole up here for a few days, give the pony a chance to rest, give your wound a chance to heal. Then we'll make for Fort Bridger."

Though he didn't say as much, Liberty sensed that he had his doubts about their chances of reaching the fort. Despite the warmth created by the fire, she shivered and drew the heavy coat close around her.

"My uncle's at Fort Bridger. He might send out a rescue party."

"Even if they find out about the massacre, they've no way of knowing there's anyone left alive," he said gently. "Winter's coming on, earlier than I'd expected. They'd be running the risk of getting caught by the snow. No one's going to come looking for us, Liberty. We're on our own.''

Matt wondered if he should have been so honest with her. Would it have been better to leave her something to cling to? There was comfort to be had in the idea that people would be looking for them—that rescue might lie just beyond the next hill.

But there was a danger in it, too. Such thinking could make you careless, could take away the edge of fear that might help keep you alive.

Liberty was silent for several seconds, her eyes blank as she absorbed his words. Matt waited, hoping he hadn't overestimated her strength. After a moment, she looked up at him, her chin set.

''Think how surprised everyone will be when we ride into the fort.''

Matt's worried look dissolved in a broad grin. ''That they will.''

If Liberty's answering smile tended to shake a little around the edges, he pretended not to notice. Better to let her retain the illusion of confidence.

He stood up and dusted his hands on the seat of his pants. ''I'd better get going.''

Liberty rose to her feet and followed him as he picked up his saddle and carried it outside to where the roan was picketed on a patch of dry grass.

''How long do you expect to be?'' She was proud of her level tone. There was nothing to give away the terror she felt at the thought of him riding off and leaving her alone.

''I'll make better time than we did yesterday,'' he said as he swung the saddle up on the roan's back.

"It'll be after dark, no doubt." He tightened the cinch and turned to look at her, his expression doubtful. "I put aside some of the rabbit and I'd some beans in my saddlebag. You can boil up a mess of those for your supper.

"There's a stream about fifty yards that way." He nodded his head to indicate the direction. "You can get drinking water there, if you need to. Best if you stay as close to the cave as possible. This is Shoshone land—Chief Washakie's tribe. They've steered clear of trouble with whites so far, but a woman alone might be a different proposition."

He drew a gun from his waistband. "Ever fired a gun?"

"My father's once."

"Point it like you would your finger and pull the trigger." She took the gun from him, trying to look more confident than she felt. "Don't worry too much about hitting what you're shooting at. If it's a man, he's probably not going to stick around to give you a chance to correct your aim. If it's an animal, the sound alone will most likely run them off."

"I probably won't need it at all."

"Probably not." He eyed her uneasily, reluctant to leave now that the moment had arrived. "I wouldn't go, but if there are any supplies left on the wagons, we need them. It was a raiding party, moving fast. They may have missed some things."

"I'll be fine," she assured him. Seeing the doubt in his eyes made her determined to show him that she wasn't quite the helpless child he apparently thought her.

"Sure." He hesitated a moment longer, wishing there was some way around the necessity of leaving her alone. Maybe the trip back to the train was a waste of time. Certainly, if the Kiowa had taken all the food, it was going to be a long ride for nothing. But anything they'd left behind would be a help. And despite his words to Liberty earlier, he needed to be sure that there were no survivors.

Still, he was reluctant to go. Leaving a young woman, inexperienced and injured, alone in the midst of a hostile country, with winter not far off, did not sit well.

With a muttered curse, he turned away from her and swung himself into the saddle. The sooner he left, the sooner he'd return. He reined the roan around, stopping next to Liberty. She looked so small, her slender figure all but smothered by the weight of his coat.

She looked up at him, her eyes wide and solemn, her chin set to show that she wasn't afraid. But he could see the fear in her eyes. He brushed the back of his fingers over her cheek.

"I'll be back." The words were a promise.

"I know." She nodded and forced a small smile. "I'll be here."

Her smile faded as he nudged the roan into a canter and moved off down the hillside.

She turned away before he was out of sight. The gun he'd given her clutched in her hand, she forced back frightened tears. He'd said he'd be back, and she knew that nothing short of death would stop him from keeping that promise.

* * *

The hours seemed to drag by, yet darkness fell all too soon. Liberty filled the time as best she could. She put on her blue calico dress, shuddering at the faint traces of rusty stain that marked the once crisp white collar. She brushed futilely at wrinkles so set in they'd probably never come out. But considering the blood-stains and the bullet hole in the side, she supposed the wrinkles were the least of her worries.

Using a pine bough for a broom, she swept the floor of the cave and then spent some time arranging their meager household goods. She brought in more branches to make thicker beds, one on each side of the fire. Since she had no matches, she was careful not to let the fire go out, feeding it bits of twig to keep the coals glowing.

Whenever she left the cave, she took the gun with her, the heavy weight of it making her feel less alone. Though she'd always been inclined toward taking solitary walks and had thought herself quite comfortable with only her own company, she realized that she'd never until now known what it felt like to be truly alone.

In Pennsylvania, there was always a farmhouse or village over the next hill or the hill beyond that. And the woods and fields were full of sound—the calls of birds, the rustle of a rabbit or mouse in the fallen leaves, the clop of a horse's hooves on a road just out of sight.

Even traveling from St. Joseph across the vast prairies, the silence of the land had been broken by the creaking of wagon wheels, the steady plod of the ox-

en's hooves, an occasional shout from one of the
drivers or the laughter of a child.

There was none of that here. No voice to break the
stillness, no rustle of life beneath the dark pines, only
rarely the call of a bird.

She stood watching an eagle soar overhead. With
one hand shading her eyes, she watched him ride the
wind currents, hardly seeming to move. She wondered what it would feel like to float so high above the
earth, to see the mountains and prairies laid out beneath like a vast map.

Her breath caught when, with shocking sudden-
ness, the eagle swooped down, disappearing behind
the shoulder of the mountain.

Shivering, she turned away, feeling a strong kin-
ship with whatever small animal it had claimed as its
victim. At the moment, she felt very small and very
vulnerable. She patted the outline of the gun where it
rested against her side, its awkward bulk reassuring.

When darkness began to fall, she retreated to the
cave, which had begun to feel very much like home.
She'd soaked the beans and then simmered them most
of the afternoon. Now she built up the fire and thrust
a piece of rabbit onto a long stick so that she could
hold it over the flames. She ate one piece but saved the
other for Matt. He'd be hungry when he returned.

She wasn't as hungry as she had been earlier in the
day. Uneasily, she checked the bandage and saw that
the wound had bled again. Perhaps she'd tried to do
too much. It might have been better to have spent the
day resting instead of trying to tidy their crude shelter. She'd also brought in more wood than they were

likely to use in a week, but at least she didn't have to worry about being forced to sit in the dark.

By the time she'd finished eating, she was so tired she could hardly keep her eyes open. Yet sleep proved impossible. At first she curled up on the buffalo coat and closed her eyes. But every sound—real or imagined—brought her lids up, her eyes straining to see into the darkness beyond the fire.

She finally managed to doze but woke with a start, terrified that the fire was going to go out and leave her in darkness. For a while she gave up trying to sleep and sat up, the gun in her lap, her senses tuned for any sound that might indicate Matt's return.

Where was he?

Despite her uneasiness, Liberty fell asleep at last. Outside, a coyote slunk past the opening to the cave, pausing to sniff at the mingled scents of wood smoke and human. It cocked its head, ears pricking forward at a sound from down the slope. Identifying the sound, it darted off, disappearing into the trees just as a horse and rider appeared from below.

Liberty came awake suddenly, starting up so quickly that pain shot through her injured side. Gasping, she pressed her left hand to the wound, her right groping for Matt's gun.

There had been a noise, something beyond the usual night sounds. Her fingers clenched around the gun's grips, Liberty stared toward the mouth of the cave, straining her ears for a repeat of the sound that had awakened her.

It could be Matt. But what if it wasn't? What if it was a grizzly that had decided this would make a good winter's den? Or an Indian? Remembering the Kiowa, she shuddered. Maybe she'd been seen today. She should have stayed in the cave, as Matt had told her to do.

If asked why an Indian who'd seen her during the day would have waited until the dead of night to return, Liberty couldn't have given an answer. Her fear wasn't a rational thing. It was a fear born of exhaustion and darkness.

She heard the sharp click of a hoof against the stone and lifted the gun, aiming it shakily toward the mouth of the cave. She wouldn't shoot until she was sure of her target. A tall silhouette appeared behind the fire and Liberty felt her heart stop.

"It's Matt," he said quietly.

Relief flooded her. Matt. He was back. She hadn't let herself realize until that moment just how frightened she'd been that he wouldn't come back, that she'd be left alone in the wilderness.

"Matt!"

Without thinking, she rose to her feet and hurried forward, skirting the small fire, which had died down to embers. Matt caught her as she all but threw herself against him. With his strong arms close around her, Liberty felt all her fears drain away. She wasn't alone anymore.

Matt held her, feeling her body tremble. He knew he'd never forget the sight of her sitting across the fire, the gun pointed at whoever was approaching, her eyes reflecting both fear and determination. She had grit, there was no denying that. He didn't doubt that she'd have fired if her visitor had turned out to be someone other than himself.

"You're here. You're all right." She pressed her face against the soft buckskin of his shirt, content to savor the reality of him.

"I told you I'd be back, and I'm not one to be breaking a promise made to a lady."

Easing her away, Matt reached up to brush the heavy weight of her hair from her forehead. Her face was flushed, her eyes a little too bright. Setting his palm flat against her forehead, he felt his heart bump uneasily. She was feverish. Not a high fever, he judged, but any fever could be dangerous.

"I thought you were going to shoot me there for a minute. And with my own gun, too." He took the forgotten gun from her hand and shoved it beneath his belt.

"I didn't know it was you," she said, taking hold of his arm as if she needed the contact to be sure he was really there and not the product of some dream.

"Who were you expecting?" he chided gently. He urged her back to her bed.

"I don't know." She gave him a shaky smile. "Just about anyone from the devil to Archangel Gabriel coming to rescue me."

"Well, I don't claim to be an angel but not many would accuse me of actually being the devil." Matt's grin hid his concern. "Sit down before you fall down."

Liberty obeyed, surprised to find that her knees felt weak. She watched as Matt moved away. He disappeared for a moment and then returned, leading the roan. The horse stood with weary patience while Matt lifted the saddle from its back.

"You reached the wagon train," Liberty said. She noted that the saddlebags, empty when he left, were now partially full.

"Yes." The clipped response seemed to be all he had to offer. She didn't ask about survivors. The fact that he'd returned alone told its own story. He began rubbing down the pony with a handful of dry grass. Leaning forward, he added wood to the fire, feeding it slowly into the embers.

She balanced the pan of beans carefully on two rocks at the edge of the fire to heat. Matt was bound to be hungry. And tired. The lines around his eyes were etched deep with exhaustion as he finished caring for the roan and came over to the fire. He sat a little back from it but held out his hands to the flames.

"Nights are cooling off," he said abruptly. "There's snow in the high country already."

"So the wagons really wouldn't have made it through before winter."

"Not unless the oxen grew wings."

"All those dreams," Liberty murmured, as much to herself as to him.

They sat quietly for a few minutes, the warmth of the fire scant protection from the chill inside. Neither of them had been very close to any of the people on the train but they still felt a sense of loss. And an awareness that their own escape was little short of a miracle. There was something humbling in the knowledge that death had spared only the two of them out of so many.

"I'd better take a look at that wound." Matt broke the silence abruptly, his voice seeming unnaturally loud.

"It's all right." Her words were automatic. In truth, the injury throbbed painfully.

"You've a fever," he said roughly, stilling any additional protest she might have offered.

A fever? Foolishly, she put her hand to her forehead. It felt no warmer than the rest of her body. But then, even if she did have a fever, she wouldn't be able to feel it herself.

"It's not high," Matt said, seeing the fear in her eyes. "But it wouldn't hurt to bathe the wound. We don't have to discuss the proprieties again, do we?" His mouth quirked with a humor that failed to disguise his determination.

"I suppose it would be pretty foolish at this late date." Her fingers went to the buttons on her dress. "After all, as you pointed out, it isn't as if you haven't seen a woman's chemise before."

He just wished this one weren't filled with such a tempting woman, Matt thought a moment later as he helped her ease the dress from her shoulders. He was bone-deep tired. He wanted nothing more than food and sleep. Yet he couldn't help but notice the softness of her skin beneath his hands, the warm, sunshine scent of her hair.

He unwrapped the bandage from her waist and eased it away from her side. Liberty sucked in a quick breath as the fabric clung to the bullet wound. A film of dried blood caked the injury. Matt poured water from his canteen onto a cloth and carefully bathed the area. The skin surrounding the wound had an angry red flush to it but there was no swelling that he could detect and no smell that might indicate the wound had begun to putrefy.

"How does it look?" There was the faintest of tremors in her voice.

"Like it hurts," Matt said, pressing a clean cloth to it and securing it. "You broke it open today."

"Maybe I did too much," she admitted as he helped her slide her arms back into her dress.

"Well, I'd say there's enough wood here to last us most of the winter," he said dryly, nodding to the stack against one wall of the cave.

"I couldn't just sit here," she protested weakly as she quickly buttoned up her dress.

"Well, it doesn't look too bad. There's no swelling and it smells clean enough. If you can stay put for a little while, I think it will heal."

He sounded more confident than he felt. The fever worried him. There were those who said a fever was a healing thing, but in his experience, it could kill as easily as it could heal.

"You must be hungry," Liberty said, breaking into his thoughts. "There's beans, and I saved a piece of the rabbit for you. It's not much but it'll help take the edge off your hunger."

"Thanks. I'll get it," he said when she moved to lift the pot from the fire. "You just lie back and rest."

Liberty obeyed his orders, curling up on the buffalo coat, her hands tucked under her cheek, her eyes heavy as she watched him. Maybe it was lack of sleep or a fever-induced delirium but it seemed to her that there was something almost domestic about the scene. If she narrowed her eyes just a little, the open fire became a fireplace and the bare stone walls could be the walls of a little house.

Matt was speaking and Liberty blinked, trying to focus her thoughts on his words.

"I found some food," he was saying. "They were in a hurry and didn't take time to search all the wagons completely. There's not a lot but it will help. There were a few other things..."

He stopped, letting his voice trail off as he looked at Liberty. She was sound asleep. Her lashes lay in dark crescents against her fever-flushed cheeks. Her breathing was slow and deep, her slender body completely relaxed.

Feeling a wave of emotion he couldn't quite put a name to, Matt laid down the fork he'd been using and moved over to her. He drew the edge of the thick coat up over her shoulder, careful not to disturb her. She sighed, her mouth curving in a sweet smile.

Matt brushed back a lock of hair from her forehead, lingering when it curled around his finger, a silken shackle. The pale gold contrasted with the bronze of his hand.

Studying her face as she slept, Matt felt worry mixed with admiration. She looked so delicate, seeming as if she'd break in the least wind, but she'd shown a core of iron these past couple of days.

Remembering how hard she'd worked during the weeks the train had been traveling across the prairies, he realized he should have known there was a strength in her that belied her fragile exterior.

He'd rarely seen her without some task at hand, whether it was minding the children or helping with one of the endless tasks that went along with keeping a home, whether it was a building with four walls and a roof or a wagon crossing the plains. A time or two, he'd even seen her walking beside the wagon, dividing her attention between the path and the scraps of fabric she was sewing together for a quilt.

When the Millers had agreed to let her travel with them in exchange for help on the journey, they'd made a better deal than they could have known.

Matt's features tightened. The Millers were dead now, dead and buried. He'd dragged all the bodies into a gully not far off the trail and caved in the sides to cover them. It wasn't much but it was the best he could manage with neither tools nor time available. The needs of the living had to come first.

He tugged the coat a little higher around Liberty's shoulder and returned to his side of the fire. All he had to do now was see that they stayed among the living.

Chapter Five

Matt woke abruptly, all his senses alert. Something wasn't as it should be. He was reaching for his Colt even as his eyes opened, his muscles tensing as if for an attack.

Across the nearly dead fire, Liberty stirred restlessly, muttering in her sleep. Matt's fingers relaxed on the gun as he recognized the sound that had awakened him. But the tension didn't leave him. Dark brows hooked together as he rose from his rough bed.

His stockinged feet made no sound as he crossed the stone floor of the cave and crouched next to Liberty's bed. Fear as great as any he'd ever known shot though him. Her face was unnaturally flushed. Reluctantly, he put his palm on her forehead, his heart sinking at the heat he felt there.

Her fever had climbed during the night. He sat back on his heels and stared at her, trying to decide the best course of action. Whatever he did in the next few hours could determine whether or not she survived the day.

He tried to remember talk around campfires about what might be done to bring down a fever. In a place and time when doctors were a rarity, folks learned to do for themselves, treating ailments with herbs and remedies handed down for generations or learned from the native peoples.

Matt himself had set broken bones, once setting his own leg after a fall from his horse. He'd then ridden fifty miles to town only to have the doctor there tell him he'd done all that needed to be done. A broken bone he could have set, a cut he could have stitched up. But this was neither.

"Matt?" While he'd been studying the problem, Liberty had awakened. She looked up at him with wide green eyes bright with fever. "I'm so hot."

"You're a little feverish," he told her, brushing the hair back from her forehead.

"I'm thirsty." She ran her tongue over her lips. "So thirsty."

Matt recalled hearing that you gave fever victims all they'd take to drink, otherwise they ran the risk of dehydration. He reached out to snag his canteen from its place near the saddle bags.

"Here." He slipped one arm under her shoulders, raising her as he held the canteen to her lips. She drank thirstily and he let her have all she wanted, thankful that water was not one of their problems.

He laid her back down on the buffalo coat and gave her a quick smile. "Better?"

"Yes. Thank you." Her tone was as polite as a child's in Sunday school. She looked up at him, her gaze too bright but completely lucid. "I'm going to die, aren't I?"

"No!" The denial was sharp. He'd buried forty people the day before. He wasn't going to let Liberty become the forty-first. "You're going to be fine," he added more quietly.

"I have a fever, don't I?"

"That doesn't mean you're going to die. You just need some rest. You'll be fine."

She looked at him a moment longer and then closed her eyes, as if accepting his reassurance. Or it could have been simply that it was too much effort to keep them open any longer.

Matt screwed the cap on his canteen and stood. Staring down at Liberty's slender figure, he vowed that she wasn't going to die. Not if he had to march all the way to the gates of hell to drag her back.

There were times in the following days when he half thought that such a march could have been no more difficult than the constant watching and worrying. By afternoon of the first day, her fever had climbed until her skin seemed to burn to the touch.

In desperation, Matt stripped her clothing from her and bathed her in cool water he'd carried from the stream. She seemed a little more comfortable after that, her sleep more peaceful. Twice in the next few hours, she woke to ask for water and he held the canteen to her lips while she drank.

Sometime in the gray hours before dawn, her fever started to climb again and Matt brought more water from the stream and stroked a damp cloth over her

feverish body. She'd been unconscious but she came
awake suddenly, sitting up so abruptly that her head
nearly collided with his.

"No!" Her eyes wide and terrified, she stared at
him, seeing some demon he could only guess at. He
jerked back, avoiding the clumsy blow she aimed at
him. She swung again and he caught her hands in his.
When she continued to struggle, he wrapped his arms
around her, pulling her against his body. With a sob,
she went limp, her body trembling with exertion.

He stroked his hand over her hair, murmuring softly
to her, his words less important than the quiet tone of
his voice. When the last of the tension drained from
her, he eased her down onto the makeshift bed. Her
eyes were closed, her breathing ragged.

His face grim, Matt picked up the folded piece of
petticoat and dipped it in the cool water. He stroked
it methodically over her body, starting with her face
and then working his way down to her feet. When he'd
completed the pattern, he turned her onto her stomach and started it over again.

He was barely aware that the body he was tending
was a young, beautiful woman's. His only concern was
to fight the fever that was draining the life from her.

At dawn, with Liberty sleeping quietly, he dared to
lie down himself. It seemed he'd barely closed his eyes
when he woke, the sound of her cry echoing in his
mind. He was beside her in an instant.

She was sitting up on the bed, her arms held stiffly
out from her sides as she stared down at herself.

"Blood," she whispered hoarsely. "I've got to get
the blood off. I have to get clean."

"Hush." Matt caught her hands in his, drawing them to his chest. "The blood is all gone." Her eyes met his, but he couldn't be sure she was really seeing him. "You washed all the blood away, Liberty, remember?"

"All gone?" she questioned childishly.

"All gone." He made his answer definite.

She blinked, and for a moment her eyes were completely rational and aware. "Matt."

"I'm here."

"I'm hot."

"You've got a fever but you're getting better." He only wished he could be sure of the truth of that. "Here. You need to get some water down." He held the canteen to her lips and she drank obediently.

"You won't leave?" She clung to his hand as he lowered her back onto the coat.

"I'll be here. For as long as you need me, I'll be here."

The promise seemed to reassure her. She closed her eyes and fell into a more peaceful sleep. She dozed off and on all day. She rarely seemed aware of him as anything more than a vague presence, but there were no more bouts of delirium and Matt began to hope that her fever was starting to go down.

But as darkness fell, the fever began to climb. In the hours between twilight and midnight, Matt bathed her constantly but nothing eased her discomfort. Several times she called out for her mother and twice she lashed out at him, thinking him an attacker.

Her skin felt fiery hot beneath his touch. Her lips were cracked and dry, and when her eyes were open, she saw only her own demons.

In desperation, Matt swept her up in his arms. Holding her cradled against his chest, he carried her from the cave to the stream, the path clear in the light of a full moon. He set her down just long enough to strip off his clothes. Naked, he picked her up and carried her into the water.

Kneeling near the center of the stream, he lowered Liberty into the cold water. She cried out as it hit her feverish skin, and she tried to lunge from his hold. Matt ground his teeth together and held her in place, cradling her against his body as if he could absorb some of her pain.

He didn't know if what he was doing was going to cure or kill her. But he knew the fever would surely be fatal if something didn't bring it down. He held her in the water until her skin felt cool and his teeth began to chatter. He made his way to the bank of the stream and gathered up his clothes. Wrapping Liberty in his shirt, he carried her back to the cave.

By his best estimate, she slept peacefully for two hours or more and then started to toss and turn as the fever began to climb again. Matt watched with something approaching despair. Did he dare take her back to the stream? The cold water had seemed to bring down the fever, at least temporarily.

She whimpered as if the heat were burning her from the inside out. Matt reached for her, intending to carry her back to the stream.

Her skin was damp.

Exhaustion had made his thoughts slow and stumbling. He drew back his hand and stared at it before reaching out to touch her again. His first thought was that she was still damp from her earlier immersion, but that wasn't possible. Only minutes ago, her skin had been hot and dry.

He stared at her, blinking stupidly at the sheen of moisture that coated her pale body. Sweating. She was sweating. The fever had broken.

Matt was too tired for elation. Instead, he felt a slow swell of relief. Her fever had broken. She was sweating. He reached out to take her hand, wondering if it was possible that her skin felt cooler already.

Fumbling with exhaustion, he bathed the dampness from her skin, forcing himself to remember that a fever could break, only to return again. But not this time. Not with Liberty. She was going to recover. He could feel it in his bones.

When the sweating seemed to have stopped, he bathed her again and then refolded the coat so that she was lying on a dry surface. He draped the blanket from his bedroll over her.

He dozed and woke to check for fever and then dozed again and woke again. When dawn began to break and there was still no sign of the fever returning, he let the creeping exhaustion take him and fell heavily asleep, one hand on Liberty's arm, the feel of her cool skin following him into sleep.

The cave was bathed with sunlight when Liberty woke. Because of the way it angled into the mountainside, very little direct light reached past the en-

trance, but the light reflected from the sandstone walls
to cast a warm ivory glow into the cavern.

She lay staring at the wall for a long time, aware that
her entire body ached. She felt as if she'd been cruelly
beaten—every joint, every inch of skin felt bruised and
sore.

She turned her head to the side, finding it almost
more than her strength would allow. Why was she so
weak? Blinking to clear the blurriness from her vision, she found herself looking at Matt. He was
slumped against the wall, his chin resting on his chest.
His jaw was shadowed by a heavy growth of beard and
there were hollows around his eyes. Deep lines were
etched on either side of his thick mustache, making
him look gaunt and worn.

She realized that he was holding her wrist, his hand
pinning it against his knee as if shackling her to him.
It took more effort than she'd have believed possible
to move her arm.

He jerked awake the moment she moved, his eyes
snapping toward her. Liberty was startled by the intensity of his look, followed a moment later by a
blazing relief. He reached out to put his hand on her
forehead, his lean face breaking into a grin when he
felt the coolness of her skin.

"Welcome back," he said, still grinning.

"Where have I been?"

"You've been sick. Feverish." Matt sat back on his
heels, seeming content to just look at her, absorbing
the miracle of her recovery.

"How long?"

"Three, four days." He shrugged. "I lost track of time."

Three or four days? Liberty frowned, trying to remember. She shook her head, unable to call up more than vague images. "I don't remember."

"Just as well." Matt touched her forehead again, as if to be sure the fever really was gone.

She started to sit up and then fell back, clutching the much too thin blanket at her throat.

"Where are my clothes?" she asked, panic making her voice sharp.

"Over there." Matt nodded to where her dress lay, her undergarments brazenly folded on top. "I had to bathe you to get your fever down and I couldn't do it with your clothing on."

"Oh." She avoided looking at him. She could feel the color coming up in her face until she was sure it must look as if her fever had returned. She was completely naked under the cover. It had been embarrassing enough when he'd seen her in her undergarments, but they'd provided at least some small amount of modesty.

"You were very sick," he said, offering her what consolation he could.

"Yes. I know." She swallowed, telling herself not to act like a silly little fool. What was needed was a certain calm acceptance—an acceptance of the necessity of his having seen her without her clothing. She swallowed again, forcing her eyes toward him.

"Thank you," she whispered, unable to bring her gaze above the level of his collarbone. "I . . . I don't remember, but I know I'm indebted to you for my life and I thank you.''

"I only did what had to be done." She saw his wide shoulders lift in a shrug. "It's thanks enough to see you doing better."

Silence fell between them. Matt couldn't remember the last time he'd been so bone-deep tired. The few hours' rest he'd had hadn't been enough to make up for the several days of short sleep rations that had gone before. For the moment, he was content to just sit and think of nothing but that he'd won the battle with the fever.

During the long hours when he'd watched over Liberty, he'd come to view her fever as a personal enemy to be faced and vanquished, a battle to be fought with cool water and determination.

He caught the anxious little glances Liberty was darting toward her clothes and shook himself, trying to dispel the urge to close his eyes and sleep a lifetime or two. He rose to his feet, arching his back to stretch the ache from his bones.

"I should look to the horse. Will you be all right if I leave you alone?"

"Yes." She didn't know whether she'd be all right or not. But she desperately wanted some privacy to don at least her chemise and pantalets. If she had to crawl to where they were, she was going to regain at least that much of her modesty.

As if he'd read her thoughts, Matt stopped and picked up her clothes. Just the sight of his large, callused hand against the white cotton of her undergarments made Liberty flush. It looked so intimate, somehow. Well, it's not as if he isn't already intimately acquainted with my person, she reminded herself and felt her flush deepen.

"You can put these on but don't tire yourself." He tossed the garments onto her lap. "You're likely to be weak as a kitten."

Liberty clutched the garments to her chest, her eyes following them as he picked up his hat and left the cave. As soon as he was out of sight, she pushed back the blanket, shivering as the cool air hit her bare skin.

She'd thought to scramble into her clothing as quickly as possible, but she soon found that Matt's prediction about her strength was accurate. Just pulling the chemise over her head left her arms trembling. The pantalets proved almost more than she could manage. By the time she'd struggled into them, she was panting as if she'd just run a race.

She lay back down, frightened by her weakness. How ill had she been? She remembered so little. Matt had gone back to the wagon train and she'd waited here for him. The last clear memory she had was of the night he'd returned. They hadn't talked much. She'd been so tired, almost light-headed. She must have fallen asleep while he was eating.

And after that?

Liberty closed her eyes, trying to remember. There was a picture of Matt's face, his eyes dark and worried. He was holding her so that she could drink from the canteen. And then another time, she had been so hot, as if she lay in the midst of a bed of coals. She'd been burning up and then there'd been the cool stroke of a damp cloth over her heated skin, soothing the fire that had threatened to consume her.

That must have been Matt, she thought drowsily. He must have carried water from the stream to bathe her. Later, when she wasn't so sleepy, she'd no doubt be terribly embarrassed by the thought of his handling her so intimately. But right now, caught in the twilight between waking and sleep, she felt cherished.

He'd saved her life so many times. Wasn't there a story that some primitive tribes believed, that when someone saved your life, some part of you belonged to them forever after? To belong to Matt Prescott... Her mouth curved in a soft smile as she drifted off to sleep.

The days that followed had an odd quality to them—a peacefulness that contrasted vividly with the turmoil that had gone before.

Liberty's recovery was slower than she had expected. For the first couple of days, it seemed as if she spent more time asleep than awake. Matt pointed out that the blood she'd lost, as well as the fever, had drained her body's reserves. It was no wonder she had so little strength.

Even when she was awake, she was content to do nothing more taxing than stare at the shadows on the walls or read from the battered volume of Plutarch's *Lives* that Matt carried in his saddlebag. She'd been surprised when he'd handed it to her.

He shrugged. "A man spends a lot of time alone out here. A good book can help to pass the time."

Three days after her fever broke, Liberty sat watching Matt carefully hone his knife, stroking the blade over the sharpening stone with smooth rhythmic movements.

Outside, darkness had fallen. Somewhere in the distance, a wolf howled, a rising note of inquiry in the call. The weather had taken a sharp turn toward winter, with the grass crisped by frost each morning. Matt had built up the fire until it snapped briskly. He'd speculated that one of the cracks in the stone ceiling must serve as a natural vent to the outside that drew the smoke up and out. If so, the cave would probably provide a damp shelter during a rain.

But it wasn't rain they had to worry about. The mountains above them had already had their first snowfall. Matt had seen the gray haze around their peaks created by the first snow of the winter. It wouldn't be long before the lower elevations also had their first dusting of white.

Liberty wasn't thinking about the possibility of snow. Her eyes drifted to Matt's chest. The lacings on his shirt allowed just a glimpse of tanned skin. She remembered seeing him without his shirt, the muscled width of his chest, the dusting of curly black hair, the strength of his shoulders.

Drowsy, she let her eyelids drift half-shut. She remembered the feel of those muscles against her shoulder, against the side of her breast. His arms had been so strong beneath her, holding her. She'd felt safe, even though the water had been painfully cold on her hot skin. Matt had held her, cradled her against his bare body, trying to ease her suffering.

His bare body.

Liberty's eyes flew open. She stared at him, frantically replaying the memories in her mind. She'd been feverish, imagining things, she told herself. Matt had said she'd been delirious. This must be some fever-induced dream.

But it was so vivid. And he had bathed her in water from the stream to try to bring her fever down. Was it so impossible that he'd also bathed her in the stream itself? And to do that, wouldn't he have had to carry her into the water, removing his own clothes before he did so?

She felt the color rise in her cheeks. She'd forced herself to accept the fact that he'd seen her without a stitch of clothing, that he knew her body nearly as well as she did herself. There'd been no one else and she wasn't so missish as to think that he should have let her die rather than try to save her life. Generally, she simply tried not to think about the intimacies he'd taken.

Really, this should be no different, she told herself briskly. Immersing her in the stream was no different from bathing her with a wet cloth.

But he'd at least had *his* clothes on then.

"I'm tired," she said abruptly. "I think I'll go to sleep now."

"Fine." Matt glanced up from his task and nodded. "I'll be doing the same before long."

Liberty smiled without looking at him and, turning her back, lay down, drawing the heavy coat over her shoulder. Staring at the back of the cave, she listened to the rasp of Matt's knife over the stone and tried to banish the mental image of the two of them, naked in the stream together.

Matt raised the knife from the sharpening stone and held it up in the firelight, testing the blade with his thumb. Satisfied, he slid the knife back into its sheath and put the sharpening stone into his saddlebag. Behind him, near the mouth of the cave, the roan shifted its weight, one hoof scraping against the rock floor.

Matt leaned forward to add a small branch to the fire. The nights were getting colder. He'd been keeping the fire going all night. He didn't dare risk Liberty catching a chill, especially not with her strength still low after the fever.

They needed to be on their way. They were more than a hundred miles from Fort Bridger. Not bad country overall. There was grass for the horse and water. Tomorrow, he'd go out and see if he could bring down a deer. If they jerked some of the meat, it would be sufficient to get them to the fort.

But it wasn't lack of food or water that was the real enemy. It was the weather they had to fear now. Autumn was fading all too swiftly. Winter was hard on its heels, so close he could almost smell it. Game was growing scarce. He'd only snared one more rabbit since the first.

If it started to snow... He frowned, letting the thought trail off. If they had two horses, they could try to beat winter to the fort. But with only one horse, they couldn't hope for speed. He was going to have to walk and lead the horse, sparing him as much as possible. They might need a quick burst of speed, if they stumbled across another raiding party.

No, the trip to Fort Bridger would be a slow one. Worrying about it wouldn't make it any faster.

He reached in his pocket for the makings of a smoke. Narrowing his eyes through the tobacco smoke, he stared at Liberty's sleeping figure.

He'd never spent so much time with a woman before, not since his mother died. He'd always been moving on, traveling over the next hill. There had never been time for more than a smile, a night or two of pleasure if the lady was willing, and then he'd be gone.

Liberty Ann Ballard was different from most of the women he'd known. He'd always made a point of avoiding women like her. They weren't the sort who allowed a man to steal a kiss—or more—and then were content to wave him on his way.

Liberty was of a different mold altogether. But these past few days, he'd found himself thinking about what it would be like to see those big green eyes warm with passion. To feel her mouth soften under his.

Muttering under his breath, he dragged his eyes from her sleeping form. He'd been doing his damnedest to forget the shape and feel of her. He'd tried to treat her as he might a younger sister.

Too bad his feelings for her weren't in the least brotherly.

He got to his feet and left the cave, making a quick check of the area. The cold night air served to cool his warm blood. Not only the chill of it but what it portended. Matt drew a deep breath, tasting the scarcely perceptible bite of snow. Not tonight, perhaps. But soon.

Chapter Six

When Liberty woke the next morning, Matt was
gone and the fire had burned down to coals. Shivering,
she reached one arm from underneath the coat and fed
twigs into the coals until flames flickered up around
them. She stayed huddled under the coat waiting for
the fire to take some of the chill from the air.

Though it seemed as if summer lay only a moment
behind, there could be no doubt that winter had nearly
arrived. Matt had said there could be a light snowfall,
followed by another spell of warm weather before
winter truly set in. But she knew he feared a heavy
snow.

Liberty slipped out from under the coat. Despite the
fire, the air was still cold and she reached quickly for
her shoes and stockings. She'd slept in her dress, as
much for warmth as for modesty. Though, considering all that had passed between her and Matt, modesty seemed a foolish concern at this point, she
admitted.

For the most part, she tried not to think about how
intimate her acquaintance with Matt Prescott had be-

come. Just thinking about him seeing her without a stitch of clothing was enough to make her whole body flush with embarrassment.

And it was no good telling herself to think of him as if he were a doctor who'd treated her when she was ill. The truth was that the feelings Matt Prescott roused bore no resemblance to the way she'd felt about Dr. Carter back home in Pennsylvania. Of course, Dr. Carter was five feet tall and nearly the same around. His hair wasn't tobacco-brown, worn just a little longer than it should have been. He didn't have golden-brown eyes and a thick mustache that gave him a wickedly rakish air.

And Dr. Carter had never knelt in a mountain stream with her naked body held in his arms, trying to draw a fever from her.

Just thinking about it made her skin warm and brought a strange tingly feeling to the pit of her stomach. No matter how much she tried to put the image from her mind, it lingered. She found herself trying to recall a clearer memory, trying to brush aside the fever-induced veil that lay between her and that night.

But no matter how she pushed and tugged at the curtain, there was no getting past it. All she had was the vague remembrance of sun-darkened skin stretched over hard muscles, the feel of that crisp mat of hair against her breasts and hands that had been at once gentle and implacable holding her in the water.

He'd talked to her. She remembered hearing his voice, clinging to it as the icy water rushed over her heated skin. But she couldn't recall his words.

Liberty shook her head and stood, favoring her injured side. If she had any proper sensibilities at all she'd be trying to forget the incident, not remember it.

It was just the enforced intimacy of their situation that was making her curiosity run in directions it had no business going.

There were cold biscuits and some bacon left from last night's supper. The Kiowa had taken most of the food from the wagon train, but in their hurry, they'd dropped a small sack of flour. It had broken open, but Matt had scraped the spilled flour from the ground and added it to their meager supplies.

Chewing on a biscuit, Liberty tried not to wonder what would happen when those supplies were gone. Perhaps Matt had gone hunting and would bring back some game. Just the thought of fresh meat made her mouth water. A thick venison steak, perhaps, sizzling hot from the pan, with biscuits and gravy.

After breakfast, she swept out the floor of the cave using a pine bough as a broom. Matt had raised his brows in silent commentary the first time he'd seen her doing the housewifely little chore. Remembering his amused look, Liberty flushed and set her chin. Perhaps it was silly to be sweeping the floor of a cave but it occupied a few minutes of her time and it gave her the feeling that she was contributing something, however unimportant.

The daylight hours passed slowly. Matt had warned her to avoid going outside the cave any more than necessary. He'd seen no sign of Indians in the area but there was no sense in taking any chances. As he'd told her once, it was the Indians you didn't see that you had to worry about. Remembering the massacred wagon train, Liberty didn't have to be told twice.

So she ignored the inviting call of the crisp weather and did her best to occupy herself. The hours dragged by, each seeming slower than the rest. She supposed it was a good sign that she was well enough to be bored, feeling too healthy to sleep the afternoon away. But it was scant consolation as the sun crept slowly across the sky.

As the afternoon wore toward evening, worry became an unwelcome distraction. Matt had been gone since early morning. Surely, if he'd expected to be gone so long, he would have wakened her to let her know.

Liberty stood in the mouth of the cave, her worried eyes going from the darkening sky to the empty slope in front of her. What if something had happened to him? He could have fallen or been bitten by a rattlesnake. Worse, he could have run into an Indian. Remembering the Kiowa brave's fierce face, she shuddered. Matt had said that the Indians in this area offered little threat, but they could change their minds.

"Don't let your imagination run away with you," she told herself, hearing her mother's voice repeating the same admonition over the years. "He's simply been delayed. No need to get yourself in a fidget about it."

The sound of her own voice helped calm her careening thoughts. Matt had spent most of his life in the west. He was no greenhorn. He knew how to take care of himself. Still, accidents could happen to anyone.

Her fingers gripped the sides of her gown, setting yet more wrinkles into the blue cotton. Her eyes strained anxiously into the twilight for some sign of the roan horse.

She was rewarded at last by a sound that could have been a hoof clicking on stone. Matt! Her heart lifted. She moved a step forward and then stopped as common sense reasserted itself. It could just as easily be an Indian.

Liberty eased back into the cave until she was hidden by the bend in the rock. She listened, ears straining. Still, Matt appeared in the mouth of the cave without her having heard another sound.

His broad figure loomed up out of the gathering darkness. Her heart bumped with fright even as she recognized him. Hearing her gasp, Matt turned, his hand dropping automatically to his gun.

Liberty hardly noticed the movement. Her relief on seeing him safe and uninjured was so great that she moved automatically, her feet flying over the rough floor.

"Matt!"

Matt's arms came up automatically, circling her slender back as her hands clutched his shoulders.

"What's wrong?" he asked sharply, feeling her tremble in his hold.

"I thought something had happened to you. I was so worried." She pressed her face against the soft buckskin that covered his shoulder.

How long had it been since someone had worried about him? Matt felt something stir in his chest, a warmth he'd never felt before. His arms tightened around her.

"I was hoping to get a deer," he said. Her hair smelled of sunshine and wood smoke. It had never occurred to him to think of those two smells as sensual but it occurred to him now.

"I'm sorry." He felt Liberty gathering herself, nudging her control back into place. Her hands pushed against his chest. Reluctantly, his arms loosened, giving her room, even as his hands lingered on her back.

"I didn't mean to be such a little idiot," she said. With her back to the fire, her eyes looked more black than green, deep mysterious pools in the pale oval of her face.

"You're not an idiot," he said automatically. Unconsciously, his fingers moved against the soft cotton of her dress, remembering the much softer feel of the skin beneath.

As she'd recovered, the intimacy of their living arrangements had made it more difficult to remember just why it was that she was off-limits. He lay awake at night, listening to her quiet breathing, and reminded himself that a woman like Liberty was the sort a man gave a wedding ring. And wedding rings weren't in his plans—not for a long time to come, if ever.

It was a difficult thought to keep in mind when she was practically in his arms, her mouth all soft and inviting and oh so close. His hands tightened, drawing her subtly closer. Liberty stared up at him, her eyes questioning.

Behind him, the roan shifted, nudging him impatiently in the back, reminding Matt that it was time to remove the annoying saddle and rub the sweat from the horse's back.

Matt's hands dropped away from Liberty as if she'd suddenly caught fire. She took a quick step backward, hiding her shaking fingers in the folds of her dress. She wasn't sure what it was she'd seen in Matt's eyes or what might have occurred if the pony hadn't taken a hand in the proceedings. And she wasn't sure whether the interruption was a relief or a disappointment, though she knew which it *should* have been.

Matt turned to tend the horse and she moved quickly to the fire, stirring up the beans she'd set to cook earlier, trying to pretend that the task took every bit of her attention.

They didn't speak again until Matt had finished rubbing down the horse. He sank down near the fire and accepted the plate she held out to him, careful that their fingers didn't touch.

When he spoke, it was of the day's failed hunting. If it hadn't been for the fact that he seemed to avoid looking at her, Liberty might have thought she'd imagined those odd, tense moments earlier. But imagined or not, they were best forgotten.

Which was easier said than done, she thought later. She watched restlessly as Matt cleaned his guns. The flickering firelight made reading difficult, and Matt was clearly in no mood to talk. There was nothing to do but watch the subtle ripple of muscle beneath the soft buckskin shirt and try to forget the feel of those same muscles under her fingers.

Annoyed with the direction of her thoughts, Liberty looked around for a distraction. Her eyes hesitated as they fell on a worn metal box that sat at the foot of her pine-bough bed.

One of the few things Matt had brought back from the wagon train, other than food, was her sewing box. By some stroke of luck, the Kiowa had missed it when they rifled the wagons. And though it was scorched from the fire that had burned most of the Millers' wagon, Liberty had cradled the metal box to her when Matt presented it, her fingers caressing the battered sides as if it contained gold.

But gold wouldn't have meant half as much to her. She'd brought very little with her when she left her home in Pennsylvania. There'd been scant room in the Miller wagon, even before they'd agreed to allow her to travel with them. Liberty had sorted through her belongings as well as those left her by her dead parents and had taken only those that were most precious.

In the midst of the devastating loss of life, the loss of her few treasures had seemed a small thing. But the sight of the sewing box, which had belonged to her mother, had brought a sharp pain to her chest, and it had taken all her self-control to keep from crying.

She'd set the box aside, unable to bring herself to open it right away. Now she reached to pick it up, feeling the familiar weight of it. Setting it on her lap, she ran her fingers over the scorch marks, knowing she'd never look at them without thinking of the

Millers and all their kindnesses to her, as well as the dreams they hadn't lived to fulfill.

Hesitantly, she lifted the lid, smiling at the familiar array of thimbles, her precious packet of needles, the scissors that had belonged to her mother, her pins. Though she knew it had to be her imagination, it almost seemed as if the box smelled of home. If she closed her eyes, she could see her mother sitting by the hearth, her needle flashing in and out of a length of cloth as she stitched some garment for her daughter or herself or worked on one of the quilts that had been her pride and joy.

Those quilts were gone now, all given to neighbors and friends, except for two that Liberty had brought with her. No doubt they'd burned with the wagon, or perhaps they were now being used in an Indian lodge. Liberty wondered if the Indian women would marvel at her mother's fine stitchery, at the care with which she'd set each piece of fabric.

Her smile trembled as she reached out to lift the scraps of fabric she'd cut before leaving home. She'd cut out the quilt and brought the pieces with her, thinking she'd have plenty of time to sew them together during the long days of riding on the wagon. There had been less time than she'd expected, and she hadn't finished more than a few blocks in all these weeks.

Her fingers smoothed over a piece of rose-colored muslin, remembering the dress it came from. She'd just turned fifteen and she'd been so proud that her mother was finally going to allow her to put up her hair. And the coarser blue cotton was from one of her father's work shirts. Her hand trembling, she reached for another piece, feeling an ache in her chest as she lifted the swatch of lavender silk from beneath a piece of piqué.

Matt made it a point to focus his attention on the guns he was cleaning, though it was a task he could have performed in his sleep. But keeping his eyes on what he was doing prevented him from looking at Liberty. Unfortunately, it didn't stop his thoughts from turning her way.

He'd nearly succumbed to the urge to kiss Liberty earlier. Perhaps that wouldn't have been such a terrible thing. But what if it hadn't stopped with just a kiss?

He'd always avoided innocent girls and not only because it was the wisest course. He preferred dealing with women of experience, women who understood the transitory nature of the encounter as well as he did. Young women had a nasty habit of expecting to exchange their virginity for commitment. It was not a trade he'd ever been interested in making.

But there was something about Liberty Ballard that drew him in a way he'd never known before. He wanted her. That much he understood. With that fall of white-gold hair and jade eyes, what man wouldn't want her? What he didn't understand—and didn't like—was the feeling he had that he wanted to protect her, to keep her safe.

Frowning, he fed bullets into the chamber on the Colt Navy revolver and snapped it into place. It was no doubt the enforced intimacy of their situation, he thought, unknowingly echoing Liberty's thinking. After all, it wasn't every day that a man handled a woman's naked body—and a delectable body, at that—and yet had to try and maintain a respectable distance from her.

A day, perhaps two, and they'd start the journey to Fort Bridger. Once they were on their way, there wouldn't be time to worry about much beyond survival. And once they arrived safely at Bridger, he'd deliver Liberty into her uncle's hands and take his own leave.

Matt slid the revolver into its holster, satisfied that he'd dealt with the problem. He reached for the rifle but his fingers had just closed over it when a sound from Liberty brought his head up. Looking across the fire to where she sat, he saw that she was fingering a square of fabric, her hand trembling.

"What is it?"

She lifted her head to look at him, and he was shocked to see her eyes brimming with tears.

"A piece of the dress my mother wore when she and my father were wed," she said slowly. "She gave it to me to put in a memory quilt. It's all I have left. My grandmother's clock, the quilts Mama made for my wedding chest, the miniatures of her and Papa— they're all gone, stolen or burned." The tears spilled over onto her cheeks.

Matt set down the rifle, but he didn't move from where he was.

"You lost a great deal," he said quietly.

"I know they were only things." Her breath caught as she tried to hold back the tears. "But they were all I had left of my family, my home."

Despite her struggle for control, new tears slipped from her eyes. Matt's fingers slowly curled into his palms. He battled the urge to go to her, to hold her.

"You have your memories," he offered in awkward comfort.

"I know." Her fingers curled over the swatch of silk. "I'm a selfish fool to be crying over a few worthless things when all those people are dead." She stopped, struggling for control. When she lifted her eyes to his, Matt could see her soul-deep feeling of loss. "It's just that I'm so alone," she said on a whisper.

He was hardly conscious of rising to circle the fire until he found himself crouched in front of her. He reached out, catching a tear on his fingertip. It was the first time he'd seen her cry. She'd weathered death and terror and illness without shedding a tear. Until now.

"You're not alone," he said, his voice husky. "I'm here."

"You told me that when I was sick, didn't you?" Liberty turned her cheek into his hand. "I remember being frightened and then you said you'd be here as long as I needed you. And I wasn't frightened anymore."

She looked at him. Her eyes were wide green pools, mysterious and inviting. Matt's fingers brushed over her cheek, feeling the dampness of her tears and the incredible softness of her skin.

"As long as you need me," he said softly, wondering if it was possible to drown in her eyes. His hand moved without conscious direction, his thumb brushing across her mouth.

Liberty's eyes widened as she felt the sudden shift in the atmosphere, the sudden change in Matt. With his back to the fire, his face was all shadowed angles, but she could feel the heat of his eyes, warming her more deeply than the fire ever could.

His thumb stroked across her mouth again and her lips parted, the invitation as clear as the innocent hunger in her eyes. Matt leaned forward, drawn to her like a moth to candle flame.

He told himself that it was only a kiss. There could be no harm in one kiss. He was only going to see for himself if her mouth was as impossibly soft as it looked. One kiss to offer comfort and then he'd go back to his own side of the fire, his curiosity satisfied.

Liberty's breath caught in her throat as Matt leaned toward her. His hand slipped to the back of her neck. Wide-eyed, Liberty watched him draw closer. He was so close that she could see the golden flecks that made his eyes more amber than brown.

He was going to kiss her. She should offer some protest, she thought, trying to grab hold of her scattered thoughts. A good girl didn't just let a man kiss her, not when there'd been no talk of commitment between them.

Her eyelids slipped downward as she felt Matt's breath on her skin, and then his mouth touched hers and the small voice of propriety trailed off, recognizing defeat.

When Billy Joe Sauderton had stolen a kiss behind his father's barn, she'd felt nothing but distaste at the sensation of his damp mouth on hers. It hadn't made her particularly anxious to sample such forbidden fruits again. At least, not until recently.

She'd thought about what it might be like if Matt Prescott kissed her, thought about it more than she had any business doing. But her imagination hadn't even come close to preparing her for the reality.

This was nothing like Billy Joe Sauderton's unwelcome salute. Matt's mouth was dry and firm, not damp and flaccid. There was nothing tentative in Matt's kiss, nothing furtive. He simply claimed her mouth for his own.

And she surrendered to that claim without so much as a whisper of protest.

Matt had told himself that he was only going to kiss her once, just taste the softness of her mouth, then draw back. A simple, innocent kiss that would serve to distract her from her hurt and at the same time satisfy his own need.

As soon as his mouth touched hers, he realized his mistake. Her lips were even softer than he'd dreamed, softer and more welcoming. Her hands came up to rest against his shirt, her fingers curling into the soft buckskin. Matt felt heat rise in his gut at her open response.

Liberty shivered in startled pleasure as his tongue came out to trace her full bottom lip. Matt took advantage of her shallow gasp, his tongue slipping between her lips to touch hers, a quick, light touch that shocked her and yet left her wanting more.

Her hands slid up his chest, feeling the ripple of muscles beneath her fingers. She had a sudden image of him without his shirt, the sun-darkened skin stretched over work-hardened muscles, the mat of curling hair that covered his chest before arrowing across his flat stomach. Her fingers flexed against his chest as if feeling the warm skin beneath his shirt.

His hand slipped to the back of her neck, tilting her head to deepen the kiss. Liberty responded instinctively, opening her mouth to him. With a groan, Matt accepted her innocent invitation, his tongue sliding deep inside her mouth, finding and tangling with hers.

Liberty's head fell back, sending an unconscious message of surrender. Her fingers gripped his shoulders, clinging to him as the world seemed to disappear beneath her.

Feeling her open response, Matt slid his hand deeper into her hair. Her hairpins had been long since lost and her hair spilled over his forearm like moon-washed silk. His other hand settled on her hip.

He knew her body as intimately as he knew his own. He'd cared for her, bathed her, seen every silken inch of her. Though he was touching only the dusty blue calico, his mind presented him with a vivid memory of pale skin and soft curves.

His hand moved upward, testing the indentation of her waist, the outward flare of her rib cage, finally coming to rest against the side of her breast. He felt her stiffen but he didn't move his hand. He drew back, meeting the uncertain green of her eyes.

Her lips were swollen from his kisses, her fair skin flushed, her eyes deep jade. Matt had never seen any woman look more desirable. He wanted her. Momentarily, there was no other thought in his head. He wanted her. Needed her. Had to have her.

Holding her eyes with his, he deliberately shifted his hand, letting his fingers trail lightly over the mound of her breast until he was touching her nipple with the tip of one finger. He heard the breath catch in her throat and her eyes widened in shock at his bold touch. But she didn't move to push his hand away.

His gaze locked on hers, Matt caught the tender bud between his thumb and forefinger, plucking it lightly until it stood up taut and hard beneath the protective fabric of dress and chemise.

Liberty felt as if she had been turned to stone, all her muscles locked in place, preventing her from moving so much as a finger. But surely, if she were stone, she'd never have been able to feel the wild sensations that were rioting through her motionless body. Her skin tingled. Her legs felt weak, and she knew that if she'd been standing she would surely have sunk to the floor in a boneless heap.

Somewhere inside, she knew she should push Matt's hand away. No doubt, she should deal him a ringing slap, too. It was wrong to sit here and let him touch her as he was. Wrong to feel her breasts grow heavy and aching. She felt the ache inside, too, lodged deep in her belly, a throbbing kind of hurt that made her press her legs together as if to alleviate the strange emptiness she felt.

Still, she didn't move, couldn't move. She could only sit there, watching as if from outside herself as he drew his right hand away from the tangled silk of her hair and reached for the buttons that marched so primly down the front of her dress. With his left hand still teasing the nipple, he unbuttoned her dress with quick efficiency.

She offered not a word of protest. In fact, she felt a quick, shameless rush of regret when his fingers left her, though it was only long enough to open her bodice. His eyes left hers at last, but only to drop to the bounty he'd bared.

The cotton chemise offered only the thinnest of shields, and Liberty felt his gaze as if it were a touch. Shuddering, she closed her eyes, hushing the frail voice of protest in her mind.

This was Matt, the man who'd saved her life more than once. He knew her body intimately. She could feel no real shame at having him look at her, at having him touch her.

And then his hand closed over her breast, cupping the heavy globe and lifting it gently. His thumb dragged across her nipple, the touch so much more acute with only her chemise between them. Liberty felt the touch all the way to her toes.

"You are beautiful." Matt's voice was hushed, almost awed. He bent close and she felt the soft brush of his mustache against her closed eyelids.

"So soft," he whispered, kissing his way along her jaw.

"So warm." His mouth slid down her throat, trailing fire every where it touched.

Liberty's head fell back, her breathing quick and shallow. Matt's lips teased at the pulse that beat so frantically at the base of her throat. Then he kissed the soft skin of her shoulders, first one and then the other. And all the while, his fingers continued to tease her taut nipple, drawing a response from her as if he were a musician and she were his instrument.

She shivered as she felt his mouth touch the upper swell of her breast. Her fingers dug into the leather of his shirt, clinging to the hard muscles beneath as the cave seemed to rock beneath her. And then his lips closed over her nipple, drawing the tight bud into his mouth, chemise and all.

"Matt!" His name escaped her on a startled gasp, her eyes flying wide with shock.

Matt's arm swept behind her, his hand pressing against her lower back, arching her so that her breasts thrust upward, offering a pouting invitation. His cheeks flexed as he drew on her. Liberty felt the drawing at her breast and again, like an echo, deep inside, tightening the ache in her stomach.

Liberty could only cling to his shoulders as sensation after sensation rocketed through her. She'd never imagined a man wanting to touch her breasts. Her innocent wondering about what might happen between a man and woman had never gone any further than the necessity of taking off her dress, a difficult enough idea.

But she felt no hesitation with Matt. She felt nothing but an intense pleasure and a feeling of rightness that made it impossible for her to question the wisdom of what was happening between them. If he chose to lay her back on the bed of pine boughs and leaves and make love to her, she wouldn't lift a finger to stop it from happening.

Matt dragged his mouth from the soft temptation of her breast, kissing his way up her throat before claiming her lips in a deep kiss that only added to the hunger burning in his gut. Their tongues met and separated only to meet again in a duel as old as time.

Liberty whimpered as he drew her onto her knees, pulling her forward until her breasts were crushed against his chest.

She was his. She didn't have to say the words. He could feel it in the pliant curve of her body, in the way she welcomed him into her mouth. She'd welcome him into her body as well. The knowledge brought an aching edge to his desire. He had only to strip the rest of her clothing away and lay her back and take her.

She wanted him as much as he wanted her. He could ease the throbbing in his loins, soothe the burning need he'd felt almost from the moment he'd first seen her; a need that had only grown stronger when they'd been forced into such intimacy after the attack on the wagon train.

In her body, he'd find release. In her sweet welcome, he'd find completion.

And what would she find?

Matt shoved the question away, slipping his hand into the heavy fall of her hair, tilting her head to deepen their kiss. But the thought wouldn't go away.

He would find completion. But what about Liberty?

Oh, he knew she'd find physical satisfaction. He had never been a selfish lover. Virgin or no, he didn't doubt that he could bring her young body to trembling completion.

But what about afterward? What about when the burning need faded and she realized what she'd done—what she'd let him do? How would she feel then? And what would happen to her later, once he was gone?

Matt dragged his mouth from hers and pressed his lips to her forehead, his brows drawing together as he tried to push the unwelcome questions out of his mind.

Take her, his body demanded. Ease the want you both feel. Tomorrow be damned. You could both be dead.

And if they weren't? the cool voice of reason asked. *If they made it to Fort Bridger despite the odds? Then what? How would Liberty feel then?*

She'd feel shamed and confused, his conscience answered with unwanted clarity. She'd have every right to expect a commitment he didn't want to give—to her or any woman.

And what if she became pregnant?

The thought hit him with the force of a blow. His own father had left his mother without a backward glance, apparently never giving a thought to the consequences of his actions. Matt had always sworn that he'd never be so careless, never leave a woman alone to bear his child.

Liberty, her senses still spinning with urges she only half understood, could sense the abrupt change in Matt. There was a sudden tension in him that had nothing to do with passion. The hands that had wrung such a shameless response from her were now still and tense on her back. Confused, she drew back, looking up into his face, seeking a reason for the change.

"Matt?" She couldn't have said what it was she was asking. Her body ached with a need she'd never felt before. But Matt's withdrawal had given her mother's years of teaching a chance to be heard.

Staring up into his taut features, Liberty suddenly saw herself as he must see her. Kneeling in front of him, her bodice lowered to her waist, the fabric of her chemise clinging damply to her swollen nipples. Her hair tumbled down her back in wanton disarray, and she knew her skin must be flushed.

"This has to stop," Matt said reluctantly.

A deeper flush rose slowly in her cheeks. But this flush had nothing to do with passion and everything to do with shame. What on earth had happened to her? She didn't know herself anymore. She couldn't possibly be kneeling half-naked in front of Matt, offering herself up to him in a completely shameless fashion.

She pulled her hands away from his shoulders as if she'd been burned. Lowering her head to avoid the contempt she was sure she'd see in his eyes, she fumbled with the bodice of her dress.

What on earth had she been thinking of? She hadn't been thinking at all, of course. From the moment Matt had taken her in his arms, intending only comfort, she'd ceased to think and had only felt. And it had felt so right to have him hold her, touch her.

But it had been wrong. She drew up her bodice, clutching it together over her breasts, wishing he'd move away. Wishing she could just die right on the spot rather than have to look at him ever again.

"Liberty." His voice was husky and she shivered, closing her eyes against the urge to hurl herself against him. "Look at me."

Matt didn't wait to see if she'd obey the quiet order. Instead, his fingers cupped her chin, tilting her face up to his. Liberty opened her eyes reluctantly, expecting to see contempt in his gaze.

"Don't look so shattered," he said softly.

There was nothing in his expression that suggested he thought any less of her. "I don't know what came over me," she whispered, half-surprised that she could get a voice past the huge lump in her chest. "I've never . . . never done anything like . . . like that."

"I know that. But you haven't committed any terrible crime." He let his hand drop from her chin, easing back on his heels, putting a few inches between them. "You were upset. You wanted some comfort. There's nothing wrong with that. It just got a little out of hand." His mouth twisted ruefully at his own understatement.

"Out of hand" didn't begin to describe the flames that had nearly engulfed them both. Even now, it would take only a touch to set the fire raging again. He could feel the need in her, see it in the soft flush that tinted her skin. And God knew, his own body ached for the release he could find in her arms.

But he couldn't do that to Liberty. She was young and innocent, with her whole life ahead of her. He wasn't going to be the one to steal that innocence and then leave her to deal with the result.

He rubbed his hands on his thighs, wishing he could rub away the memory of how she'd melted so sweetly at his touch. She'd lowered her head and was fumbling with the buttons on her bodice. Catching a glimpse of white cotton against her pale skin, Matt swallowed hard and pushed himself to his feet.

"I'll go make a check outside," he said. He turned away and then hesitated, glancing back down at her kneeling figure. "Are you all right?"

"Yes." Her voice was hardly more than a whisper.

Matt sought something he could say that would ease her embarrassment, something to reassure her that a few stolen kisses were not quite the sin she'd probably been raised to believe. But nothing came to mind. With an inaudible sigh, he walked away, leaving Liberty alone in the cave.

Once he was gone, Liberty fumbled the remaining buttons back through the appropriate slots and then ran shaking hands over her hair, smoothing away the tangles put there by Matt.

She stopped suddenly and pressed her fingers to her cheeks, squeezing her eyes shut. Somehow—and she couldn't imagine how—she had to forget the past few minutes.

Miles of wilderness lay between them and civilization. Miles during which she had to depend on Matt Prescott for her survival. She had to force herself to remember only that she needed him to survive and to forget the way his mouth had felt on hers.

Chapter Seven

While forgetting proved impossible—for both of them—Liberty and Matt did manage to put aside what had happened and rub along reasonably well together. Or, at least, so they told themselves.

If they didn't look at each other any more than was absolutely essential; if they were careful not to allow even the merest brush of fingertips; if Matt left before Liberty was awake and didn't return until dark— then it was possible to pretend that neither of them gave a thought to those passionate moments they'd shared.

Though Liberty would have sworn that she hadn't slept a bit, she must have dozed off sometime before dawn. When she woke, Matt was gone, for which she was devoutly grateful. Lying awake, her ears tuned to every move Matt made, she'd determined to treat their unfortunate embrace and her even more unfortunate—not to mention enthusiastic—participation in it as if it had never happened.

A sensible decision but one that would be considerably easier to stick to if she didn't have to look at

Matt. Even without him there, she found her memory
all too clear. She had to guard her thoughts carefully
to prevent them from turning in directions she was
determined they would not go.

She did her best to keep herself occupied, tidying up
their living quarters, bringing in a few fresh pine
boughs to replace those that had grown dried and
brittle. It occurred to her that, when she'd imagined
herself taking care of her first home, she hadn't pictured it being under quite these circumstances.

Instead of airing feather ticks, she was laying out
pine branches. Her meal preparations were severely
limited because there was only one pan available, not
to mention a frighteningly low store of food to cook.

After tidying up, she broke her night's fast with a
cold biscuit. She wasn't particularly hungry but it was
important to keep up her strength. She was almost
back to normal and she didn't want anything to delay
her recovery. The sooner they left the cave the better.
Judging by her actions the night before, it was more
than time for her to get back to civilization lest she
forget everything she'd ever learned about proper behavior. But she'd already decided not to think about
that—or about Mr. Matt Prescott.

Easier said than done. When she went to the stream
to get water, she thought of Matt bathing her fevered
body in its waters. When she ate a small plate of beans
at noon, she thought about Matt crouched on the
other side of the fire, carefully cooking pieces of rabbit the first day they'd spent in the cave.

How long ago that seemed. Liberty picked at her
dinner, a faint frown pleating her forehead. How long

had it been since the massacre? Two weeks? Three, perhaps? Her perception of time had been skewed by the period when she'd been ill. There were no clocks or calendars to mark the passing hours and days.

By now, word of the massacre must have reached Fort Bridger. Her uncle would surely believe her dead. Would he be sorry or simply relieved not to be burdened with her? She hadn't seen Harland and Marybelle Swanson since they'd moved west, more than ten years ago. She remembered her uncle as a slightly round gentleman who smiled a great deal and his wife as an even rounder woman who tended to flutter at the least disturbance.

They'd invited her to live with them, but there was no way of knowing whether it was duty or desire that had led them to do so. She sighed and addressed herself to her meal. There was no sense in worrying about it now. Though Matt hadn't said as much, she could guess that he had serious doubts about his ability to take them both safely to Fort Bridger. She could have survived the massacre only to die in the wilderness that lay between them and the fort. Only she wouldn't die alone.

Which brought her thoughts full circle to Matt again. She shook her head and stood, reining her thinking to another direction. She just needed to keep herself busy, give herself something else to think about.

Liberty was only marginally successful in disciplining her thinking for the rest of the day. True, she frequently went as much as half an hour without thoughts of Matt intruding, but intrude they inevitably did.

It was absurd to feel relieved when the object of her thinking returned in the late afternoon, but somehow, having Matt there in the flesh was better than spending quantities of time trying not to think about him. At least now she had a legitimate reason to allow him back into her thoughts.

"Got a deer," Matt offered by way of greeting as he entered the cave.

"Thank heavens." The news made Liberty's mouth curve in a genuine smile.

"We'll dry and smoke the meat as best as we can. It may be enough to get us to Bridger. We should leave as soon as possible," he continued. "The first snows will be here before you know it."

Unspoken between them was the thought that cold weather was no longer their only concern. Ironically, the fire that had been kindled last night was nearly as dangerous as the snow that could block their path.

"How soon do you think we can leave?" Liberty asked without looking at him.

"A week. Ten days at most. I want to make what preparations we can for the trip."

"Yes." Liberty nodded her agreement. She turned to add more wood to the fire, preparatory to cooking supper. Behind her, she heard Matt leave and she allowed a relieved breath to escape her. The difficult hurdle of facing him for the first time had been successfully negotiated. From now on, it would be easier.

* * *

The next few days were busy ones. There was meat to be cut and smoked, and smoking required plenty of firewood. Since the windfalls nearby had been largely depleted, gathering wood meant ranging farther from their camp. Matt was no longer as worried as before about their presence being discovered by Indians. Now, the weather was the enemy he was most concerned with.

Matt had brought back the meat in chunks that he'd bundled in the animal's hide. While Liberty was busy cutting the meat into strips and hanging it on the framework Matt had built over a firepit, he set to work to cure the hide.

Since she was now uncomfortably cold even during the day unless she was standing in direct sunlight, Liberty didn't have to ask why he was working on the skin.

Matt made another framework out of saplings he'd cut down and stretched the hide on it, using sinew to pull it taut. Then he set to work carefully scraping the bits of fat and flesh from the surface. He'd chipped an edge on a fist-sized rock and used that as his scraping tool.

Liberty tried not to let her eyes linger on him as he worked, tried not to notice how the muscles in his shoulders rippled beneath the soft buckskin of his shirt. She knew just what those muscles felt like beneath her hands, just how strong his arms had felt around her.

Sensing her gaze, Matt looked up. Golden-brown eyes met jade green. The distance was too great for her to read his expression but she feared her own thoughts must be written bold as brass on her face.

Flushing, she dragged her eyes back to the strips of meat, aware that her fingers were not quite steady. So far, her resolution not to think about the kisses they'd shared was a rousing failure. It might have been some consolation if she'd thought Matt was having an equally difficult time forgetting, but she doubted that was the case.

As he'd told her once, she didn't have anything he hadn't seen before. To him she was, no doubt, nothing more than one of many women he'd known. The thought stung but she forced herself to confront it squarely. Only a fool blinded herself to the truth just because it hurt. And contrary to her recent behavior, she was not a fool.

Matt probably saw her as little more than a burdensome female who was slowing him down. Once he'd delivered her safely to her uncle, he'd walk away without a backward glance and probably never give her another thought. Undoubtedly, he'd dismissed their embrace as simply a momentary weakness on his part and had all but forgotten the incident already.

Actually, Matt would have given much to be able to forget it as easily as she expected. Instead, he had only to look at Liberty's mouth to remember how soft it had felt under his. He found his gaze falling to her breasts and his fingers would curl into his palms, remembering the sweet weight of them in his hands.

Never in his life had a woman lingered in his thoughts the way Liberty was doing. Generally, he had no trouble banishing any woman from his thinking almost as soon as she had left his bed. But Liberty wouldn't be so easily banished. Perhaps if he'd actually bedded her, she'd be easier to forget, he thought cynically.

But there was a niggling little voice of doubt that suggested it wasn't that simple. The trouble with respectable young women was that they were too much trouble. He'd made the right decision and he didn't regret it for a minute. But knowing that didn't ease the twisting ache of desire he felt every time he looked at her.

Grinding his teeth together, he finished scraping a section of hide and shifted it on the frame so that he could reach a fresh area. A quick gust of wind blew through the small clearing, cold enough to remind Matt that he had more important things to worry about than the unaccountably strong attraction he felt to Liberty.

He glanced up at the sky, finding no reassurance in its cloudless blue arc. It might not snow today or tomorrow, or even the next day, but it would soon. He bent to work on the hide again, his face tight with worry.

If they'd had two horses, they could have tried to race the coming winter to Fort Bridger, using speed as their defense. But that option was closed to them, so they were forced to delay their departure longer than he liked in order to prepare for the cold that would almost certainly catch up with them somewhere between here and Bridger.

With care and a helping of good luck, they'd make it.

It was nearly ten days before Matt decided they'd done the best they could to prepare for the trip. It had been a busy time, with survival taking precedence over the awareness that still hummed between them.

The deerskin had been fashioned into a crude coat for Liberty. Matt had cut the scraped hide, following Liberty's directions, and she'd sewn it together into something resembling a Mexican poncho. The venison had been smoked and packed into Matt's saddlebags, along with the few remaining supplies from the wagon train.

They left early in the morning before the sun had completely revealed itself. The roan had cropped most of the grass that grew in front of the cave but what remained was coated with a thick layer of frost, a crystalline reminder of the winter now hovering over their shoulders like a chill specter.

Looking at the gold-rimmed gray sky, Liberty suddenly thought of the morning she'd slipped away from camp to watch the sunrise. She'd watched the sky lighten in the east without any idea that her entire life was about to change forever.

Shivering, she wrapped her arms around her waist and turned away from the sunrise. Matt was gathering the last of their things from the cave. Liberty wasn't concerned that she might have left anything behind. Other than her sewing box, she was wearing every belonging she had in the world.

Looking at the cave mouth, she stifled the urge to go back inside and suggest that they just stay where they were. It wasn't simply that she was frightened of the journey that lay ahead, though certainly that was part of it.

More than that, she felt as if she was leaving behind everything that was familiar. In some odd way, the cave had become home and she'd lost too many homes this past year to give up even so crude an example without a pang.

First, her parents' death had taken from her the home in which she'd grown up. Then, during the long weeks of travel west, the wagon had become a home; the other members of the party forming something nearly approaching a little village, albeit one that never rested in one place for more than a day or two. She'd started to think of the Millers as a sort of family, and had settled into her place in their ranks, enjoying the security of belonging. But the attack by the Kiowa had left her without home and family yet again.

Spending these past few weeks with Matt, she'd begun to think of the cave as a home—primitive and lacking any civilized amenities but providing shelter and protection. Now, she couldn't help but feel a tug of regret at leaving behind its comforts, scant though they were.

Leaving the cave behind didn't frighten her as much as the fact that their going brought closer the day when Matt Prescott would walk out of her life. That thought brought with it a chill that had nothing to do with the temperature.

"That's everything." Matt strode toward her, his boots crunching on the frost-coated grass. He cast a quick look at the sky. "We'll ride this morning and then walk as much as we can," he announced.

"I don't mind walking now," Liberty told him, determined not to be a burden.

"We might as well ride while the horse is fresh," he said.

Liberty moved to the horse, uncomfortably aware of her most unconventional attire. Her dress had been turned into a riding garment by the simple expedient of splitting the skirt down the middle and then stitching each side together to form a sort of pant leg.

It had been Matt's suggestion and she couldn't argue its practicality, but she still felt awkward and exposed in the new garb. But she had to admit that it was considerably more sensible than riding with her skirt rucked immodestly up around her knees.

Matt swung into the saddle behind her and reached around her to lift the reins from where they'd been looped about the saddle horn. Clicking his tongue, he nudged the roan with one heel.

Liberty resisted the urge to crane her head around for one last glimpse of the cave mouth. They were on their way, and the only sensible direction to look was forward.

She'd been injured and in shock on their swift journey from the site of the massacre to the shelter they'd found in the mountains. Her memories of that trip were vague impressions of what had seemed a nearly endless ride. Over the following days, she learned the meaning of "endless."

They traveled at a steady but not too rapid speed. Matt didn't want to risk an injury to either themselves or the roan, so he set a pace that covered ground but didn't push either animal or humans to the point where exhaustion might lead to a misstep. An injury to any one of them could be fatal to all three.

At first, Liberty tried to keep her spine rigidly straight, determined not to lean back against Matt. He tolerated this for a few miles and then he flattened his hand against her stomach and pulled her back against his chest.

"Relax. I'm not going to bite."

It wasn't him she was afraid of, she thought uneasily. With the hard wall of his chest pressed to her back, the muscled length of his thighs against hers and his arms circling her, he was practically embracing her. The intimacy of their position stirred uneasy remembrances of a time when they'd been even more intimate. Matt might be able to ignore her even when she was all but plastered against him, but she was not quite so disciplined.

But after a few hours, discomfort had pushed her awareness aside. Her legs ached from the unaccustomed strain of riding astride. Matt's saddle had not been designed to hold two people and her spine ached from the awkward position. She was grateful when Matt announced that it was time to stop. Walking would be a relief.

That first night, dusk found them out in the open, with no obvious shelter in sight. Matt found a place where a flash flood had cut a gully in the land. He worked to deepen a natural hollow, providing some shelter form the wind that cut across the open prairie, carrying a bitter chill with it.

When he'd deepened the area as much as was practical, he stood up and dusted the dirt from his hands. He turned to look at Liberty, who stood nearby, all but swaying on her feet from exhaustion. She'd walked with the wagon train but it had traveled at a slower pace. Between the morning's ride and the afternoon's walk, it seemed as if every muscle in her body was making its unhappiness known.

"I don't want to risk a fire," Matt said slowly. "It would be too easily seen."

Liberty nodded, too tired to speak. She stumbled forward and crouched in the shelter he'd made. Just being out of reach of the wind made her feel warmer. She huddled her arms under her deerskin wrap.

Outside, Matt unsaddled the roan and rubbed him down thoroughly before picketing him where the bank of the gully would provide some shelter. Carrying the saddlebags and the buffalo coat, he ducked beneath the overhang, dropping on his heels beside Liberty.

She'd been half-asleep but she roused enough to open her eyes and blink sleepily at him. Looking at her, seeing her tiredness, the pallor of her skin, Matt changed his mind about a fire. True, there was some danger if anyone should happen to see it. But there was a greater danger in letting their physical reserves drop too low.

Without a word, he went out and began gathering what fuel he could find in the short time left before darkness fell completely. Once back beneath the overhang, he built a small fire and then nudged Liberty awake. Her hands stretched eagerly toward the heat.

They had no coffee but Matt heated water and dropped some of the smoked venison into it, creating a sort of weak broth with chunks of meat. Liberty ate first, more because he insisted than because she felt hunger. The hot food warmed her from the inside out.

The meal over, Liberty became aware of the cold again. She wrapped the deerskin closer around her shoulders and drew her knees up to her chest, huddling for warmth.

"We'll sleep together tonight," Matt announced abruptly.

She blinked. *Together?* What did he mean? She watched him spread a blanket on the ground at the back of their shelter.

"Come here." He held out his hand and Liberty reached to take it automatically, letting him draw her forward. She balked as she suddenly realized just what he intended.

"Together?" Her voice rose questioningly. She tugged her hand from his, her green eyes slanting from the blanket to his face, revealed in the soft glow from the fire. "That's not necessary," she said, scooching back hastily. "I'll be just fine over here."

"No, you won't." Matt caught her hand and pulled her toward him. "I'm going to put out the fire and you'll freeze. The temperature's going to drop below freezing tonight, and that hide isn't enough to keep you warm. Shared body heat is one of the best ways to stay warm."

Of course what he was saying was completely right, completely practical. But Liberty hung back, uneasily aware that she wasn't as reluctant to share a bed with him as she should have been.

"Look, I'm not going to ravish you," Matt said bluntly. "I just want to make sure that neither of us freezes solid before morning."

"I know." She let him pull her forward and onto the blanket. He put out the fire before joining her there.

Liberty had curled up facing the dirt wall of their shelter and she couldn't prevent herself from jumping when she felt his hard body against her back. She closed her eyes, concentrating on keeping her breathing slow and steady so that Matt wouldn't sense her disturbance.

He stirred around for a moment, tugging the buffalo coat over the two of them. She'd almost managed to convince herself that she'd been foolish to be disturbed by the idea of sharing a bed with him when his arm came around her waist, pulling her back against his chest, his thighs coming up beneath her own until they were curled together spoon fashion.

All her sleepiness had vanished from the moment she'd realized that they were going to be sleeping together. Now she stared at the blackness of the wall in front of her, her eyes wide, her entire body tense.

"Relax." Matt's breath brushed her ear. He flattened his palm against her stomach, settling her more comfortably into the cradle of his body. "This is just for warmth."

Warmth? Feeling the flush that seemed to cover her entire body, Liberty half wondered if her fever had returned. At the moment, warmth was the least of her problems. She certainly could never fall asleep this way.

Behind her, Matt felt her relax. Beneath his hand, he felt her breathing slow and steady as she drifted off to sleep. He lay awake for a long time, feeling her heartbeat beneath his fingers.

Chapter Eight

Matt and Liberty kept to the pattern they had set that first day. They rode in the morning, not stopping until it was time to take a short break for the noon meal. After a cold dinner, they walked, with Matt leading the roan.

As the sun started to sink, Matt would look for a likely spot for the night's camp. If he located a place with fuel and shelter to prevent a flame from being seen, they heated water and boiled some of the smoked venison to make a primitive soup.

If he couldn't find a place that offered enough shelter, then they dined on cold smoked venison and water from his canteen. By nightfall, Liberty was generally too exhausted to care what she ate, but the heat of the fire was a welcome respite from the cold.

It seemed as if winter had followed them down from the mountains, nipping at their heels as if taunting them for being foolish enough to think they could escape its clutches. Though the sun shone during the day, the temperature didn't rise enough for her to get truly warm except at high noon.

Liberty had difficulty separating one day from another. Each was much like the one before. She no longer hesitated about sleeping in Matt's arms. As he'd said, it was the most practical way to keep warm. And sleeping in Matt's arms, it was possible to believe that everything was all right. In fact, she couldn't remember anything ever feeling quite so right as being in Matt's arms.

She'd lost track of how many days had passed since their journey began. It seemed as if she'd been traveling forever, though she knew it couldn't have been more than a few days.

She glanced over at Matt, who was leading the roan and saw him looking at the sky, his face tight and expressionless. Following his gaze, Liberty felt her stomach drop. The sky that had been a clear pale blue when they stopped at noon was now iron-gray. The sun had disappeared behind the heavy clouds bearing down from the north.

"Snow," Matt said flatly, the single word as bleak as the sky above.

Liberty shivered and drew her deerskin coat closer about her. She didn't need Matt to tell her what snow could mean to them. They were perhaps two days, maybe less away from Fort Bridger, but that estimate was based on dry ground. A heavy snowfall could double or triple that time.

Or it could ensure that they didn't reach the fort at all.

"There's a cabin a few miles from here," Matt said. "Or there was three or four years ago. I hadn't planned to go there because it's out of our way, but if we get more than a flurry or two, we'll be better off there than out in the open.''

They mounted the roan and Matt nudged him into a trot. As if the storm had only been waiting for them to recognize its presence, the temperature started to drop, though no snow fell. Matt opened the buffalo coat and drew Liberty back against him, shielding her as much as possible from the chill wind that had kicked up.

He estimated they were only a mile from the cabin when the first white flakes began to drift from the sky. Muttering a curse under his breath, he resisted the urge to nudge the pony to a faster pace. By the time they reached the ramshackle building, the snow had increased to the point where visibility was limited.

''Get inside,'' he told Liberty as he lowered her to the ground. ''I've got to take care of the horse.''

Liberty didn't need to be told twice. She hurried into the shack. Years of abandonment had left the little building in disrepair. But the walls were sturdily built of stone and served to block the wind. There were only two small windows that might have been covered with isinglass at one time but had since been boarded over, leaving the interior black as night.

Once her eyes had adjusted to the dimness, she saw that there was a fireplace on the wall opposite the door and the remains of a table and two chairs under one of the boarded-up windows. Everything was covered with a thick layer of dust.

When Matt came in, he had the saddlebags slung over one shoulder and a bundle of wood in his arms. It wasn't long before he had a fire going in the fireplace, which still drew quite well. The fire took the worst of the chill from the air but it was still cold enough that Liberty kept her poncho on, though Matt shrugged out of the heavy buffalo coat.

They talked little as they ate a hot meal of broth and venison. Though this was the most comfortable accommodation they'd had since leaving the cave, neither of them could find much joy in that thought.

Twice Matt got up and went to the door to stare out into the night. The grim set of his expression told Liberty that it was still snowing. The longer it snowed, the more difficult travel would be.

Liberty spread out the blanket at a little distance from the fire and sat on it, watching the flames while Matt paced restlessly back and forth behind her. He was like a caged animal, seeking a way out of a trap.

"Pacing isn't going to make the snow go away," she said at last, when she could bear his restlessness no longer.

Matt stopped in front of the door, glaring at the hand-hewn panel, as if he could see the snow through it.

"Maybe it will only snow a little while," Liberty said.

"Maybe." He realized that his actions could only be adding to her anxiety and turned away from the door.

Seeing the deep lines that bracketed his mouth, the bleakness of his eyes, Liberty felt her heart ache for him. She was frightened but her fear was softened by a gut-deep belief that Matt would take care of her. Matt had no one to ease the burden he carried.

She wanted to smooth the lines from beside his eyes. She wanted to put her arms around him and tell him not to worry. She wanted to tell him that she loved him.

The thought slipped in so quietly that it took a moment for its implications to strike Liberty. She caught her breath, staring at Matt as if seeing him for the first time.

Of course she was in love with him. How could she not have realized it sooner? She'd worried about her shameless response when he'd kissed her, had wondered how she could behave like such a wanton. But it had felt so right to have him kiss her, touch her.

And why not? She'd loved him even then. That was why she'd welcomed his touch and felt a guilty sense of loss when he'd been the one to pull back.

Matt moved to the door again, his hand reaching for the latch before the fingers curled into his palm and his arm dropped to his side. He turned away, his frustration palpable.

"Come to bed." Liberty heard the suggestiveness of her words and flushed but she didn't lower her eyes from his. Matt's brows rose as if he sensed something of the change in her. With a last glance at the door, he crossed the dirt floor to where she'd spread the blanket.

"We might as well try to get some sleep," she said, trying to sound calm and unemotional and not as if she'd just come to the shattering realization that she'd fallen in love with him.

"You're right." He sighed and ran his fingers through his hair. "Watching it fall isn't going to stop it." He set one of the chairs in front of the door. It wouldn't prevent anyone from entering but it would make a racket if the door was opened.

He crossed the dirt floor to where she sat, pausing to add a few more pieces of wood to the fire before he unbuckled his gun belt and laid it on the floor next to the blanket.

The past few nights, sleeping in Matt's arms had grown to feel so natural that Liberty barely gave it a thought when the time came to settle in for the night. Tonight, she thought about it. She thought about it while she watched Matt tug off his boots. She thought about it as he lay down and automatically turned on his side to gather her close.

She lay there, eyes wide, staring at the flickering shadows on the stone walls. Nothing was different tonight, she reminded herself. Nothing had changed. But everything was different and everything had changed.

She'd managed to suppress her awareness of him as a man, to pretend that she didn't feel anything when he touched her, when he held her in his arms. But realizing her true feelings for him made that pretense impossible.

A gust of wind rattled the door. Liberty shivered in response to the sound, thinking of what it must be like outside. Matt's arm tightened around her, offering silent reassurance.

What if it was still snowing in the morning? She'd heard stories of the fierce blizzards that could rage across the western lands. If this was the beginning of such a blizzard, they wouldn't be able to travel until the storm abated. And perhaps not then if the snow was too deep. How long would their meager supplies last?

They'd come so far, survived so much, yet they could still die here in this forgotten little cabin. Since they'd undoubtedly been presumed killed with the others on the wagon train, no one would ever know what had truly become of them.

She was eighteen years old, and in the past year she'd lost both parents and her home. She'd ventured westward, full of dreams, traveling with people who had dreams of their own. In the course of an hour, she'd seen all those people die and their dreams with them. She'd been shot and nearly died from the resulting infection.

She'd learned something of the passion that resided in her own body but she might not live to taste the full range of that passion. The man she loved lay pressed against her back. She didn't know how Matt felt about her, though she was not so foolish as to believe that, just because she'd realized her love for him, he had to feel the same. They could both die in the next few days, victims of cold or hunger.

Something stirred inside her, an angry denial of that possibility, a hunger to know something more of life before she faced the thought of surrendering it.

Uncertain of just what it was she was seeking, Liberty shifted tentatively until she was lying on her back.

"Can't sleep?" Matt came up on one elbow and looked down at her. Liberty was vividly aware that the hand that had rested on her hip was now lying on her stomach. She could feel the imprint of it burning through her dress.

"I don't seem to be very sleepy."

"Worrying isn't going to make it quit snowing, any more than my glaring at the door would." Matt's mouth curled in a smile.

"No." She lifted one hand to brush back the lock of hair that had fallen onto his forehead. "Your hair needs cutting," she murmured, hardly aware of what she was saying. She let her fingers slide into his hair, looking at the way her pale hand contrasted with his dark hair.

"Liberty." Matt's smile faded.

"Kiss me, Matt," she whispered, her eyes meeting his.

"You don't know what you're asking," he told her huskily. She felt his fingers move caressingly on her stomach.

"Yes, I do. Please, Matt. Kiss me and I won't ask for anything more."

The trouble was that her eyes were already asking for a great deal more than a kiss. And God help him, he wasn't sure he could stop at a kiss. How many sleepless nights had he lain awake thinking about what it would be like to hold her, to feel her skin heat at his touch?

He leaned toward her, telling himself he'd only brush a kiss on her mouth. He could offer her that much comfort. He realized his mistake the moment his lips touched hers. Her mouth softened under his, her fingers curling into his hair to draw him closer.

Matt was lost. His hand slid under her, flattening against her back and arching her into his embrace. His lips opened over hers, his tongue sliding into the honeyed welcome of her mouth.

He could no longer remember a time when he hadn't wanted her, when thoughts of her hadn't haunted his sleep. She felt like heaven in his arms, soft and warm, melting at his touch.

Her hunger matched his own, and he could no more stop himself from taking what she so sweetly offered than he could have sprouted wings to fly them safely to the fort. All his commonsense arguments as to why he should keep his distance from her faded, unwanted and unheard.

This time he was listening to the gut-level instinct that said that this was what was right. This was what was meant to be.

In a matter of minutes, she lay bare beneath him, the light of the fire dancing over her body, painting shadows and highlights as if she were a canvas for its artistry.

But if she was a canvas to be filled, Liberty knew that Matt was the one who could make her complete. Only Matt could fill the emptiness she felt inside, both physical and emotional.

She felt no shame in lying naked beneath him; no doubts about the wisdom of what she was doing. This was what was meant to be. And whether they reached Fort Bridger or died here in the wilderness, she would not regret taking this night.

And then Matt's hands cupped her breasts, and rational thought evaporated like dew before a bright summer sun. He stroked and caressed her, sweeping her senses away with every touch.

She twisted beneath him, hungry for something she couldn't have defined but only knew she had to have. With every kiss, every caress, the hunger built until it threatened to consume her.

When he pulled the buckskin shirt off over his head, Liberty's fingers buried themselves in the thick mat of hair on his chest, feeling the ripple of hard muscle under his skin. Her fingers found his flat nipples, brushing over them. She felt the muscles in his stomach jerk in reaction to the light touch. She lifted her eyes to his face, which was all hard planes and angles in the firelight.

"Witch," he murmured, his voice thick.

Liberty smiled, liking the sound of that. She liked the thought of bewitching him.

The slow sensuality of her smile hit Matt like a kick in the gut. God, was it possible that he'd ever wanted anyone else? Certainly he'd never wanted another woman the way he wanted her, not with this soul-deep need that drove him past the bounds of reason.

His fingers unsteady, he stripped off his pants, and settled back against her. Liberty's eyes widened when she felt him against her hip, hard and hot. He could see no fear, no hesitation, but he retained just enough sanity to give her a chance to change her mind.

"Are you sure, Liberty?" he whispered, his hand unconsciously tracing soft patterns on her flat stomach.

"I'm sure." Her fingers moved restlessly on his shoulders as her hips arched upward.

Looking into her wide green eyes, Matt heard a small voice inside, telling him he should stop this before it went any further. Even if it meant spending the night in the lean-to with his horse, he should put some distance between himself and Liberty.

But he smothered the nagging words. Never in his life had anything felt more right. He'd never been much of a believer in fate, but at this moment it seemed as if his entire life had been leading to this place, this instant, this woman.

He rose above her and Liberty parted her legs in instinctive welcome. She felt no fear, no uncertainty about giving herself to this man. This was what was right. This was what was meant to be.

If there was pain, it was only for a moment and the pleasure that followed soon made the pain a rapidly fading memory. With Matt's possession, she was complete in a way she'd never dreamed possible.

Matt gritted his teeth, feeling her innocent response jeopardize his control. She fit him so perfectly, as if she were made for him alone. There was an honesty in her response that he'd never experienced before. She didn't hold back anything, didn't pretend to feelings that weren't there. She was all fire and passion, taking everything he had to offer and returning it with sweet abandon. He held back, wanting to prolong the delicious torment, needing to see her reach complete fulfillment.

Liberty trembled beneath him, her body racked with feelings she'd never known, never imagined. The heat inside her increased with Matt's every move. Her fingers clung to his shoulders, feeling the sweat-dampened muscles shift and ripple.

She felt herself rushing toward some goal she couldn't quite see, some deep fulfillment that would assuage the burning ache that had begun deep inside and slowly spiraled out to encompass her entire body. She felt as if she were going to shatter into a million pieces before she could attain that unseen goal.

And then she found that the shattering *was* the goal. She arched against Matt, her nails biting into his shoulders, her body taut, her eyes flying wide with shocked pleasure.

Matt felt the delicate inner contractions caressing him and allowed his own control to slip, following her into the spinning vortex.

It was a long time before Matt could gather the strength to roll to the side. Liberty murmured a protest that trailed off when he swept one arm beneath her to draw her close against his side. She rested her head on his shoulder, liking the feel of his hard body the length of hers.

She felt warm and relaxed, completed in ways she'd never known before. She felt no regret about what she'd done, no uneasiness about what the future might bring. Whatever happened, she knew she'd made the right choice. If Matt were to disappear tomorrow, she wouldn't regret what had happened. She rubbed her face against his shoulder, letting the warm contentment lull her into sleep.

Matt felt her slip into slumber, her slender body lax against him. Even now, she felt like heaven on earth.

He'd never known such completion, never lost himself so completely in a woman's body.

He frowned up at the darkened ceiling. Unlike Liberty, he couldn't quite forget tomorrow. She'd come to him so sweetly tonight, eager and sensuous and innocent. She'd been sure of what she wanted and he'd wanted her so much he'd managed to shut out the voice of caution.

He laid his forearm over his eyes. How would she feel tomorrow? And if—no, *when*—they made it to the fort, how would she feel then?

Matt stifled a groan. He didn't even know how the hell *he* felt. How could he possibly guess what Liberty would think or feel?

Beside him, Liberty slept the sleep of the innocent while Matt lay awake long into the night. His thoughts circled restlessly until his body's need for rest finally overrode his mind's need to worry the problem and he fell asleep sometime before dawn.

Outside, a stiff wind kicked up, swirling the fallen snow into low drifts. Overhead, the clouds departed with sullen slowness. They'd served their purpose. They'd announced the change of seasons. Winter had arrived.

Matt was gone when Liberty woke. Though she felt neither regret nor shame for what she'd done, she was glad to have a few moments of privacy in which to struggle into her awkwardly altered dress and to run a comb through her tangled hair. Tangled by Matt's fingers, she thought.

Her own fingers grew suddenly clumsy as the door was pushed open and Matt entered on a wave of cold air. Past his shoulder, she saw a slice of pale blue sky.

"The snow has stopped!"

Startled that those should be her first words, Matt glanced over his shoulder as if needing to confirm their truth.

"Sometime last night," he said, shutting the door behind him.

Liberty suddenly realized that there were, perhaps, other things she should have said to the man who was now her lover. But the moment had passed and she was abruptly overcome with shyness.

"That's good," she mumbled, lowering her head to hide the blush that had come up in her cheeks. She fumbled with the leather thong he'd given her to tie back her hair and sought for something intelligent to say.

"Here. Let me do that," Matt said gruffly. He took the thong from her and moved to stand behind her, gathering her hair at the nape of her neck and securing it there with the leather strip.

"Thank you." Liberty raised her eyes to meet his, dismayed by the grim set of his features. *Was he regretting what had passed between them? Did men regret such things?*

Matt's eyes skimmed over her face, seeing the slight trembling of her mouth, the flush of color in her cheeks and the soft uncertainty of her eyes. Damn, but she was beautiful. And he'd been a fool to take her.

"You're not to worry about last night," he said abruptly.

"I'm not worried." She set her hand on his forearm, feeling the knotted muscles there. "I thought you might be regretting it."

He wanted to regret it. It had been wrong. He'd had no business taking **an** innocent girl, no matter how sweetly she'd offered herself, no matter how achingly he'd wanted her. He should have had more control.

The hell of it was that he still wanted her. Looking down into her jade-green eyes, Matt acknowledged the truth. He wanted her as much as ever. And if he didn't get her out of this cabin, he'd no doubt compound his sins by pulling her down onto the blankets and taking her up on the invitation he wasn't even sure she knew she was offering.

"I don't regret it," he said softly, knowing he was probably damning his soul to hell with the admission. He brushed a stray lock of hair back from her forehead. "I should," he admitted, his mouth twisting ruefully. "But I don't."

"And you're not to think that I'll expect . . . anything from you if we reach Fort Bridger," she told him awkwardly.

"*When* we reach Fort Bridger," he corrected her. Before she could pursue the question of her expectation, he bent to kiss her, a slow, hungry kiss that made Liberty forget what she'd been about to say, just as he'd intended it to do.

When he lifted his head, she blinked up at him, her eyes smoky green and filled with an innocent hunger that Matt felt in his gut. He swallowed hard and forced himself to move away from her before he gave in to the urge to pull her into his arms and kiss her properly.

"We need to get on our way." He crouched beside the fire, and for the first time Liberty realized venison was bubbling in broth on the hearth. "The sky's clear now," he continued, "but it smells like another storm might be on the way."

Liberty settled on the floor and accepted the mug of thin soup he handed her. She wasn't really hungry. She was too conscious of what had happened between them, too aware of Matt only a few inches away. But she drank the broth and then fished the pieces of venison out with her fingers.

She chewed doggedly, trying not to notice the smoky taste of the meat. Glancing up, she caught Matt's eyes on her, something in them she couldn't quite define. Swallowing, she gestured with the mug.

"I don't think I'll ever be able to truly enjoy venison again," she said lightly, hoping to ease the strained silence.

"It does get a bit tiring," Matt agreed. He looked at her a moment longer and then stood abruptly. Muttering something about wanting to check on the horse, he told her to meet him outside when she was done.

Liberty watched him go, wishing she could fathom something of his thoughts. Shaking her head, she popped another piece of venison in her mouth. She hoped Matt had believed her when she'd told him that she felt no regrets about last night. Whatever the future might hold, she couldn't be sorry that Matt had been her lover. It was impossible to regret something that had felt so right.

A few minutes later, she'd scattered the embers inside the fireplace, knowing that the fire would die out soon enough once it no longer had anything to feed on. Matt had rolled up the blanket they'd shared the night before and removed every sign of their presence except the pan and mug she'd used and her deerskin wrap.

Liberty drew the hide over her head and picked up the utensils. She paused at the door to look back on the shabby little cabin. The walls were plain stone, the floor was dirt and the windows were boarded over. But she'd remember the place as beautiful. Smiling at her own fancy, she stepped out and pulled the door carefully closed behind her.

Matt strode toward her, looking bigger than ever in the thick buffalo coat. He took the utensils from her and moved to where the roan stood. Shoving the items in the saddlebags, he turned back to Liberty.

"There's a cloud bank to the north that looks like trouble," he said abruptly. "I think yesterday's storm was just a warning."

Seeing the lines that pleated his forehead and bracketed his thick mustache, Liberty cast a worried glance northward. There were clouds piled up over the mountains. She didn't see anything to indicate that they offered any particular hazard but she didn't doubt Matt's concern.

"Should we stay here and wait it out?" she asked. The stone cabin suddenly seemed like a wonderfully safe haven.

"No." Matt was already shaking his head. "We don't have enough supplies to sit out a real storm. We're going to try to beat it to Bridger."

"But you said it was another two days to the fort." Liberty put her foot in the stirrup even as she offered the protest. Matt boosted her up into the saddle before swinging up behind her.

"Two days at the pace we've been going. We'll ride straight through. We won't stop for anything short of an entire Indian tribe blocking the path."

"Do you think we might run into Indians?" Liberty asked, clutching at the saddle horn as he nudged the roan into motion.

"Not likely. They're able to read the signs as well as anybody. Most Indians are too smart to be caught out in the open with the heavy snow coming."

"But it might not snow?" she questioned hopefully.

"Might not but I'm not taking any chances." He urged the pony into a fast, ground-eating walk and pointed it south.

Liberty could never remember the ride that followed with any real clarity. If she'd thought the previous days of travel were tiring, this day gave new meaning to the word. True to his word, Matt didn't stop the roan.

He kept the pace steady throughout the morning. The noon pause was only long enough to allow her to stretch her legs and retreat to the privacy of a rock outcrop for a moment. When she returned, Matt gave her a handful of smoked venison and boosted her back into the saddle. Liberty bit her lip against a groan of pain as her body protested.

If they made it to the fort, she was never getting astride a horse again as long as she lived. But she didn't voice her complaint to Matt. She could feel his tension where her back rested against his chest.

Late in the afternoon, the roan slowed as tiredness set in. Matt didn't push him to a faster pace but Liberty felt his urgency. The clouds were still behind them, though they'd drifted closer throughout the day. As if they cast a kind of shadow ahead of them, the temperature had dropped rapidly. When a sharp wind kicked up, Liberty couldn't prevent a shiver.

Without a word, Matt unfastened the buffalo coat and drew her back against him, drawing the sides of the coat as far around her as they'd reach. Liberty snuggled back, warmed as much by his concern as she was by the protection of the coat.

When dusk approached and they'd not yet sighted Fort Bridger, Liberty was sure Matt would stop and they'd camp for the night.

"It's a full moon tonight," he said, as if reading her thoughts. "As long as the clouds hold back, there'll be light enough for the pony to see."

It might have been light enough for the mustang roan to see, but Liberty's eyes were certainly not up to the challenge. To her, the landscape was all treacherous shadows once the last of the daylight had faded. The clear moonlight only seemed to make everything look more mysterious and otherworldly.

But the pony picked his way carefully through the shadows, his pace slowed as much by tiredness as by the lack of light. Several times, Matt leaned around her to stroke the roan's neck, murmuring to him. Whether it was Matt's encouragement or that the horse didn't want to spend another night out in the cold, Liberty couldn't guess. But he kept moving.

Though she wouldn't have believed it possible, she must have dozed off, or more likely, passed out from exhaustion. She didn't know how long she'd been unconscious when an exclamation from Matt brought her awake.

"What is it?" She lifted her head.

"We made it, by God!" Matt's voice was hoarse with exhaustion.

"We did?" Liberty blinked stupidly at the lights she could see ahead of them. Lights in buildings, she realized after a moment.

"Just a few more minutes, sweetheart." In the midst of realization, neither of them noticed the endearment.

"Fort Bridger?" she questioned, hardly able to believe in the reality of it. How long had it been since she'd set out from Pennsylvania with this as her goal? Years seemed to have gone by.

"Fort Bridger," Matt confirmed, his tone laced with triumph. As if sensing that they were nearly at the end of their journey, the exhausted pony suddenly picked up his pace to a jolting walk.

Liberty watched the buildings approach, trying to take it in. She was here. They'd really made it. When Matt drew up the horse in front of one of the one-story buildings, she could only sit and stare stupidly at the light spilling from its windows.

Matt reached up to lift her down but her knees gave out the minute her feet touched the ground. She clutched at his arms, trying to force strength into her joints but Matt didn't bother to wait. He swung her up in his arms as if she weighed no more than a feather and strode up to the door. He opened it by the simple expedient of putting his boot to the panel.

Matt stepped into the room and Liberty was immediately assaulted by both light and warmth. The light seemed much too bright and the warmth made her frozen cheeks burn. Also, there seemed to be a hundred startled faces turned in their direction.

After so much time with Matt her only companion, Liberty felt the impact of their gazes like blows. Afterward, she learned that there were really only half a dozen men at the sutler's when she and Matt made their dramatic entrance.

"What the hell!" That exclamation came from a big blond man sporting a straggly beard. He lunged up from a table, his hand automatically dropping to his gun, though it was obvious that there was no danger. "That's a woman!" he added, in case anyone else might have failed to notice the length of pale blond hair that spilled over Matt's arm.

With a muffled whimper of fright, Liberty turned her face into the shelter of Matt's chest and let exhaustion sweep her away into the welcoming darkness.

Chapter Nine

"Now, Liberty, I'm really not at all sure you should be getting out of bed so soon." Marybelle Swanson waved her hands in delicate little fluttering motions, indicating distress.

In the past thirty-six hours Liberty had learned that her aunt also fluttered when she was happy or when she felt strongly about something. Truthfully, Aunt Marybelle seemed to have a flutter for every occasion. And Liberty loved every one of them.

It was impossible not to love her aunt. After ten years in the west, Marybelle managed to look as if she had just stepped out of an elegant drawing room in some eastern city. Her clothing was not more than a year or two behind the very latest fashions.

Her graying blond hair was styled in fashionable ringlets that made her look like a rather plump, aging shepherdess. Her skin was lily-white and smooth as a baby's bottom; clearly the hot western sun was never allowed to shine on her unprotected face.

She spoke in quick breathless bursts and her hands were constantly in motion. If they weren't occupied with some of her endless tatting, they were fluttering aimlessly in front of her, lending even the most commonsense remarks a slightly helpless air.

Any concerns Liberty might have had about whether her aunt and uncle truly wanted her had evaporated in the warmth of their welcome. They took her to their hearts immediately, seeming to regard her more as the daughter they'd never had than as a niece.

"I'm fine, Aunt Marybelle." Ignoring her aunt's uncertain little hand movements, Liberty pushed back the covers and swung her legs over the side of the bed.

"I do think you're rushing things, Liberty, dear. After all, you went through quite an ordeal. It's never a good idea to hurry a recovery, you know."

"I wasn't ill. Only tired," Liberty pointed out, reaching for the wrapper that lay across the foot of the bed. "I slept for nearly twenty-four full hours after we arrived, and you've scarcely allowed me to set foot out of bed in the day and a half since then. The only thing wrong with me is that I'm getting *too much* rest."

"Well, if you're sure." As always, Marybelle was quick to surrender to a stronger will.

"I'm sure." Liberty gave the older woman a reassuring smile as she rose and tied the wrapper at her waist.

Though she would never admit it, she still felt quite weak, and she didn't protest when her aunt insisted that she be seated while Marybelle brushed her hair.

Seated on a plain stool, Liberty stared at the bare wall opposite and let her thoughts wander. She'd been at the fort two and a half days. Though the accommodations were stark by the standards of more settled areas, after weeks on the wagon train and then in a cave, she found them almost luxurious.

The room she was in now was in the home of one of the fort's officers, who'd graciously given up his quarters so that Liberty and her aunt and uncle would have a place to stay.

Out the window, she could see a patch of clear blue sky. The threatened snow that she and Matt had raced to the fort had turned out to be nothing more than the lightest dusting of powder. By the time Liberty had awakened from her twenty-four-hour sleep, the sun had been shining as if it planned never to stop.

Matt. An uneasy frown creased her forehead. She hadn't seen him since she'd so foolishly fainted in his arms the night of their arrival. Her aunt had told her that Matt had refused to get any rest himself until he'd been assured that she was only asleep and not ill. Marybelle also said that when Matt woke from his own much needed rest, the first thing he'd done was to check and make sure that Liberty was all right.

Surely, he must know that she was awake, she thought. But he hadn't been to see her. If it hadn't been for her aunt's reassurance, she might have thought that Matt had left the fort without bothering to say goodbye. But Aunt Marybelle said that Matt was still at the fort.

Liberty tugged restlessly at the sash of her wrapper, which belonged to her aunt. Her nonexistent wardrobe had been the cause of much distressed muttering on Marybelle's part, though there was a gleam of pleasure in her eye when she began to discuss the need for a whole new wardrobe.

Liberty was not particularly concerned with her lack of attire. She was more interested in the reason Matt hadn't come to see her. Surely, he didn't think that she would cling to him or beg him to marry her. She'd made it clear that she had no such expectations. She'd made her choices with her eyes wide open and she had no regrets. And so she'd tell Matt, if only she got the chance.

"Brandy, Mr. Prescott?" Harland Swanson lifted the decanter questioningly.

"Thanks." Matt nodded. His expression held a touch of wariness as he watched Liberty's uncle pour the amber liquid into two snifters.

Bathed and shaved, his thick mustache trimmed, Matt looked considerably better than the trail-battered man who'd ridden into the fort two days before. The sutler had provided fresh clothing, and Matt now wore a soft blue bib-front shirt, tucked into his own Levi's, which had been washed by one of the laundresses who lived in shanties at the edge of the fort.

But he still felt a great deal like a wolf who'd tumbled into a trap.

"I'm sure the captain won't mind if we make use of his liquor cabinet. He's already loaned us his house." Harland's smile was just a little too hearty, and Matt felt the wariness increase.

He swirled the brandy absently, keeping his eyes on the aimless movement. When he'd gotten the message from Harland asking him to come to the house the Swansons were occupying with their niece, he'd had a pretty good idea what it was the older man wanted to discuss. He'd been more than half expecting the summons since he woke from the twelve-hour sleep that had claimed him as soon as he'd been assured that Liberty was all right.

But expecting it and being prepared for it were two separate things. Just how was he going to respond to the questions he could see in Swanson's eyes?

"Well." Harland cleared his throat uneasily. "Well, well." He paused again, his round features distinctly unhappy. Matt waited, neither encouraging nor discouraging.

"Well, first of all, I'd like to thank you again for what you did for my niece, Mr. Prescott. I don't mind telling you that my wife and I were devastated when we heard that the Indians had wiped out the wagon train. Liberty is our only surviving relative and when we thought she'd been killed by savages we were heartbroken. Absolutely heartbroken." He shook his head, his face drawn into lines of heartbreak that sat oddly on his cheerful features.

"It must have been difficult. I regret that we couldn't have reached the fort sooner and saved you some of that pain."

"No, no. You did all you could, Mr. Prescott." Harland seemed distressed by the idea that he might have sounded in some way critical. "You've done nothing to regret."

Matt let the statement lie, though he wasn't as positive of the truth of it as his host seemed to be. He took a sip of brandy, letting the ice and fire of it burn his throat.

"My wife and I are both grateful to you, Mr. Prescott. More grateful than I can express. The Lord didn't see fit to bless us with children of our own. When Liberty wrote to tell us that her father had died and that my dear sister had followed him only a short time later, we knew immediately that the good Lord intended her to come to us, to be the daughter we might have had."

Harland stopped, his voice choked with emotion. Matt felt something akin to panic stir in his gut. Damn, did the man have to be so nice? He knew what was coming, but he'd been braced for anger and demands, not gratitude and near tears.

"I know Liberty—Miss Ballard," Matt corrected himself, annoyed at the slip, "was looking forward to joining you." Actually, he suspected Liberty had had more than a few doubts about her welcome, but those doubts must surely have been eased by now.

He'd asked around about the Swansons, and so far, he'd heard nothing to make him think that Liberty wouldn't be happy with them. The worst anyone could say about them was that they were Easterners, not having adopted the more casual speech and manners of most Westerners. That was hardly a damning flaw.

He swallowed more of the brandy and told himself that he could leave Liberty with her aunt and uncle and ride away with a clear conscience.

That same conscience reared up in protest. Was he a man like his father, then? Anxious to walk away from his responsibilities?

There was more to be considered here than the fact that Harland and Marybelle Swanson were nice people who were eager to welcome their orphaned niece into their home. That night in the cabin had left a great deal more to be considered.

Grimacing down at the remaining brandy, Matt realized that Harland was speaking again. He forced his attention back to the conversation.

"Liberty has told us most of what happened, of course," he was saying. "But I was hoping that I could hear it in your own words."

"I don't think I could add much to what Miss Ballard has said," Matt said cautiously. *Just what had Liberty said to her aunt and uncle?*

"Indulge me, if you would." Harland's smile was friendly but there was a surprising amount of steel in his tone.

Matt realized he'd underestimated the other man. A foolish thing to do. It should have been obvious that there had to be more to Harland Swanson than his jolly looks and precise way of speaking had led him to believe. A man didn't live ten years in the west and keep both his scalp and his land without having a considerable amount of iron in his backbone.

Matt lifted the snifter and tossed off the last of the brandy, setting the snifter on a side table before he spoke. He kept his voice even, almost in a monotone, as he related how he'd seen Liberty leave the wagon train and had followed her to make sure she was safe. The massacre and the ensuing fight with the Kiowa were dealt with in quick, dull sentences.

Harland listened without comment, his gaze on his own brandy—brandy he hadn't touched, Matt noted.

It wasn't until Matt mentioned Liberty's fever that he showed any interest.

"Liberty mentioned that. Said she would have died if it hadn't been for you taking care of her."

"I did what had to be done," Matt said, shrugging.

"My mother died of a fever," Harland said. "Be interested to know what you did for Liberty."

Matt saw the trap yawning wide at his feet and ground his teeth together. But there was no way to avoid it, short of refusing to answer. And he was damned if he'd do that. He'd done nothing to be ashamed of—at least not then.

"I bathed her in a stream to try to bring the fever down," he said evenly.

"Ah." The word could have meant anything or nothing. "I imagine that would have been awkward to manage with her clothes on," he said to no one in particular.

"I imagine it would have been, if I hadn't taken them off." Matt's gaze held the other man's steadily.

"Ah." Harland didn't seem to have anything to add to that. His eyes dropped to the snifter. Aimless movements set the brandy swirling in amber patterns inside the glass.

Matt let the silence stretch, determined that he wouldn't be the one to break it. He didn't answer to Harland Swanson for his actions. If anyone had the right to take him to task for what he'd done, it was Liberty.

But Harland was responsible for Liberty now, his conscience nagged. *Didn't he have a right to question what might have happened?*

"Why don't you say what's on your mind, Mr. Swanson?" he said abruptly, tired of the cat-and-mouse game they were playing.

"All right." Harland set down the untouched brandy and fixed Matt with cool green eyes—eyes remarkably like his niece's, Matt suddenly realized. "Since the death of my sister and brother-in-law, my wife and I are Liberty's only relatives, the closest things to parents that she has. I don't want to see her hurt, Mr. Prescott."

"And you think I've hurt her?"

"I don't know. My wife thinks that Liberty's in love with you."

"Did Liberty say that?" Matt asked.

"No."

The answer didn't ease the tightness in Matt's chest. Though he'd been reluctant to admit as much to himself, he knew Liberty's aunt was right. Liberty *was* in love with him or at least she *thought* she was. She wouldn't have given herself so sweetly if she didn't feel deeply for him.

"Now, I've never had daughters of my own," Harland said. "But I'd be a fool if I thought that, just because Liberty thinks she's in love with you, it means she really is. She's young and you saved her life—more than once. It's only natural that she should fancy herself in love with you."

"Why do I get the feeling that there's more on your mind than whether or not your niece loves me?"

Harland grinned but the expression didn't quite reach his eyes. "Because there is, Mr. Prescott. There is, indeed."

But he didn't seem in any hurry to expand on what else there might be. Reaching into his shirt pocket, he drew out a pipe and a leather tobacco pouch. He tugged open the pouch and dipped the pipe into it.

Matt watched impassively while the older man closed the pouch and dropped it back in his pocket before he began to carefully tamp the tobacco in the pipe. Swanson's movements were slow and deliberate. He might have nothing more important on his mind than getting his pipe ready to light. Matt knew better and his reluctant admiration increased. The older man knew how to play a waiting game. But he wasn't the only one.

Matt waited, his thumbs hooked in the pockets of his Levi's, his expression calm. He looked the picture of ease.

Harland's eyes met his over the flame of his match and Matt saw a gleam of something that could have been amusement. In a moment, the pipe was lit and fragrant smoke wafted into the air between the two men. Harland puffed a few times to make sure the tobacco was properly lit.

"Do you smoke, Mr. Prescott?"

"I picked up the habit of rolling my own while I was in Sante Fe," Matt admitted, not protesting the diversion.

"My wife thinks it's a filthy habit," Harland said with a sigh. "I daresay she's right." He puffed again.

Matt waited, determined that he wouldn't be the one to force the conversation back to the real subject matter. Shooting Matt another quick glance from those disconcertingly aware eyes, Harland took the pipe from his mouth.

"I'll be frank with you, Mr. Prescott."

"I'd appreciate that, Mr. Swanson." This time it was Matt's smile that failed to reach his eyes.

"My wife is worried about Liberty."

"She's not sick, is she?" Matt's sharp question brought a gleam of satisfaction to the older man's eyes—a gleam he quickly concealed by lowering his gaze to the pipe.

"No. Physically, she seems to be in excellent health, a fact for which we are well aware we have you to thank."

Matt shrugged, uneasy with Swanson's gratitude—gratitude his conscience insisted that he didn't really deserve. He might have kept Liberty alive but he'd taken unpardonable advantage of her vulnerability. And the fact that she'd wanted him to make love to her was no excuse.

"Quite honestly, my wife has expressed some concern about the length of time you were alone with Liberty."

It was no more than Matt had expected, and now that the moment was there, he felt surprisingly relaxed and completely clear about what he had to do. But that didn't mean he had to tell Harland Swanson his decision quite yet.

"It was a little difficult to come up with a chaperon under the circumstances, Mr. Swanson." The words were dry, revealing nothing of his thoughts.

"True enough. Even Marybelle has admitted as much, and I don't mind saying that my wife isn't always the most practical of women, especially when it comes to proprieties. She holds suchlike quite dear."

He stopped to puff on his pipe, the smoke veiling his genial features—deceptively genial, Matt acknowledged ruefully. He could have ended the conversation there and then by telling the other man that he'd decided to marry his niece. But he had to admit to a certain curiosity about Harland's approach to the subject.

"But Marybelle was willing to admit that it would be unreasonable to hold the lack of chaperoning against either of you, the circumstances being what they were."

"Then I fail to see the problem," Matt said coolly.

"The problem is my niece's feelings for you, Mr. Prescott." Harland's eyes narrowed, the geniality fading. "A girl who thinks she's in love will do some foolish things. One who thinks she's in love and also thinks she and the man she loves may not live to reach civilization..." He shrugged. "Well, there's just no telling how something like that could overset her common sense."

Though Matt's expression didn't change, inside he flinched from the blow Harland had wittingly or unwittingly delivered. Her uncle had hit on exactly what Liberty must have felt. And he, like a callow boy, had taken advantage of those feelings. He would have stopped the game then, but Harland was already speaking again.

"What I'd like to hear from you, Mr. Prescott, is a reassurance that nothing happened between you and my niece that need cause her aunt and myself any worry." There was hard demand in the look he shot Matt. Matt didn't doubt that he had a shotgun handy, ready to protect Liberty's honor if necessary.

"Have you asked Liberty?"

"She tells her aunt that you were a perfect gentleman and that there's not a thing for us to concern ourselves with."

"You don't believe her?"

"I believe she'd lie to protect you, Mr. Prescott."

Yes, she would, Matt thought, feeling something close to pain in his chest. The little fool, telling them there was nothing to be concerned about. Had she considered the possibility that she might be carrying his child? It wasn't likely that she knew otherwise.

Harland grew impatient with his silence.

"Bluntly, Mr. Prescott, I'd like your reassurance that you didn't touch my niece."

Matt's first instinct was to protect Liberty, to tell her uncle that he hadn't laid a finger on her. But if he then suggested marriage, would Harland go along with it? Or would the man want better for his niece than a drifter with little more than a good horse to his name?

"I can't tell you that, Mr. Swanson," Matt said at last. He saw anger flare in the other man's eyes. Anger but no surprise, he noted.

"You'll marry her, by God!"

"Yes." Matt didn't add anything to the flat agreement—no excuses, no apologies. Any excuses and apologies he had to make belonged to Liberty.

"Make the arrangements." He started toward the door but Harland stepped in front of him with surprising agility in one of his bulk.

"You'll be there." The words were more threat than question.

"I'll be there," Matt said coldly. He didn't like having his word questioned. But then he could hardly blame the man for doubting his honor. An honorable man would have turned away from the sweet temptation Liberty had offered.

Without another word, Matt left the small house, stepping out into the crisp air. He'd picked up his denim jacket on the way out and now, standing on the narrow plank porch, he shrugged into it.

He'd just agreed to get married.

Staring unseeingly at the low buildings that comprised the fort, he waited for the impact of the words to strike him. When they didn't seem about to knock him to his knees, he left the porch and strode toward the building where the roan was stabled.

As he walked, he startled to whistle. Odd, but he suddenly felt something remarkably close to relief. He'd been wrestling with his conscience for days now. Every time he'd almost managed to convince himself that he could simply ride away without a backward glance, two images had come to mind: Liberty's wide green eyes looking at him with such trust, and the shame his mother had lived with after his birth.

Until Will Prescott had married her and taken her six-year-old son as his own, there wasn't a day went by that Addie Bellar hadn't paid for the sin of having a child out of wedlock.

If Liberty was pregnant, his child would bear his name. And if she wasn't pregnant? Matt paused to lean against the roan's flank. If she wasn't, he couldn't honestly find it in him to regret his decision to marry her.

True, he'd never really planned to wed, but perhaps that was a foolish boy's notion. As he'd told Liberty before the Kiowa attacked the wagon train, the people who sank down roots and built something worthwhile were the ones who were going to truly settle this land.

He'd roamed the west for ten years now and had nothing to show for it but a worn-out saddle and more close calls than he cared to remember. He owned a ranch in Arizona that he'd never seen, won in a poker game in San Francisco two or three years back. He'd started out to see it more than once but always managed to get sidetracked before he got there. For all he knew, it could be nothing but desert, but there was some good land in Arizona, places a man could raise horses, some cattle.

The idea held more appeal than he would have believed a few short weeks ago. Matt shook his head and threw a blanket over the roan's back before picking up his saddle. Seemed like just the idea of getting married tended to tame a man.

But a man could do worse than settle down with a woman like Liberty. She had spirit and fire, as well as a gentleness of spirit. She'd come west, uncertain of her welcome but determined to build a good life for herself. It looked as if they'd be building it together.

"But I don't understand, Uncle Harland. Why didn't Matt stay to talk to me?" Liberty linked her hands in her lap, making a conscious effort to prevent her fingers from twisting together.

Only a short while ago, she'd been wondering why Matt hadn't been to see her. Now her uncle was telling her that Matt had been here while she was with her aunt, and that during that brief visit he'd said he wanted to marry her. And now he was gone without her getting so much as a glimpse of him.

"He was riding out with a hunting party, Liberty," Harland said soothingly. "I'm sure he'd have stayed to talk with you if he hadn't been needed elsewhere."

Liberty dropped her gaze to her hands, trying to sort out her thoughts. For almost two days, she'd been wanting to see Matt, while at the same time dreading that he might stop by only to say goodbye. Despite the current spell of good weather, winter was so close, even she could smell it. No doubt he'd want to be on his way before snow made travel difficult.

She'd been braced to say goodbye and not to lose her dignity while doing it. Instead, here was her uncle telling her Matt wanted to marry her. Marry her! When not a word of such a thing had been spoken between them!

"Did Matt say why he wanted to marry me?" she asked at last, lifting her eyes to her uncle's face. But it was her Aunt Marybelle who responded first.

"What kind of foolish question is that, Liberty Ann?" Marybelle Swanson's tatting shuttle never faltered as she lifted pale blue eyes from her work and fixed her niece with what should have been a stern look. Since she was very nearsighted and much too vain to wear spectacles, the sternness was largely dissipated by her squint as she attempted to bring Liberty's blurry figure into focus.

"What reason should he have for wanting to marry you except the one most men would have for wanting to marry a charming, beautiful girl?"

"None." Liberty realized that she'd begun to knot her fingers together and forced her hands to stillness. She could hardly explain that she was afraid Matt might have offered to marry her because he felt guilty about making love to her. Aunt Marybelle would probably have a heart attack at the very thought. And Uncle Harland, for all his mild seeming ways, just might take after Matt with a shotgun, making her a widow before she became a bride.

A bride. She lifted her hands to press them to her suddenly flushed cheeks. Married to Matt Prescott. The thought started a fluttering low in her belly. How many times had she fantasized about just that?

Even before that night in the little stone cabin, hadn't she sometimes thought that they were living much as a husband and wife? Even before the Kiowa raid had thrown them into each other's company, the man in her secret little dreams about the future had started to change.

He had no longer been a gallant but faceless presence in her fantasies. He'd taken on shape and form,

grown taller, harder. His hair had darkened to a rich
tobacco brown and his eyes were no longer sky blue
but brown tinged with gold. He'd grown a thick mustache and taken to wearing buckskins and smiling at
her quite wickedly.

The past few weeks had made those dreams seem
pathetically childish, but they'd also served to replace
the harmless fantasy with a more dangerous reality.
Matt was much more than she ever could have imagined. And what she felt for him was considerably more
than the gentle emotion she'd always imagined love to
be.

Marriage. She hadn't even really let herself think of
it as a possibility. But she didn't want it if it wasn't
marriage for the right reasons. She didn't want a husband who'd married her because he thought he had to.
She was young, but she was old enough to know that
a marriage based on duty was doomed before it began.

"Did Matt say anything to you, Uncle Harland?
Anything about...about his feelings for me?" She
flushed as she asked the question but her eyes remained steady.

Harland Swanson tamped tobacco into his pipe
while he debated his answer. Had Matt Prescott said
anything about his feelings for her? Well, that all depended on whether you only listened to what a man
said with words or if you also listened to his actions.

Though he hadn't been at the fort to see Matt carry
Liberty into the sutler's, there had been plenty who
were anxious to tell him the story; anxious, too, to tell

him about how Matt had refused to get any rest himself until he was assured that Liberty was all right.

And he'd seen the look in Prescott's eyes when he'd mentioned that Liberty's aunt was worried about her; he'd heard the sharp bite of fear in Prescott's voice when he'd asked if she was ill.

He didn't know all that had gone on between the two of them, but he was no fool and he could probably guess most of it. Two healthy young people, isolated from the usual constraints of society, left to depend on each other... Well, he would certainly be the last to cast any judgment on them.

As long as he saw his niece safely wed, it didn't much matter that they'd no doubt anticipated the wedding night.

But looking at his niece, he knew he had to weigh his answer carefully. In the set of her chin, he saw more than a trace of the stubbornness that had made him love his sister, even as he sometimes cursed her strong nature. He should have guessed that Ann's daughter would have her strength.

Ann had been capable of spitting in the devil's eye if she believed it was the right thing to do. And heaven help the poor soul who tried to convince her to do something she thought was wrong.

He didn't doubt that Liberty loved Matt Prescott. And he strongly suspected that Matt felt the same way about her, though he doubted the boy had the good sense to recognize that fact. But if Liberty thought that Matt had offered to marry her out of guilt— which he damn well should have done, Harland thought with a flare of anger—then nothing short of binding and gagging her would get her to the wedding.

"Matt doesn't strike me as a man to reveal his feelings easily, Liberty," he said at last. "But he also doesn't strike me as a man who'd do something he didn't choose to do."

That was certainly true enough, he thought, pleased with the way he'd managed to avoid the question, answering without answering.

"But did he say anything of what he felt for me?"

Damn, but she reminded him of her mother when she was the same age. Beautiful and stubborn. The thought reminded Harland of how much he missed his sister and hardened his determination to see that her daughter was properly cared for.

"He didn't have to say anything of how he felt," Marybelle chimed in. "Any fool could see it in his eyes. The boy's in love with you."

The novelty of hearing Matt referred to as a boy softened the impact of her aunt's announcement. But only for a moment.

"Do you really think so, Aunt Marybelle?"

"Of course, dear." Marybelle looked up from her tatting and squinted at her niece. "It was as plain as the nose on your face."

Since Harland suspected his wife couldn't even *see* the nose on Liberty's face, he considered this a poor choice of comparison. But Liberty didn't seem to agree. Her cheeks were flushed and her eyes were smoky green with a mixture of hope and uncertainty.

"If I could be sure," she murmured, half to herself.

Blessing his wife for seeing the proper way to handle things, Harland accepted her lead. "I never saw a man more concerned than he's been about you, Liberty. Sometimes, you have to judge a man's feelings more on what he does than on what he says. And it's not likely he'd tell me how he felt, now is it?"

"No," she agreed slowly. She tried to think clearly, knowing that the decision she made in the next few minutes was going to affect the rest of her life. She *wanted* to marry Matt, but only if it was truly what he wanted, too.

"But why didn't he ask me? Why did he ask you and then leave without even talking to me?"

"I *am* your guardian," Harland reminded her. "It's proper that Matt should ask my permission. I think he wanted to get everything settled before he left on this hunting trip. I had the feeling that perhaps he had a reason to think you'd accept him," he added slyly.

Her color deepened and her eyes dropped back down to where her fingers were once again knotted together in her lap. Yes, she supposed Matt did have good reason to think she'd accept. From the way she'd all but thrown herself at him, he couldn't have had much doubt about her feelings.

"The hunting party should be back day after tomorrow. I thought that would be a fine day for a wedding." Harland had calculated his words carefully, hoping to switch her attention to plans for the wedding, rather than worries about whether or not there would *be* a wedding.

"Day after tomorrow!" Liberty and her aunt both voiced the same exclamation.

"But what will I wear?"

At Liberty's age-old feminine question, Harland relaxed and took a contented puff of his pipe. There would be a wedding. If he hadn't believed that Matt Prescott would make his niece a good husband, he wouldn't have forced the issue. On the other hand, he suspected that if Matt hadn't been willing to marry Liberty, no force could have been brought to bear to make him.

The two of them would do just fine together.

Chapter Ten

In all her girlish daydreams, Liberty had never imagined her wedding day quite as it turned out. She'd thought her parents would be there, of course, and her friends. She'd be wearing a dress that she and her mother had made together and her father would be waiting to give her away.

The ceremony would be in a church—in spring. She'd have flowers to carry, something sweetly scented. And afterward, she and her new husband would take a short wedding journey, perhaps only a day or two but long enough to cement their identity as a couple.

None of her dreams had included a stark little ceremony in a small four-room house that was about the best the fort had to offer. Her parents were dead and buried a thousand miles away. Her friends had also been left behind. The only family she had to stand up with her was an aunt and uncle she barely knew, though they'd taken her to their hearts as if she were their own.

As for the groom...well, he bore little resemblance to her vague imaginings. Matt wasn't a fair-haired, blue-eyed knight on a white steed. But that image paled in comparison to the reality. Matt was real and vibrant, a man unlike any other she'd known.

And she loved him. If she was nervous and jittery, that was just because everything had been so rushed. It wasn't because she had any doubts about marrying Matt. How could she doubt the rightness of that step? She'd given not only her heart, but her body to him. When she'd offered herself to him in the little stone cabin, she'd made a commitment as strong as any vows spoken before God.

If only she'd had a chance to talk to Matt before the ceremony, she thought. Her hand trembled on her uncle's arm as they walked down the short hallway. She could hear the slightly scratchy sound of a fiddle—the only instrument the fort had to offer besides a trumpet.

Liberty bit her lip, uncertain whether she wanted to laugh or to cry. She'd never pictured herself getting married to the sound of a fiddle. The door loomed up ahead and her shoes suddenly seemed to be filled with lead, weighting her footsteps.

What on earth was she thinking of? How could she possibly marry Matt Prescott? She barely knew the man. She'd spent weeks alone with him, shared intimacies she could certainly never share with another man, but that didn't mean she could commit the rest of her life to him.

"I can't do it," she whispered suddenly, coming to a stop.

"Of course you can, my dear." Uncle Harland's hand patted her fingers. "You're just feeling a perfectly natural nervousness."

"I have to talk to Matt," she said. "I have to be sure this is what he wants, that it isn't just because he feels guilty over what happened."

She was unaware of how much her words revealed. Her only thought was that she needed to talk to Matt. What her uncle heard was a confirmation of what he'd already suspected. Matt Prescott had saved Liberty's life but he'd also taken her innocence. Harland's determination to see her safely wed hardened.

"Of course this is what he wants," he told her firmly. "He loves you."

"How can you be sure?" Liberty's eyes, wide and uncertain, looked at him, asking for reassurance. Reassurance her uncle gave her without hesitation.

"He said as much, my dear. I saw him only this morning and he said as much. Now, I don't think he changed his mind between then and now, do you?" he said with a twinkle in his eye.

"No," she breathed. "He said he loved me?"

She didn't seem to require a response, for which Harland was grateful. Having uttered the lie once, he was not particularly anxious to repeat it.

Seeing the radiance bloom in his niece's face, he told himself he'd done the right thing. After all, he was nearly positive that Matt *did* love her. Was it such a terrible thing to stretch the truth to reassure her? The important thing now was to get the two of them married. If, nine months from now, he was to become a great-uncle, there would be no reason for anyone to count on their fingers and come to any unpleasant conclusions.

"Your groom is waiting," he said, smiling down at her and smothering the niggling twinges of his conscience.

"Yes." Feeling new confidence, Liberty moved toward the door and the future that awaited her beyond it—a future as Matt's wife.

Matt stared out into the darkness, his fingers drumming restlessly on the windowsill. There was nothing to be seen beyond the windowpane but the slow drift of the falling snow. But he wasn't really interested in scenery at the moment.

He was married.

He reached up to loosen his collar, though he knew that the choking sensation had less to do with the heavily starched linen shirt than it did with the ceremony that had taken place a few hours before.

Married.

Thrusting his fingers through his hair, Matt turned away from the window. Liberty was in the bedroom just across the narrow hall, preparing for her wedding night. Matt crossed the room with quick strides. Picking up the heavy decanter that sat on a low table, he poured himself a stiff shot of Scotch. Lifting the glass, he downed the contents in two swallows, feeling the liquor burn its way down his throat.

Shuddering, he rolled the empty glass between his palms, debating the wisdom of a second drink. But getting drunk on his wedding night was hardly the best way to start off his marriage. Besides, what was he so nervous about? Wasn't it the bride who was supposed to be jittery?

Glass met table with an annoyed snap. Shoving his hands in his pockets, Matt turned away from the table, intending to go back to the window. But he stopped with the movement only half-completed. His bride stood in the doorway and Matt felt his breath, as well as most of his wits, desert him.

How was it possible that her beauty could still surprise him? He'd thought she looked beautiful in the ivory silk gown she'd worn as a wedding dress, a garment of her aunt's that had been quickly altered, she'd told him shyly when he'd commented on it after the ceremony. But seeing her now, wearing a simple white cotton wrapper, was like seeing her for the first time all over again.

Her hair spilled over her shoulders like a moonlight-colored cape. The light wrapper hinted at curves he knew only too well. Matt felt desire rise in him, wiping out any doubts he might have about finding himself a married man.

He didn't love Liberty, but he wanted her as he'd never wanted any woman in his life. He couldn't imagine the time ever coming when he didn't want her. Marriages had been based on less.

The look in Matt's eyes sent a nervous shiver up Liberty's spine. During the brief ceremony that had made them husband and wife, she'd stolen glances at him, searching for some sign that he loved her, as he'd told her uncle he did. All she'd seen was a rather stern expression that had made her wonder if he was already regretting the step they were taking.

But seeing the way he was looking at her now, she felt her doubts melt away. Too inexperienced to know that desire and love did not necessarily go hand in hand, she saw the warmth of Matt's gaze as confirmation that he loved her.

When Matt crossed the room to take her hands, her eyes skittered away from his, unable to sustain the burning heat of his gaze. His look made her feel like a particularly succulent sweetmeat that he was thinking about devouring.

"You look beautiful," he said, his voice husky.

"Thank you. One of the officers' wives gave me the wrapper as a wedding gift. She seemed to think it most improper that I had nothing to wear on my wedding night," she added.

"*That* sounds even better to me." Matt's hand slid up her arms, drawing a tingling awareness in their wake.

"I thought you might feel that way." She cleared her throat, suddenly doubting the wisdom of what she'd done. "That's why I left the nightgown off," she admitted in a voice so low he had to strain to hear it.

She felt the sudden tension in the fingers on her shoulder, heard the quick breath Matt sucked through his teeth. Fearing he might be angry, might think her too bold, Liberty dared a quick glance at him through her lashes.

His eyes were closed, his expression almost pained. But when his lashes lifted, it wasn't anger they revealed. Liberty felt her knees buckle under the burning heat of his look. His eyes seemed more gold than brown, their touch almost physical as they drifted downward to where the wrapper closed over her breasts.

Trembling, she kept her gaze on his face as his hands slowly slid down the collar of the wrapper to where the belt looped about her narrow waist. She felt the brush of cool air on her skin as the belt dropped to the floor and the wrapper fell open. But then Matt's hands were on her, cupping the soft weight of her breasts and she felt anything but cool.

Liberty's hands settled on Matt's lean hips, clinging for support as his thumbs brushed over her nipples, teasing the sensitive buds to hardness.

"You are so beautiful," he whispered against her throat.

"I love you." The words simply couldn't be held back a moment longer. Saying them was as necessary as breathing, as right as the feel of his ring on her finger. "I love you."

She felt a sudden stillness in Matt, as if he were surprised. She waited, hardly breathing, for his response. He hadn't given her the words before, but now that he knew she loved him just as he loved her, he'd say what was in his heart.

But whatever was in Matt's heart, he didn't seem inclined to let her know. For the space of several heartbeats, he didn't move, hardly seemed to breathe. And then, so suddenly that Liberty felt the breath catch in her throat, he bent to sweep her up in his arms. Liberty's arms clung to his neck as he carried her across the hall into the bedroom and laid her on the bed.

He tugged the wrapper open until it lay on the bed around her, a soft frame for her slender body. His eyes were like molten gold pouring over her, his hands tracing the path scarcely a heartbeat behind his look.

Stunned by the sudden rise of passion, Liberty arched into his touch. Her pulse pounded in her ears, drowning out the small voice that questioned his lack of response to her words of love.

"I want you," he whispered against her breast.

The tiny voice of doubt was stilled. He said he wanted her. What she heard was that he loved her. Only two hearts fully in tune could produce the sensations rioting through her.

Matt's clothing was stripped away, tossed to the floor and forgotten. He'd planned to make their lovemaking last all night. After all, she was his wife now. They had all the time in the world. But then she lifted her arms to him and looked at him with those incredible eyes full of love, and all he could think of was the need to be a part of her, to confirm that she was his.

He retained enough control to keep from plunging his aching hardness into her. Though she was no longer a virgin, she was far from experienced. He eased into her slowly, the pace a sweet torture that left him burning with hunger.

A hunger only she could satisfy. She clung to him as he began to move, her hips lifting in the rhythm he'd taught her. Her hands moved up and down his back, seeking something to cling to as the world started to spin around them.

Matt watched her face, seeing passion's flush warm her cheeks, the heavy-lidded need in her eyes. The sight, he discovered, was nearly as powerful an aphrodisiac as the feel of her holding him, drawing him deeper into her.

He felt a new tension enter her and knew she was nearing her peak. He increased the pace, clinging to his thinning control, needing to see her reach her own fulfillment as much as he needed his own.

Liberty's eyes suddenly snapped wide open, her fingers digging into his shoulders as she arched against him. Matt felt the delicate contractions ripple around him, felt his climax approaching, but still he held back, wanting—needing—something more. Something he couldn't define.

"I love you." The words came out on a cry as she shuddered beneath him.

As if that was the signal he'd been awaiting, Matt released the last tenuous hold on his control and let the powerful waves of completion wash over him.

When Liberty woke the next morning, she was aware of a feeling of contentment unlike anything she'd ever known before. It was more than simply the physical relaxation of a body that had been very well loved. It was the deep contentment that came with knowing that Matt's ring was on her finger.

Smiling, she stretched, aware even without opening her eyes that Matt wasn't in the bed. But he'd been there last night. Her smile took on a sensuous curve. He'd awakened her twice, bringing her to shuddering fulfillment almost before her eyes were open each time. He'd been insatiable.

"You look like a cat who's just had a big saucer of cream."

At the sound of Matt's voice, Liberty's eyes flew open. She sat up in bed, hardly noticing when the covers fell down around her waist. But Matt noticed. His eyes dropped to her breasts. Her hair, tangled from sleep and loving, fell over her shoulders, creating a partial veil for her sleep-warmed body.

Despite the promise he'd made himself to keep his distance from her, Matt felt his loins tighten. God, what was it about her that tied his gut in knots and made him forget everything but the need to hold her?

"Is that coffee?" Oblivious to the picture she presented, Liberty referred to the cup Matt held.

"Yeah." Matt made a conscious effort to drag his gaze from her body. "I thought you might like some."

"Thank you."

Because she was looking at him expectantly, he crossed the room. He was just going to hand her the coffee and then walk away, he told himself. He knew exactly how things would end up if he stayed close to her.

But when he handed her the cup, she lifted her face expectantly. Of course he had to kiss her good-morning. It would only hurt her feelings if he didn't. Her mouth softened under his, her lips parting. Matt sank down on the bed. One arm came around her back to draw her closer, and he felt her breasts press against his chest, seeming to burn through the fabric of his shirt.

Left sitting on the floor, the coffee grew cold.

* * *

More than an hour later, Matt stood in front of the dressing table preparing to shave. He could see Liberty in the mirror as she buttoned up her dress. It was another garment given to her by the wife of one of the officers at the fort, and it was a little too big for her slender frame. He saw her faint moue of annoyance as she tugged at the loose waist.

Actually, he was somewhat grateful for the gown's poor fit. He seemed to have lost his self-control when he'd slipped a ring on her finger. Or was it when he'd heard her say she loved him? Frowning, he dragged his gaze back to his reflection and dabbed shaving cream on his cheeks.

The words didn't really mean anything, of course. She was young. He was her first lover—her *only* lover, he thought possessively. It was natural that she should think she was in love with him. Women had a tendency to think that physical fulfillment and love went hand in hand.

That wasn't necessarily the case, but there was no need to explain that to Liberty. They were married now and it made no difference if she thought she was in love with him. Just as well, really.

Matt frowned at his reflection, hearing the passion in her voice when she'd told him how she felt, seeing it in her eyes. To tell the truth, he liked hearing her say it. Absently, he dabbed more shaving cream over the layer already on his face.

He liked it more than he particularly wanted to admit. The words seemed to speak to something deep inside him, some part of him he'd never known was there. Just hearing them made something strong and warm well up in his gut.

Yeah, lust, you idiot. You want her, that's all. And who wouldn't? She's a beautiful woman. And she's yours.

Matt's gaze drifted again to Liberty's reflection in the mirror. She was making the bed, humming a soft tune to herself as she worked. She'd pinned her hair up on top of her head. The soft style suited her, bringing out the delicate bone structure of her face.

Matt felt some emotion he couldn't quite define. A mixture of possessiveness and need. He wanted to protect her and he wanted to throw her back on the bed and make love to her again, to hear her cry out his name, hear her say she loved him.

He realized that Liberty was looking at him, her eyes meeting his in the mirror, their expression questioning. Suddenly aware that he was standing there like a statue, the razor clutched in his fingers, Matt looked away from her and dipped the blade in the bowl of steaming water.

It must be getting married that had temporarily addled his brain. For a moment there, he'd almost started to wonder if he could be falling in love with his wife.

Chapter Eleven

Liberty watched Matt begin to shave, feeling wonderfully content. Glancing down at her left hand, she admired the way the sunlight caught on the plain gold band that adorned her left hand. The ring had belonged to Matt's mother. She'd been surprised and touched when he told her where it came from. It seemed an oddly sentimental gesture for him to have kept it all these years. She didn't think sentiment came easily to Matt.

Which was no doubt why he hadn't yet told her he loved her. She tried to ignore the little ache in her chest. She was being foolish to even think about it. As Uncle Harland had said, you just had to read some men's feelings from their actions, not their words.

And Matt's actions had surely proved that he loved her. A man couldn't make love to a woman the way he'd made love to her the night before unless he loved her. Still, it would be nice to hear the words, she thought wistfully. Perhaps what he needed was an opening. She reached for her stockings, which she'd draped across the bed.

"It's stopped snowing." As a prelude to coaxing a declaration of love from her husband, it seemed safe enough.

"Yes." Matt stroked the razor down his cheek.

"You know, everything happened so quickly, we haven't had much time to talk."

"Umm." Matt rinsed the blade and carefully shaved around a sideburn.

"I mean, we haven't talked about anything," she persisted. "I don't know where we're to live or how we're going to get there. Nothing at all."

"I've got a ranch in Arizona," Matt said slowly, almost as if reluctant to part with the information. "I haven't seen it myself. Could be nothing but desert, but it could be decent range."

"Is there a house?" Liberty asked, already arranging her kitchen in her mind.

"I'd guess there's some kind of house but I doubt it's much."

"It can always be fixed up."

Liberty pulled one stocking over her foot and then stopped and looked at him again. She didn't really want to talk about their house, appealing as that topic was. What she really wanted to talk about was how he felt about her. Obviously, she needed to try another angle.

"When Uncle Harland told me that you'd asked to marry me, I didn't know what to think." If Liberty hadn't been watching him so closely, she might have missed the expression that flickered across Matt's face. She might not have seen the quick, involuntary jerk of surprise, gone almost before it happened.

"I'm relieved you made up your mind," Matt said, after a barely perceptible pause. His fingers were steady as he stroked the razor down his cheek.

"You did ask Uncle Harland if you could marry me, didn't you?" she asked, wishing the words unsaid as soon as they left her mouth.

"We discussed it," he said evasively. Matt's eyes met hers in the mirror for an instant before he bent to rinse the razor in the bowl of water before him.

In that quick glance, she read the truth he hadn't said. Their marriage hadn't been his idea. It must have been her uncle's. Which meant Uncle Harland had lied to her, by omission if not directly. And if he'd lied about that, what else might he have lied about?

Let it go, you little fool, she thought. *You're married. What difference does it make how it came about?*

Liberty finished pulling up the first stocking, trying to ignore the sudden flood of unwelcome thoughts. So many things were suddenly made clear. Her uncle saying that Matt hadn't taken time to ask her to marry him because he had to leave and wanted everything settled before he went. The fact that he hadn't made any effort to see her before the wedding.

Of course he hadn't asked her to marry him. Because he hadn't wanted to get married at all. And why should he worry about seeing her before the wedding? He'd known he was going to be stuck with her for the rest of his life. Why see her any sooner than he had to?

Her fingers were shaking by the time the second stocking had been smoothed over her calf. She didn't have to close her eyes to hear Uncle Harland telling her that Matt had said he loved her. Words Matt had yet to speak himself.

Because it wasn't what he felt, she thought bleakly. He *hadn't* married her for love. He'd married her out of guilt and perhaps even because of some threat from her uncle. Uncle Harland must have guessed what had happened between them, not a difficult feat, really. A blind man could have seen how she felt about Matt.

So her uncle had made sure that she and Matt were married, worried no doubt about the possibility that she might be pregnant. And he'd sensed that she wouldn't marry Matt unless she believed he loved her, believed that he *wanted* to marry her. So Harland had told her what she wanted to hear and she'd fallen for it like the veriest child.

Liberty closed her eyes, feeling hurt and humiliation well up inside. Her tumble from sweet contentment to despair was made all the harder by the sense of betrayal she felt. She'd trusted her uncle and he'd lied to her.

But worst of all was what Matt had done. Oh, he'd never said he loved her. But he'd let her go on and on like a lovesick fool, when all the while he'd known he didn't care for her.

Her chest ached as if a fist had closed over her heart and was squeezing the life from it. In her mind's eye, she saw herself as she'd been last night, wild with passion, melting in his arms.

And prattling about love like a stupid child.

I love you, Matt.

God, how many times had she said those words? And when he hadn't offered vows of love in return, she'd told herself it was just because he was a man and found it difficult to express what he felt.

Especially when he didn't feel anything at all.

Liberty picked up a shoe and jerked it on with force enough to nearly rip the leather. What an idiot he must have thought her. Protective anger started to well up, smothering the hurt. He'd let her make a fool of herself, encouraged it, really. It must have amused him no end to listen to her prattling on about love.

Maybe he'd even been glad to hear the words, thinking it might make her a more biddable sort of bride, less likely to argue with him. She jerked on the other shoe, feeling her temper climb. No doubt, he thought he'd married a silly little female, one who had no more sense than to fall in love with a man who didn't care a fig for her.

And why shouldn't he think as much? she asked herself furiously. She'd all but thrown herself into his arms, nearly begged him to make love to her. Of course, she'd thought that they were probably going to die, but that didn't make her feel any less the fool.

"It wasn't your idea to get married at all," she said bleakly. "Was it?"

Matt was patting his face dry and he didn't bother to lower the towel to see her expression before he answered. If he had, he might have chosen a different response than the one he did.

"What difference does it make whose idea it was? It's done."

His words reflected nothing more than a normal male reluctance to hash over events that couldn't be changed. To Liberty, it sounded as if he were saying he was resigned to his fate.

Her temper flared hotter. How dared he make marriage to her sound one step above a prison sentence! As sure as she had been moments ago that she loved him, she was now equally sure that she'd never hated anyone the way she hated Matthew Prescott.

Somewhere inside she knew that her anger was unreasonable. After all, it was her uncle who'd lied to her, not Matt; her uncle who'd said Matt wanted to marry her, that he loved her. It wasn't Matt's fault if Harland Swanson had said he felt things he didn't.

But she wasn't in love with her uncle. She was in love with Matt. She'd married Matt thinking that he loved her. The pain of finding out how wrong she'd been cut deep and hard. Her anger was a protective measure against the pain. If she got angry, maybe it wouldn't feel quite so much as though her heart had just broken into a hundred pieces.

"Whether the wedding was your choice or not makes a difference to me," she said evenly.

This time, Matt caught the tightness in her voice. Dropping the towel, he turned to face her. Though she looked as cool as the snow outside, something in the stillness of her expression warned him that a wise man would choose his words carefully.

"Your uncle brought it up first," he admitted. "But the thought had been in my mind."

"Why?"

"Why?" Matt had been reaching for his shirt, but the stark question made him stop and turn to look at her. "Why what?"

"Why did you think about marrying me?" Liberty had risen from the bed and she now stood next to it, her hands linked together in front of her, her eyes steady on his.

"What difference does it make why I thought about it?" Matt asked, his voice taking on an irritated edge. In his mind, there was no reason to discuss *why* they'd gotten married.

"I want to know why."

A glance at the stubborn set of her jaw told Matt she wasn't going to let the topic go without a fight. Annoyed, he picked up his shirt and jerked it on.

"I think it should be obvious why I was thinking about it," he told her shortly. God, why was it that women always had to make things so complicated?

"Because of what happened in the cabin?" Her tone made it half statement, half question.

"That's right." Matt buttoned his shirt, hoping she would just let the whole subject go.

"I told you then that you didn't have to feel obligated to me."

"You thought we were going to die. Hell, *I* thought we were going to die."

"So the only reason you . . . made love to me was because it wouldn't matter if we were both about to die?"

"Well, it wouldn't have made any real difference if we were going to freeze to death, now would it?" Something in her tone made him feel as if he were on the defensive, a position for which he had no liking. The feeling put an edge to his tone that he hadn't really intended.

"If I'd had the sense of a prairie chicken, I would have slept in the lean-to with the horse," he muttered, tucking his shirt into his Levi's.

"And then you wouldn't have had to marry me," she finished. This time, the hurt showed through the anger. Hearing it, Matt felt something twist in his chest.

"Look, I don't know why you're ragging at this," he said. "We're married. Isn't that enough?" He reached to take her hands but Liberty drew back as if stung.

"I thought the marriage was your idea."

"It would have been if your uncle hadn't gotten to it first." Matt made an effort to keep his impatience from showing in his voice.

"I told you I loved you," she said accusingly. "And you let me!"

"What should I have done?" he asked. He watched her, his eyes unfathomable.

If Liberty had held out any hope that he might say he loved her, it died beneath that cool look. He couldn't possibly look at her like that if he cared for her. The ache in her chest was almost unbearable.

"You let me make a fool of myself," she cried. She skirted the bed, wanting to put more distance between them. "You must have been laughing at me all the time."

"No." Matt rejected the idea that he'd found her declaration of love amusing. "I wasn't laughing."

If Liberty hadn't been blinded by pain, she might have heard the protest in his voice, might have seen the gentleness in his eyes as he reached for her. But her hurt went too deep to allow her to see anything beyond it.

"Don't touch me!" She jerked away from his touch, stumbling past the corner of the bed.

"Fine." Matt's arms dropped back to his sides, his expression shuttered.

"I wouldn't have married you if I hadn't thought you cared about me."

"Of course I care about you," he said impatiently. "I married you, didn't I?"

"Because you thought I might be pregnant," she snapped. "You wouldn't have married me otherwise, would you?"

"Why worry about what I might have done?" he asked, trying to sidestep the gaping hole she'd opened at his feet. "We're married now."

"Would you have wanted to marry me if you hadn't thought I might be carrying your child?" she asked, her voice like iron.

For the space of several heartbeats, the room was dead quiet. Liberty waited for Matt's response, hope flickering in her, despite the anger that stiffened her spine. If only he'd say that he loved her...

Matt knew exactly the words that would heal the breach between them. All he had to do was to say yes. Yes, he'd have married her one way or another. But it would have been a lie. And he didn't like the way she'd backed him into a corner, hammering at him as if he'd done something to feel guilty about.

She was his wife. That should be enough. He wasn't going to go down on his knees and beg her to forgive him for lies he hadn't told.

"No." The word fell into the silence like a stone into a pond. "No, I wouldn't have married you if there was no possibility of a child."

Though she'd already known it, Liberty felt the words strike her with the force of knives. The pain was so sharp, she wouldn't have been surprised to see blood flowing from half a dozen wounds.

She closed her eyes for a moment and when she opened them again, they were as bleak as the snow-bleached landscape outside.

"Get out." The words were flat and expressionless and had more impact than if she'd shouted them.

"We *are* married, Liberty," Matt told her, trying to rid himself of the feeling that he'd just destroyed something very precious. "You're my wife. You could be carrying my child. What difference does it make *why* we wed?"

"It makes a difference to me. I was stupid enough to think you loved me. But you can't even *like* me if you'd just let me make a fool of myself the way I did last night."

"I didn't think you were making a fool of yourself," he snapped. "I thought you were... That it was...nice." The bland word hardly began to describe the way he'd felt when she'd said she loved him.

"I'm sure it was very *nice* to think you'd married a lovesick little fool who'd be happy to do your bidding and expect nothing in return but a few scraps of your attention."

"That's not what I thought." Matt realized that he was nearly shouting and stopped. Thrusting his fingers through his hair, he tried to understand how everything had changed so quickly. It wasn't that long ago that she'd been melting in his arms. Now she looked as if she hated him.

"I don't care what you thought," she said, even as her heart whispered that she was lying. "I want you to go away. I don't want to see you ever again." She half turned away as if the sight of him was more than she could stand.

Time, Matt thought. Time apart was the best thing right now. And more than a few hours, he decided, looking at her set profile. This was more than a simple snit that she was going to recover from in an afternoon. The hurt went deep.

He rubbed one hand over the back of his neck, feeling suddenly very old and very tired. A short while ago he'd been holding a warm and very willing woman in his arms. He'd just about decided that marriage wasn't such a bad thing overall and was starting to look forward to taking Liberty to Arizona, to building something there together.

"I'll go for now," he said at last, his voice as weary as he felt. "I'll go to Arizona, check out the ranch. I'll come back in the spring."

"Don't bother."

"You're my wife, Liberty."

"Yes. But I won't live with you. There's no reason for you to come back." Liberty could feel her heart breaking with every word she spoke. Part of her—the part that loved him no matter what—wanted to say that it didn't matter if he loved her. Her love would be enough for both of them.

But her hurt and anger were stronger. She felt humiliated and betrayed. The knowledge that he didn't feel anything more than regret when she felt as if acid were eating into her vitals only added to her rage. She wanted—needed—him to feel just a small portion of her pain.

"What if you *are* carrying my child?" Matt asked evenly.

"Then I won't be for long," she said, her tone all the more harsh for the pain the question caused her. If she'd hoped to get a reaction from him, she was successful. Matt moved as quickly as a striking diamondback, his fingers hard on her upper arms as he jerked her to face him.

"What are you talking about?"

"There are ways for a woman to rid herself of unwanted burdens," she said recklessly. She had no idea if it was true. She just wanted to hurt him.

She got her wish. She saw the impact of her words in the way his eyes darkened, in the way the skin tightened over his cheekbones. He looked as if he'd been struck. She was glad if she'd hurt him, she told herself. Glad. Which didn't explain the fact that she seemed to be dying inside.

"If I thought you meant that, I'd take you with me and keep you chained to my side."

"I do mean it!" But something in her eyes must have given her away. Matt's bruising hold eased on her arms. Shaking his head slowly, he released her and took a step back, visibly regaining control of his temper.

"No, you don't." He shook his head. "You don't mean it, but if you were hoping to make me go, you've got your wish."

"Good."

Matt picked up his hat, his tight hold creasing the brim. "You're hurt and you're angry," he said, turning to look at her. "But you're still my wife. I didn't plan on getting married but, having done it, I don't plan on having a wife who lives apart from me, either."

"Then you'll have to change your plans," she flung at him.

"No. I'll be back in the spring. If you're pregnant, we'll wait here for the birth before heading south. But pregnant or not, you're my wife and I'll be back to claim you."

"I won't be here," she threatened, feeling panic well up inside.

"Then I'll come find you," he told her flatly. He settled his hat on his head and fixed her with a cool look. "You're my wife, Liberty. And I'll be back for you."

He strode from the room without another word. Liberty listened to the sound of his boots in the hallway and then the opening and closing of the front door.

She stood there for a long time.

Chapter Twelve

Six Years Later

Though the calendar said it was spring, the weather held more of winter's bite than spring's soft caress. Matt swung down from the roan's back and looped the reins over the hitching rail in front of the saloon.

A breeze cut around the corner of the false-front building, causing him to hunch his shoulders under the worn denim jacket. Boot heels echoing on the wooden slats, he crossed the boardwalk and pushed open the saloon's door.

It was the middle of the afternoon and the clientele consisted of two old men playing a desultory game of poker at a table near the potbellied stove, a drunk passed out at another table and half a dozen men standing at the bar. There was a piano in the corner, and Matt guessed that the place would be pretty lively once the sun went down.

He wasn't particularly interested in lively at the moment. All he wanted was a shot of whiskey to warm away the chill of a long ride, and some information. Though, to tell the truth, he wasn't quite sure just what he'd do with the information if he got it.

Six years was a long time. If he had any sense, he'd have his drink, get back on his horse and head south, back to a place where spring didn't have such a bite to it.

But for six years, a pair of jade-green eyes had lingered in his dreams. Six years, and he still couldn't forget the woman who'd been his wife for less than twenty-four hours before she'd thrown him out of her life.

He wouldn't think of her for weeks and then he'd see something that would bring her image to his mind as sharp and clear as if he'd seen her only the day before. He couldn't have said what it was that had made her so difficult to forget. She'd made her wishes clear enough on that long-ago winter day.

He'd told her he'd be back and he'd meant it, but he hadn't expected to take six years to fulfill that promise. Or had it been a threat? he wondered ruefully. A little of both, perhaps. He'd been nearly as angry as she that day. Her anger had been born of hurt. And his? Well, no man liked to hear his bride of one day telling him to get out of her life.

Shaking his head, Matt downed the last of the whiskey and signaled for another. He'd planned to come back that spring, just as he'd told her he would. Had she looked for him? Had she been just the smallest bit disappointed when he hadn't shown up? Or had she felt nothing but relief?

He cupped the fresh drink between his palms. If war hadn't broken out in the east, would he have come back for her? Or would he have decided to take her at her word and stay out of her life? It was impossible to say now.

War *had* broken out, and he'd traveled to Pennsylvania to enlist, to fight for the preservation of the Union, a cause that had meant little to him until its existence was threatened. He'd spent some time in uniform, but his skills as a tracker and scout had been deemed more valuable than his presence in a regimental lineup.

Five years of fighting. The Union had been saved, but Matt was no longer sure the cause had been worth the terrible price it had cost. He'd mustered out after Lee's surrender and headed west, going home, though there was nothing that really deserved that name waiting for him. A year of wandering and somehow he'd found himself heading north with the spring, chasing after a dream he didn't want to admit he had.

Grimacing at his foolishness, Matt downed the second whiskey in two gulps and set the glass on the bar. There was no sense in delaying. Either he was going to ask if she was still in the area or he was going to go out and get on the roan and head south.

"I'm looking for Liberty Prescott," he said, to no one in particular.

There was a moment of silence while the others digested the piece of information. One of the old men playing poker looked up from his hand, squinting rheumy blue eyes at Matt.

"There's a Liberty Prescott runs a place north of here. The Swanson place."

"She runs it?" Matt wasn't sure whether to be glad or sorry that his question had been so easily answered.

"Has since her uncle was bushwhacked a year or more ago. Though she did a lot of work around the place afore that."

"What about her aunt?"

"Went back east right after they buried Swanson. Said she'd only stayed because of him, anyway. Heard she tried to get the niece to go back with her, but she wasn't havin' none of it. Said her uncle wouldn't have quit and neither would she. Done a right good job of things, too, from all I hear."

"How would I get to the Swanson place?" Matt asked, half thinking that he could still turn and ride away.

"I wouldn't bother going out there." That was one of the men at the bar, a slender young man with eyes that seemed too old for his face.

"Why is that?" The look Matt turned on him was cool and disinterested.

"Liberty Prescott's going to marry John Randall, and he's not likely to appreciate strange men turning up on her doorstep."

Matt had been reaching into his pocket for the money to pay for his drinks but the other man's words made him freeze for an instant. Slowly, he withdrew his hand and tossed the necessary coins on the bar.

"I don't think so," he said pleasantly.

"You don't think what?" the other man demanded.

"I don't think she's going to marry John Randall or anybody else," Matt said calmly.

"And why not? Just who the hell are you to be saying that?"

Matt settled his hat more firmly on his head and gave the man a cool glance. "I'm Matt Prescott. Her husband."

Matt got the directions he needed from the hostler at the livery stable. Though common sense suggested that he find a place to spend the night and think about what he wanted to do next, he ignored it. The doubts he'd had about seeing Liberty had vanished the moment he heard someone say that she was engaged.

What the hell was she doing getting engaged when she still had a husband? Did she think he was dead? Did she think that, after six years, it no longer really mattered?

Wanting to reach the ranch by nightfall, he nudged the roan into a slow canter. Really, he had no right to be angry, he told himself. He was the one who'd disappeared for six years. If Liberty had assumed herself to be a widow, he had only himself to blame.

But that didn't change the fact that she was far from being a widow. And she had no right to get herself engaged.

If it occurred to him that his anger was out of proportion to the crime, Matt dismissed the idea. Just as he'd consistently refused to look too closely at the reasons she'd haunted his dreams, even after six long and bloody years.

The sun was low in the sky when Matt turned the roan onto the roughly marked road that should lead to the Swanson ranch. The word *road* was an exaggeration. It was little more than a vaguely defined set of ruts in the grass.

He'd gone less than half a mile when the trail curved around an outcrop of rock. Matt drew the horse to an abrupt halt when he saw the rider waiting in the middle of the path. It wasn't the presence of the man alone that impressed itself on Matt. It was the rifle that was resting across his thighs, its muzzle pointed with deceptive casualness right at Matt's gut.

Matt was careful to keep his hands in plain sight. Something in the way the other man held the rifle, as well as in the cool gray of his eyes, said that he wouldn't hesitate about firing.

They studied each other in the light of the dying sun. Matt saw a man who was probably not yet twenty-five but looked ten years older. His hair was sandy and cut short over his ears. He wore a sheepskin-lined denim jacket and blue uniform pants, tucked into worn black boots.

"Is this the way to the Swanson place?" Matt asked at last, when it seemed as if the other man was content with the silence.

"It could be." The words held the slow drawl of Georgia.

"I'm looking for Liberty Prescott."

"You got any reason in particular?"

"She's my wife."

If Matt had hoped for a quick change in attitude, he was disappointed. Other than a slight widening of those cool gray eyes, there was no reaction at all.

"Well, I suppose that's reason enough to want to see a lady," he said after a while. "She didn't say anythin' about expectin' you, though."

"Should she have?" Matt asked coolly.

"Well, I reckon she would have, seein' as how I'm her foreman." The other man pushed his hat back on his head and gave Matt a slow smile that didn't come near his eyes. Matt also noticed that the rifle barrel didn't move.

"Do you also screen her visitors?"

"Not exactly. I just try to make sure we don't get too many unwelcome surprises. Saw you comin' from up on the ridge," he said, nodding to the north. "Since we weren't expectin' anybody, thought it wouldn't hurt to mosey on down and see what you were doin'."

"Well, I thought I was coming to see my wife," Matt said.

"I suppose there's nothin' wrong with that," the man said, with another of those cool smiles. "I'll just ride along and make sure you don't get lost."

It wasn't a suggestion and Matt didn't mistake it for such. He nudged the roan forward, aware that the other man had fallen in just slightly behind him and to the right. The muzzle of the rifle was now pointed at his spine. They rode in silence for a mile or two.

"Are you just naturally suspicious, or has there been trouble?" Matt asked conversationally.

"A little of both." The foreman didn't seem inclined to expand on the statement and Matt decided not to push. He could add it to the growing list of questions he had for Liberty.

"You have a name?" he asked after a while. "I always like to know the name of someone who's pointing a gun at me."

"A right understandable feelin'. Hank Benteen, late of the Second U.S. Volunteers."

"A Galvanized Yankee," Matt said, recognizing the name of the regiment. The Second was one of two regiments recruited from among Confederate prisoners. Given the promise that they wouldn't be asked to fight against their former comrades, many Southerners had chosen to join the army and had been sent west to deal with the Indians.

"That's one name I've been called," Hank said agreeably. "Did you join in the late conflict?"

"I was a scout under Grant."

"It seems a long way away out here."

"That it does."

No more needed to be said. Whatever might occur between them in the future, the fact that they'd fought on opposite sides in the war between the States would not be a factor. That time was over and done, and they, like most of the country, wanted only to put it behind them.

It was nearly dark when Matt saw the lights of a house ahead. He and Hank had spoken little since that one brief spate of conversation. The Southerner seemed a man of few words, which suited Matt just fine. The closer he came to seeing Liberty again, the more he doubted the wisdom of it.

Seeing her again could only make the memories sharper, could only imprint her more deeply in his thoughts. When he heard she was engaged, he should just have ridden south and put her out of his mind once and for all, the way she'd obviously done with him.

The house was a low, one-story building, simply but solidly built. Matt could make out other buildings in the twilight—a barn, a bunkhouse, a couple of sheds. Even in the poor light, the place gave off a feeling of being clean and well run.

The door opened as their horses stopped in front of the house. A woman's figure was momentarily silhouetted against the light and then the door shut, leaving her a shadow against the bulk of the house.

"Hank? Is everything all right?" The sound of her voice ran down Matt's spine like liquid gold. His doubt about the wisdom of coming vanished beneath the need to see her.

Ignoring Hank and the rifle that still pointed in his direction, he swung down off the roan. The movement must have made her realize that the foreman was not alone. He saw her head turn his way as he walked toward her. His boot heels drew a hollow sound from the wooden planks of the porch. He stopped in front of her and reached up to take off his hat, hearing the sharply indrawn breath that said she'd recognized him.

"Hello, Liberty."

Matt!

Liberty felt her senses spin, and she shut her eyes,

for one moment close to fainting. It wasn't possible. She'd long since given up any thought of seeing him again. She'd more than half believed him dead. But when she opened her eyes again, he was still standing in front of her.

"Matt." His name was a whisper. "Is it really you?"

"In the flesh." One corner of his mustache kicked upward in a half smile, the expression sweeping her back six years.

A jumble of memories flooded over her—Matt smiling at her, worried over her injury, relieved when she woke from the fever. And then, sharper still, the look in his eyes as he leaned over her in the firelight, the feel of his muscled shoulders under her hands, the soft brush of his mustache on her skin.

There were so many thoughts tumbled together in her head that she could only stare at him, trying to absorb the reality of his presence. Matt didn't seem inclined to speak but only stood there, watching her with hooded eyes, his expression unreadable. It was left to Hank to break the silence.

"Saw him comin' up the road," he said, still sitting his horse. "Said he was your husband."

Liberty blinked and dragged her eyes from Matt's face to look at the foreman. He was little more than a silhouette in the darkness.

"Yes," she said slowly. "Yes, he is."

Beside her, she sensed an infinitesimal easing of tension in Matt and wondered if he'd thought she might deny his claim. To tell the truth, she'd been so shocked by his presence that it hadn't even occurred to her.

"Then I reckon the two of you have some catchin' up to do," Hank drawled. "I'll see to your horse, Mr. Prescott." Hank reached over and unlooped the reins from the saddle horn.

"It's Matt. And thanks."

Just hearing his voice made Liberty feel as if she'd stepped back in time. It felt almost as if the past six years hadn't happened. But that wasn't the case. Time had passed and she was no longer a girl of eighteen. She was a woman of twenty-four, a woman who'd been single-handedly running a ranch for nearly a year.

Reminding herself of all that had changed helped her regain her control. No matter how incredible it seemed, Matt was standing here in front of her, real and solid. When she'd come out to greet Hank, she'd thrown a wool wrap over her shoulders as protection against the chill in the air. Now she drew the shawl tighter, seeking to wrap her accustomed self-control about herself along with it.

"You might as well come in," she said, the words sounding more grudging than she'd intended.

Liberty sensed, more than saw, Matt's brows go up, but she chose not to soften the tone. After all, he'd arrived on her doorstep without so much as a breath of warning. After six long years of silence, he couldn't really expect her to do a jig over his arrival.

She pushed open the door and stepped into the hall, aware of Matt following her. She hesitated in the entryway, uncertain which direction to turn. Finally, she went right, toward the kitchen.

"There's coffee," she said, moving toward the stove. "And bread and meat left from supper, if you're hungry."

"Coffee sounds fine," Matt said.

Liberty got a cup from the cupboard and poured coffee from the pot that always sat on the back of the stove. Though she avoided looking at him, she was aware of Matt's every move. He hung his hat on one of the hooks near the back door and then moved to the big oak table that served as both work and dining surface.

Liberty set the cup in front of him and then sat down across the table. She stared at her fingers, linked together on the tabletop, and tried to think of something to say. Just what did you say when the husband you hadn't seen in six years suddenly appeared out of the night? She'd be willing to bet that even Aunt Marybelle would have been stumped by that question of etiquette.

"You've changed." It was Matt who broke the silence.

"Yes." Liberty lifted her eyes, really looking at him for the first time.

In the light of the kerosene lantern, it seemed at first as if he looked just the same as he had six years ago. But looking more closely, she could see that the fine lines at the corners of his eyes were deeper. And the lines that bracketed his mustache were harsher, making him look older, more stern.

There was a scar high on one cheekbone that hadn't been there before and a certain weariness in his eyes that she didn't remember. When he bent his head to blow on the hot coffee, she saw that silver now threaded the tobacco-brown hair at his temples.

Matt glanced up, his eyes catching hers. She looked away, feeling her cheeks warm. But she didn't have to look at him to know that he was studying her with as much interest as she'd studied him. She curled her fingers together, resisting the urge to reach up and check her hair.

Matt could have told her that her hair looked fine. He'd said she'd changed and it was no more than the truth. But he could also have added that she was even more beautiful than he'd remembered. He'd hoped to exorcise her from his thoughts by seeing her again. But if the girl she'd been had proved difficult to forget, he knew the woman she'd become would be impossible to forget.

Her hair was the same pale, moonlit gold he remembered, though he'd most often pictured it tumbling over her bare shoulders and it was now drawn back from her face and confined in a thick braid that trailed down her back almost to her hips.

The face that had been lovely six years ago had matured into real beauty. Her eyes seemed bigger than he remembered, the jade color a striking contrast to her fair skin. She was wearing a plain dress of dove gray that covered her from throat to wrist but the severe style only served to make her beauty more obvious.

Looking at her, the coffee forgotten in his hands, it came to Matt that he'd been an almighty fool to leave her six years ago. He'd told himself it was because he didn't love her, but he'd had a long time to question the truth of that belief. He still couldn't say whether or not he loved her, but she'd proved unforgettable, something no other woman had ever been.

But perhaps he'd been as big a fool to come back as he had been to leave. This wasn't a woman a man could walk away from twice.

"You've changed, too," Liberty said suddenly, needing to break the silence.

"You mean this?" He reached up to touch the scar on his cheek.

"I wasn't thinking of that, exactly. You look older."

"Six years." His eyes skimmed her face, a look that might almost have been hunger in their depths. "You've grown more beautiful," he said quietly. "I didn't think that was possible."

Liberty looked away uncertainly. She might be a grown woman now, but he could still make her tremble with no more than a look from those golden-brown eyes. The realization made her angry. She was not a foolish girl anymore. This was her ranch, her kitchen, her table he was sitting at, and she wasn't going to let any man overset her balance, not even Matt Prescott. Most especially not him.

"Why are you here?" Her eyes met his, making no apology for the abruptness of the question.

Matt let the question lie for a moment, choosing an answer. "I don't exactly know," he said at last. "You've lingered in my mind."

"And I have all your letters to prove it," she shot back. She refused to admit to the twinge of pleasure his words brought her. She certainly had no interest in lingering in his mind. None at all.

"I suppose I should have written," Matt acknowledged.

"It didn't matter," she lied, shrugging.

"Considering the way we parted, I can't say I thought you'd be all that anxious to hear from me."

"I wondered a little when you didn't come back that spring." Not for anything would she admit the way she'd watched for him, nor how she'd cried when she'd finally had to accept that he wasn't coming for her.

"Your uncle wrote and told me there was no child."

Liberty's head jerked up, her surprise obvious. "Uncle Harland wrote you?"

"He didn't tell you?"

She shook her head. "He never said a word."

"Maybe he thought you wouldn't care."

"Why would he write to you?" she asked, sidestepping the question of whether or not she'd cared.

"Because I asked him to."

"Why?"

"I wanted to know if there was a child before I went east and enlisted."

"Oh." Liberty traced aimless patterns on the table with the tip of one finger, keeping her eye on the movement. "He told me that he'd heard you'd enlisted," she said finally. "When I didn't hear from you again, I thought . . ."

"That I'd been killed?" Matt finished the sentence for her.

"It occurred to me."

There was nothing in her tone to suggest that the thought of his death had caused her any real grief. Matt stared at the dregs of coffee in his cup, thinking again that he'd been a fool to come here.

"I'm glad you're all right," she said quietly.

"Are you?" Matt's mouth curved in a rueful smile, his eyes lifting to hers.

"Yes." The smile she gave him was shy, reminding him of the girl he'd married. "I was angry with you six years ago but I never wished you dead."

Liberty reached across the table to touch the back of his hand. She jumped when he moved, catching her fingers in his.

"Thank you."

She liked the feel of his hand on hers, she admitted to herself. It made her feel as if she wasn't alone anymore. As if there was someone she could depend on, someone who could help shoulder some of her burden.

But she was thinking like a foolish girl again, not a grown woman. Matt had shown up out of the blue. He could disappear against just as quickly. She tugged her hand away and tucked both of them safely into her lap.

"You're welcome to stay the night," she said, trying to pretend that he was nothing more than a casual visitor.

"Only the night?"

She glanced at him and then away. "Of course not. You're welcome to stay as long as you want. I just assumed . . ." She let a shrug finish the sentence.

"That I'd traveled all this way to say hello and then leave again?" he questioned, his smile not quite reaching his eyes.

"I don't know." She suddenly felt weary. "I don't know how far you've come. Or how long you planned to stay. Or why you're here at all."

When Liberty stood, Matt rose also, and the kitchen seemed suddenly much too small. Unless she wanted to dart out the back door as if she was running away, she'd have to brush past him to leave. She'd almost forgotten the breathless feeling that just being in the same room with him could bring.

"I'd answer that question if I could, Liberty," Matt said quietly. "I don't know why I'm here. Except maybe that you're my wife. I can't quite forget that."

"You didn't have any trouble forgetting it for six years," she snapped.

"I never forgot."

"You can't come here and expect to pretend that you've been here right along." Despite her determination to seem in complete control, she found herself edging a little away from him.

"I don't expect that. I don't expect anything. I just want—" He broke off and thrust his fingers through his hair, groping for words. But how could he find the words to tell her what he wanted when he didn't even know what it was himself?

"You want what?" She was watching him uneasily, her green eyes suspicious.

"I don't know," he admitted. He shook his head. "I don't know. War changes a man, Liberty. It makes him look at where he's been and where he might be going. I had plenty of time to consider both. And I realized that a man should have more to show for his life than the miles he's traveled."

"The war's been over for a year." Liberty had to steel herself against letting his words soften her toward him.

"True enough. It took me a while to admit that something was pulling me back here. We've unfinished business between us, Liberty. Whether you want to admit it or not."

He'd moved toward her as he spoke and now stood much too close for her peace of mind. He smelled of sun and leather and horse. She'd moved as far back as she could; further retreat was blocked by the edge of a counter. Unless she wanted to start moving sideways, there was nowhere to go.

Liberty looked up at him, seeing the man she'd married, the man she'd loved. He was older, harder perhaps, but he still set her pulse to racing.

"I don't know of any unfinished business between us," she said, wishing she didn't sound quite so breathless. "Unless you want to annul the marriage."

"We can't annul it. It was consummated, remember?"

Remember? It wasn't something she was likely to forget.

"Divorce, then," she suggested. "We can't have anything else to discuss."

She started as he reached out and caught her left hand in his.

"You're still wearing my wedding band. The marriage must mean something to you." He rubbed his thumb over the gold band, his gaze holding hers. "Would it be so impossible to be my wife?" he asked softly.

Liberty felt as if she were suffocating. The intensity of his look made it difficult to breathe. Impossible to be his wife? At the moment, it seemed like the most natural thing in the world. With him standing in front of her like this, holding her hand, looking at her as if she meant the world to him, it was possible to believe that no time at all had passed since they'd been together.

"Yes." She pulled her hand away and edged around him, no longer as concerned with seeming to retreat as she was with putting some distance between them. Once safely on the other side of the kitchen, she turned to face him again.

"Yes, it is impossible. You can't just ride in here and pretend that the past six years didn't happen. I'm not the same foolish child I was then."

"I never thought you were foolish," Matt said quietly.

"No? Well, I was. I was foolish enough to give my heart to a man who didn't want it. Foolish enough to marry a man who was only marrying me because he had to.

"I haven't fought in a war but I've changed, too, Matt. I've grown up, gotten the stars out of my eyes." Her hands curled into fists at her side and she lifted her chin, her eyes challenging.

"Maybe we do have unfinished business. But I'm not rushing into anything. You can stay here, if you want to. I'll not deny your right to share a house with me. But that's all we'll share."

"Agreed." He nodded, biting back a smile as he watched shock flicker over her face. She'd been braced for an argument but he had no intention of giving her one.

"You can sleep in the bedroom my aunt and uncle used," she said after a moment. There was a touch of belligerence in her words, as if she was still expecting a protest.

"Fine. It's been a long time since I slept in a decent bed." He gave her an easy smile, enjoying the quick play of emotions across her face.

"I'll get some linens," she muttered.

Matt's smile faded with her departure. He still didn't know exactly what it was that had drawn him back here. But he wasn't going anywhere until he either got Liberty out of his system once and for all.

Or made her his forever.

Chapter Thirteen

Knowing Matt was sleeping just across the hall made
sleep elusive. Liberty tossed and turned, determined
not to let his presence disturb her. But when she heard
her aunt's precious mantel clock strike twelve, she gave
up the pretense. It was foolish to pretend that Matt's
arrival meant nothing.

For the first time since her wedding night, she was
sharing a house, if not a bed, with her husband. A
husband she'd more or less assumed was dead. A
husband she'd certainly never expected to see again.

With a sigh, Liberty sat up. Drawing her knees up
to her chest, she stared broodingly at the door. Why
had he come back? He'd said it was because he
couldn't get her out of his mind. Was he telling her the
truth? Was it possible that he'd found her as difficult
to forget as she'd found him?

Lord knew she'd tried to forget him. When she'd
sent him away six years before, she'd been sure that
she hated him, that she never wanted to see him again.
Yet she'd shed bitter tears when she found out she
wasn't pregnant. And still more tears when she'd fi-

nally had to accept that he wasn't coming back for her as he'd promised—threatened really, she thought.

Of course, he'd had no reason to think she'd welcome his return—if, as he'd said, Uncle Harland had seen fit to tell him that he didn't have to worry about abandoning a wife *and* child. Only a wife who'd said she never wanted to see him again.

Would it be so impossible to be my wife?

She shivered and closed her eyes. *Impossible?* What had proved impossible was *forgetting* she was his wife. Opening her eyes, she stared at the gold band on her left hand. How many times had she told herself she was going to take it off, going to put her foolish marriage behind her? After all, she'd been married less than twenty-four hours when her husband left. Why should she stay tied to a man who'd clearly forgotten her?

But she'd never gotten around to removing the ring. Just as she'd never managed to forget Matt the way she'd told herself she should.

How was it possible to forget the man who'd saved her life, who'd nursed her through a fever, who'd been the first man she loved? The *only* man she loved. Who'd been her first and only lover.

Liberty had asked herself a thousand times what would have happened if she hadn't found out so soon that he didn't love her, if she hadn't felt the need to try to prod him into confessing what she'd thought he felt for her? Would she have gone off to Arizona with him, happy with her false belief that he loved her? How long would it have been before she realized that the love was all on her side?

She sighed and lowered her chin to rest atop her updrawn knees. By then, she might have been carrying his child. She might have come to terms with what he could give her.

Love might have grown between them, given time. Six years older and wiser, she no longer believed that love had to strike like a bolt out of the blue. It could be like a seed planted in warm ground and carefully tended, finally growing to be a strong, healthy plant.

If she'd been a little older, if she hadn't lost so much in such a short span of time, perhaps she wouldn't have been so quick to feel betrayed, or quite so quick to speak angry words.

But she *had* been young and hurt. And she'd felt a deep betrayal. And she'd struck out, wanting to hurt Matt as deeply as he'd hurt her. And he'd gone, just as she'd told him to. He'd gone from her life. Forever, she'd thought.

But here he was again, saying that he hadn't been able to forget her any more than she'd been able to forget him. And she wanted to believe him, she admitted. Alone in the darkness, she was able to acknowledge just how much she wanted to believe him.

Would it be so impossible to be my wife?

The question implied that he wanted her to be his wife, that he'd come back to see if they could make their marriage something more than a piece of paper.

If that was what he wanted, he was going to have to work for it, she thought on a wave of anger. It was all very well and good for him to walk back into her life and announce that he'd never forgotten her, but she was not going to open her arms—or her bed—to him until she had reason to believe that they could build something deep and lasting together.

Liberty slid back down between the covers. Six years was a long time and he wasn't the only one who'd changed. She was willing to have him stay. Willing to entertain the idea of a real marriage with him. But he needn't think that she was simply going to fall back into his arms, grateful that he'd returned.

And so she'd tell him, first thing in the morning.

But she didn't get the chance. By the time she'd dressed—in what just happened to be a particularly flattering outfit—Matt was already up and gone. If it hadn't been for the few dishes on the counter that showed he'd made himself breakfast and the fresh pot of coffee keeping warm on the back of the stove, he might have been a figment of her imagination.

Maybe he'd left, she thought, feeling her heart bump with something that came perilously close to panic. The thought had her hurrying back down the hallway to thrust open the door of the room she'd prepared for him.

The bed was made, but the clothing Matt had worn the day before lay in a heap on the floor. His razor was on the fine maple dresser her uncle had brought west for his wife—a touch of home, he'd said.

Liberty leaned in the doorway, relief making her knees weak. Matt wouldn't have left his things behind if he was gone for good. He was probably down in the barn or out somewhere with one of the hands. She straightened slowly, shaken by the intensity of her reaction.

For someone who was determined not to rush things, she was letting her feelings get out of hand.

Liberty didn't see Matt until halfway through the morning. She'd changed out of the soft lavender dress into her more accustomed garb of crisp white shirt paired with a full split skirt of dark brown. Calf-high boots and a flat-brimmed black hat completed the outfit.

Aunt Marybelle had been scandalized the first time she'd seen her niece in the costume, but Uncle Harland had only chuckled indulgently and taken her out on the range with him. It was a long time since Liberty had given any thought to what others might think of the outfit. But when she set the hat on her head and looked at her reflection in the mirror, she suddenly wondered what Matt would think.

As soon as the thought popped up, she dismissed it with a toss of her head. Her wardrobe was certainly no concern of Matt Prescott's. And so she'd tell him if he mentioned it.

Matt had just finished rubbing down the roan when he sensed Liberty approaching. He lowered the hoof he'd been checking and straightened as she swept into the barn. She came to an abrupt halt when she saw him.

"Hello." Matt offered an easy greeting and bent to lift another of the gelding's hooves, glad to have something to look at besides his wife. Was it possible that she'd grown more beautiful overnight?

"Hello." Liberty hesitated in the doorway a moment before continuing into the barn. "That's the same horse you had six years ago, isn't it?"

"Yup." He released his hold on the gelding's hoof and straightened. "We've been through quite a bit together." He patted the roan on the neck and received a rough nudge in return.

"He certainly saved our lives six years ago." Liberty came to stand in front of the roan and held out her hand. He looked at her, his ears twitching inquiringly and then stretched his neck to snuffle her palm. "Do you suppose he remembers me?" she asked a little wistfully.

"Of course he does. He'd never forget a beautiful woman." Matt patted the gelding on the rump and sent him trotting through the open barn door and into the corral beyond.

"You were up early this morning," Liberty said.

"I think the bed was too comfortable. I had a hard time sleeping." He grinned and shrugged. "I guess I've gotten used to sleeping on the ground."

"I could scatter a few rocks on the sheets," Liberty suggested. "Make it seem more what you're accustomed to."

"That's all right. I'll try to adjust."

She was surprised to find herself returning his smile. This wasn't how she'd pictured their next meeting. The last thing she'd expected was to find herself smiling with him.

"Are you going riding?" he asked, nodding to her clothing.

"Yes. Hank and I are going to check the north pasture. He's saddling a horse for me now."

Matt hooked his thumbs in his back pockets and rocked back on his heels, his eyes in shadow as he looked at her. Liberty shifted uneasily under that enigmatic regard.

"That outfit looks better than the one you wore into Bridger six years ago."

She'd been braced for him to voice some complaint. Instead, his words brought back memories of the calico dress that had been turned into a crude riding skirt. The memory made her smile.

"It wasn't exactly high fashion, was it?"

"It looked good to me." He reached out, catching a lock of her hair between his fingers. "I used to wonder if I'd dreamed the color of your hair," he said softly.

When had he moved so close?

"Did you?" The only reason she wasn't moving back was that she didn't want him to think that he intimidated her, she told herself. And it was annoyance that made her pulse a little too fast.

"The color of corn silk." His voice was husky. He was so close that she could feel his breath on her forehead.

"I could remember the way it spilled through my hands like silken moonlight."

She closed her eyes and swallowed hard, reminding herself that she didn't intend to let him back into her life so easily.

He released her hair and his fingertips settled on her cheek. She could feel the roughness of calluses. It swept her back six years to the feel of his hands on her breasts.

"I was a fool to leave." Matt's words were hardly more than whisper.

Liberty's lashes lifted, her smoky-green eyes staring up at him. How could she have thought to keep him at a distance when the lightest touch of his hand was enough to set her pulse pounding and scatter her resolve to the four winds?

Did he lower his head or did she rise toward him? All she was sure of was that his mouth was hardly more than a whisper away from hers. His fingers were cupping the nape of her neck. Her hand rested against his chest, feeling the strong beat of his heart through the cloth of his shirt.

All thoughts of keeping distance between them were forgotten. Years of loneliness were about to come to an end. Her mouth softened in anticipation of his kiss.

"Got your horse ready, Mrs. Prescott." Hank's voice was like a dash of ice-cold water. Liberty's eyes, which had been drooping shut, flew open. She stared up at Matt for a shocked instant, suddenly aware of what had almost happened.

She dropped back down on her heels, only then realizing that she'd risen on her toes to get closer to Matt. Her hand jerked back from his chest as if she'd been burned.

When Hank stepped into the shadowy barn, Matt was bending over to scoop Liberty's hat up from the floor and Liberty stood still as a statue staring down at him. Hank's gray eyes shifted from one to the other, seeing more than either of them would have wished.

"You ready to go, ma'am?" was all he said.

Liberty turned toward him, her eyes not quite focused. "Yes. Yes, I'm ready."

"Don't forget this." Matt held up the hat she didn't remember dropping. She took it from him, her gaze meeting his for a fleeting moment before she turned away.

"Thank you," she whispered. She walked toward Hank, suppressing the urge to run from Matt as if the devil were chasing her.

Obviously, it wasn't going to be as easy as she'd thought to keep him at a distance. Her own senses were too quick to betray her.

Matt leaned back against a shelf of rock and looked at Hank. He'd worked with the other man for the past week and had learned a great deal about the ranch. It was not a large operation but it was well run.

Besides the foreman, there were three hands. One of the men was married and his wife did the cooking, preparing meals in the big ranch house kitchen for Liberty and the men. He'd learned that the men respected Liberty and felt no uneasiness about working for a woman.

He'd also learned that Liberty worked as hard as any of them, spending most of her days in the saddle. She was just as likely to be pulling a new calf from a mud hole as she was to be overseeing the work. He frowned and reached for his tobacco pouch. She worked harder than she should, doing work that was not only strenuous and dirty but occasionally dangerous.

Matt tapped tobacco into a neat line on the paper. He understood that she'd earned the men's respect with her willingness to turn her hand to any task. But now that she had it, wasn't it time for her to retire to more suitable pursuits?

Only yesterday, he'd seen an old mossy horn steer turn on her when she was trying to haze it back into the group they were moving to summer pasture. If her pony had been a little less quick, she could have been badly injured.

"How long have you worked the Rocking S?" Matt asked Hank, his voice breaking the comfortable silence.

"'Bout a year, I'd guess," Hank said. He reached up to tilt his hat farther back on his head. "Swanson hired me when I mustered out."

"So you knew Liberty's uncle?"

"I'd been here a month or two when he was killed. Good man. The missus wouldn't stay without his bein' here. Said she'd only stayed for him. Tried to get Liberty to go east with her. Sell the place."

"She wouldn't go?"

Hank shook his head. "Said she didn't belong in the east anymore. Told Mrs. Swanson she'd run the place for her. She'd worked with her uncle and knew the ranch purty near as well as he did. She's got grit."

Matt caught the look the other man slid him and felt a stab of irritation. He didn't need the foreman to tell him Liberty had grit. She'd had it six years ago—more grit than he'd have expected to find in a girl of eighteen.

"What happened to Swanson?" he asked, changing the subject.

"Bushwhacked." Hank reached out and pulled a blade of grass. Pleating it between his fingers, he stared out across the valley. "Shot in the back."

"Any idea who did it?"

"I've got my own opinion." Hank shrugged. "No proof so there was no arrest."

"Who was it?"

"Fella by the name of John Randall." He caught Matt's surprised look. "You heard of him?"

"More or less." Matt stubbed out the cigarette. "The night I rode into the fort, I stopped for a drink and asked after Liberty. A man at the bar took it on himself to warn me away from her. Said she was going to marry a John Randall."

"Young fellow with fair hair and hard eyes?" Hank asked. "Slim, not too tall?"

"He fit that description," Matt agreed. "When I told him Liberty wasn't likely to be marrying John Randall or anyone else, he demanded to know who I was." He lifted one shoulder in a half shrug. "I told him."

"I'd have given a month's pay to see his face," Hank said. For the first time since they'd met, Matt saw his lean features break into a grin. "Sounds like John's boy, Curly. He's young but he's mean clear through. He and his old man moved into the area round about three years ago, from what I hear tell. Started buyin' up land or just usin' if it was available. They've got a big spread north and east of here.

"But Swanson, he filed on some of the best land hereabouts—good water year round, grass to cut for winter. He knew what he was doing. When Randall had spread about as far as he could go, he ran smack up against Swanson's land. He tried to buy, but the old man wasn't interested in sellin'."

"Then Swanson turned up dead," Matt finished for him.

"I ain't got proof." Hank shrugged. "Randall, he come to the funeral and he drew his face down real regretful-like. But that son of his didn't look regretful. Matter of fact, he seemed right pleased with himself.

"Right after the funeral, Randall came to the house and offered to buy the ranch from Mrs. Swanson—said he knew she wouldn't want such a burden."

"And she refused to sell?" Matt asked.

"It was Liberty who refused him. Told him her uncle wouldn't sell and neither would she. Mrs. Swanson let her have her way."

Matt stared into the distance, picturing the scene in his mind. Yes, he could easily imagine Liberty standing up to Randall, telling him the ranch wasn't for sale. He felt admiration mixed with a touch of anger. Had she considered what could have happened to her? If Randall had killed her uncle, who was to say he'd draw the line at killing a woman?

"So Randall backed off?"

"Not exactly. After Mrs. Swanson went back east, he took to comin' around every so often, said he was just a concerned neighbor." Hank's tone made it clear

what he thought of that excuse. "Truth is, he came
courtin' Liberty."

"And how did Liberty take that?" Matt was surprised to hear how calm he sounded. Inside, his blood
was simmering at the thought of another man
"courting" his wife. Not that he had any business
getting hot and bothered, he admitted. He hadn't been
here to protect her.

"She was polite but she made it clear she wasn't interested. He keeps comin' around, though. Figurin' to
wear her down, I guess."

Hank slanted Matt a speculative look. "Of course,
I guess that'll change. Now that you're here. If you're
stayin', that is."

Matt met the other man's eyes, his own hard.

"I'm staying."

Any thoughts he'd had of leaving had vanished, replaced by a determination to persuade Liberty to be
his wife in fact as well as in name. He wanted more
than his wedding ring on her finger. He was hungry to
have her in his bed. But he also wanted her standing
beside him, looking toward a future they'd build together.

"Why don't you stay at the ranch house today?"

Matt's question made Liberty lift her eyes to his
face. They were sitting across the kitchen table from
each other, just as they had every morning for nearly
a week. They shared breakfast before the day's work
began, but that had been about all they'd shared.

Other than a polite exchange of greeting each
morning, they'd barely spoken. For a man who'd said

he wanted their marriage to be more than words on a piece of paper, he didn't seem in any hurry to change things.

She'd expected to have to resist his advances. Instead, she'd hardly seen him. Aside from the fact that he slept in the main house instead of the bunkhouse, he might have been one of the hired hands, rather than her husband. But the look he was giving her now was very husbandly. She'd seen her Uncle Harland give Aunt Marybelle that same frowning look more times than she could remember.

"Why would I stay at the house?" she asked, puzzled. "We're going to start moving the cattle onto the summer range today."

"The men and I can handle it," Matt said irritably. "There's no reason for you to be out on the range."

"I always go out with the men," she said.

"That doesn't mean you have to go today." Matt pushed back his chair and stood, his frown deepening. "There must be things you could do around here." He glanced around the kitchen as if looking for a likely project.

"I suppose there are," Liberty said slowly. "But they'll have to wait."

"There's no need for you to go out."

"Why don't you want me to go out with the men today?" She stood and faced him across the table.

"I don't think it's necessary."

"*You* don't think it's necessary?" she asked.

Matt caught the edge of temper in her voice and his jaw tightened. "There's no reason for you to work like one of the hands now that I'm here."

"So, now that you've decided to grace my life with your presence again, you expect me to do as you say?" Her tone was ominous, but no more so than the fire that had started to simmer in her eyes.

"I'm not ordering you—"

"How nice," she murmured sweetly.

"I'm asking," Matt said, though his gritted teeth made it seem something less than a polite request.

"How dare you!" Liberty spun away from the table, her split skirt swirling around her booted calves. She spun back just as abruptly. "Who are you to ask me anything?"

"I'm your husband." Matt's temper rose to meet hers.

This past week had been as close to torture as he ever hoped to come. Seeing her during the day, so sweetly desirable and so out of reach was nothing compared to sleeping in the same house with her, knowing she was only a few feet away. He hadn't had a decent night's sleep since his arrival.

"My husband?" Liberty repeated contemptuously. "You're not my husband. You're a man I shared a bed with for a couple of nights when I was younger and considerably more foolish."

She spun toward the door, but Matt moved with a speed she hadn't expected, catching her hand and spinning her to face him.

"If that's all I am, then why are you still wearing this?" he demanded. He raised her left hand until the wedding band was in front of her eyes.

Seeing it, Liberty thought of all the foolish dreams she'd had when he slipped that ring on her finger. And the even more foolish tears she'd shed over it when she'd thought he was dead.

"Stupidity," she snapped. "That's the only reason I'm still wearing it." She wrenched her hand away and began tugging on the ring, intending to snatch it off and throw it away, just as she should have done years ago.

"Don't." Matt's hands caught her wrists, jerking her forward. Off balance, she stumbled against him.

"Let go of me!" She threw back her head to glare up at him.

"No. We're going to get this all out of the way. Go ahead and tell me how angry you are that I left. Tell me what a fool I was to stay away so long."

"You're certainly a fool," she said, tugging uselessly against his hold. "But I wasn't angry when you left. And I didn't care if you ever came back."

"Liar." Matt's anger had gone, leaving him feeling nothing but regret for the years he'd wasted.

His calm only added fuel to the fire of Liberty's temper. How dared he look so cool when she felt anything but? This wasn't about whether or not she should work with the men. It was about the years he'd been gone and the tears she'd shed.

He'd said he'd been a fool to leave, but words weren't enough to soothe the hurt he'd dealt her—first by not loving her and then by not coming back for her. It had taken her years to get over that pain, and he'd brought it all rushing back.

And then he stood there looking at her so coolly, making her feel like a foolish, hot-tempered child. If only he'd felt half the hurt she had.

"The only reason I continued to wear that ring was because I thought you were dead," she spit. She gave up the futile struggle to free her hands and glared at him. "It's a pity I was wrong."

The words fell between them like stones dropped into a pool. Liberty saw the ripple of their impact wash over Matt. The lines around his mouth deepened. Pain flared in his eyes for an instant before being quickly concealed. His eyes became dark mirrors that reflected nothing but her own image back at her.

Triumph washed over her. Finally, she'd gotten some of her own back. If only for an instant, Matt knew something of the hurt she'd felt when she realized he didn't love her.

He released her wrists and took a step back, putting distance between them. There was an odd pallor under his suntanned skin.

And she suddenly knew she'd made a terrible mistake.

Hurting Matt wasn't going to change what had happened between them six years ago. If she were honest, she had to admit that the source of her anger was more the fact that he hadn't loved her than the years that had passed.

She was still angry with him over something that couldn't be helped. He couldn't love her just because it was what she wanted. Any more than she could stop loving him just because her mind told her heart it was the best thing to do.

He turned away and she knew he was leaving, not just the room, but the house. And her. She'd told herself that was what she wanted. All she had to do was stay still and he'd be gone again.

"Matt."

He stopped in the doorway but didn't turn. The rigid set of his shoulders was less than encouraging. Liberty bit her lower lip. She took a step toward him and then stopped.

"I didn't mean that," she said finally.

"There's no reason you shouldn't mean it." He kept his back to her. "No reason at all."

"I was angry."

"You've reason enough," he said flatly.

"Perhaps. But that doesn't excuse what I said."

He shrugged as if to say it didn't matter. But he still didn't turn to look at her.

Liberty stared at his broad back, her teeth worrying her lower lip. Something in the set of his shoulders told her that her apology held less weight than the words that had gone before. He shifted, as if to continue his exit. If he left now, he'd never come back. She wasn't sure what she wanted but she knew she didn't want him to leave.

Without giving herself time to change her mind, she covered the distance between them with hurried steps. Though she didn't doubt that he'd heard her approach, Matt didn't turn toward her. She had to move around him to look up into his face.

What she saw there made her heart ache. His expression was bleak and empty, full of hard loneliness. There was regret in his eyes but no anger. She realized suddenly that, as much anger as she felt toward him, it was no more than he felt toward himself. If she'd wished him dead, he felt it was no more than he'd earned.

"Matt, I never wished you dead."

For a moment, she thought it was too late, that her words had bitten too deeply. Slowly, some of the tension eased from his shoulders. His eyes grow less bleak.

"When I decided to come find you, I didn't give much thought to how you must have felt," he admitted. "I only knew I couldn't get you out of my head." He lifted one hand to touch her cheek.

Liberty felt that light touch shiver down her spine, trailing awareness in its wake. It had been six years, but she hadn't forgotten the feel of his hands on her skin; the way it had been when she was in his arms. Never before or since had she felt so completely alive, so wholly female.

She swallowed and forced her thoughts into focus. "You can't have thought that we would simply pick up where we left off," she said. The words lacked any real force.

"I didn't expect anything." His fingers edged along her jaw. "And if we were picking up where we left off, we wouldn't be sleeping in separate bedrooms," he reminded her pointedly but without heat.

His thumb settled at the base of her throat, feeling the pulse that pounded there. She saw awareness flare in his eyes.

"Your heart's beating too fast," he said softly.

"I . . ." She stopped, groping for something to say to defuse the tension that suddenly lay between them. But her mind was blank.

When Matt's head started to lower toward hers, she raised her hands and set them against his chest—to push him away, she told herself. But somehow her fingers were curling into the fabric of his shirt, clinging to him as his mouth settled on hers.

It was everything she remembered and more. It was as if the years that had gone before were no more than the blink of an eye. It couldn't possibly be six years since he'd held her like this, six years since he'd kissed her.

She'd told herself that she'd gone on with her life, put Matt where he belonged—firmly in the past. Yet, he had only to touch her for her to realize that she'd lied to herself. She hadn't really been living. She'd only been marking time, waiting for this moment.

Feeling her response, Matt slipped his arms around her, one hand flattening on the small of her back, pressing her closer. His head tilted, his mouth hardening over hers, demanding a response she was more than willing to give.

Liberty's hands slid up to his shoulders, her fingers digging into the hard muscles there as she opened her mouth to him, inviting him to taste the sweet warmth of her response.

It wasn't what either of them had expected. So much time had passed, it didn't seem possible that the fire still lay so close to the surface that a single kiss could send it blazing to life.

How far that kiss might have taken them was something they weren't destined to discover. Matt's fingers had just tangled in the thick braid of her hair when someone began to pound on the front door.

The moment was shattered. Matt lifted his head and stared down into her eyes for a moment, his own dark and searching. Liberty looked away, half-afraid of what he might find. Her hands left his shoulders to press against his chest, forcing some distance between them.

"Someone's at the door," she said, when he didn't seem inclined to release her. A second round of knocking punctuated her words.

Matt's hands dropped to his sides, leaving her standing on her own. Though it was what she'd wanted, Liberty felt suddenly bereft. She moved back a step, smoothing her hands over her hips, her eyes focusing somewhere to the side.

She should say something, she thought. Something light and witty to show that she didn't think the embrace they'd just shared meant anything. The problem was that she seemed to be fresh out of light, witty remarks.

"Mrs. Prescott?" The voice was Hank's, coming through the solid wood of the door.

Drawing a quick breath, Liberty moved past Matt and into the foyer. She was aware of Matt following. Pulling open the front door, she hoped it wasn't obvious that she and Matt had just been locked in each other's arms.

But looking at Hank's face, the grim coldness in his pale eyes, she knew she had more to worry about than whether he knew she'd been kissing her husband. Glancing over his shoulder, she felt her stomach sink as she saw her neighbor, John Randall, and his son, sitting on their horses just beyond the porch steps.

Chapter Fourteen

"Hello, Liberty." Randall doffed his hat and bowed from the saddle.

"Mr. Randall." Though he'd asked her to call him John on more than one occasion, Liberty had no desire to share even such a small intimacy with him. The man had made her flesh crawl even before she'd had reason to suspect him of killing her uncle.

There was nothing in his square-jawed features to hint that he was anything other than what he appeared—a successful rancher who was carving his success out of a hard land. With his thick dark hair and ready smile, she supposed there were those who'd even consider him a handsome man. But the chill blue of his eyes was what she always noticed about him.

"Just thought we'd stop and make sure you were all right," Randall continued when neither Liberty nor Hank moved to break the silence.

"Is there reason to think I'd be anything but fine?" Liberty asked coolly.

"Now, don't get your back up, Liberty. I know you pride yourself on being able to take care of yourself."

Randall chuckled richly. Beside him, his son's mouth curved in a smile as cold as his eyes.

"I've done quite well, so far."

"Of course you have. I wouldn't dream of implying otherwise. No doubt you'd skin me alive if I did."

Liberty didn't bother to return his indulgent smile, but only watched him out of cool green eyes. Hank stood a few feet away, one hand resting on his hip, only inches away from his holstered Colt. Matt hadn't stepped out of the house. She could sense that he was just inside the door, watching and waiting.

When she didn't respond, Randall's smile faded. For a moment, anger flickered in his eyes and then was quickly smoothed over. His expression became serious and concerned.

"The truth is, Liberty, I had cause to be worried about you. Curly was at the fort a few days back when a stranger rode in. This man asked after you and when Curly asked his business, the fellow claimed to be your husband."

"Why would your son feel it was any concern of his who might be coming to see me?" Liberty asked.

The icy question was not what Randall had been expecting, and it threw him momentarily off balance.

"Well, naturally, knowing of our connection, he knew I'd want to know."

"Our connection?" Liberty raised her brows. "Do you show equal concern for all your neighbors, Mr. Randall?"

"Of course not." Randall stopped and drew a slow breath, easing the anger from his features and voice.

"You are a woman alone. Of course, I'm concerned for your safety."

"That's very kind of you but unnecessary. I have several men who work here and give me any assistance I need."

"I'll rest easier knowing that," Randall got out, his polite tone strained. "About this man Curly saw at the fort," he continued. "It was my understanding that you were a widow."

"Was it?" Liberty offered nothing beyond that. Knowing that Matt was just behind her, for the first time, she felt comfortable in letting her dislike for Randall and his reptilian son become plain. "I'm very busy, Mr. Randall. Did you call for a reason beyond inquiring into my marital status?"

Randall stiffened, his hands tightening on the reins, making his horse dance uneasily a moment before he brought it under control again.

"There's no need to take that tone," he snapped. "You'd do well to remember that out here neighbors need to depend on one another."

"The way my uncle depended on you?" The question was delivered in a pleasant tone, no hint of her suspicions allowed to color it.

Randall's face paled beneath his tan, his big body stiffening. But the reaction was gone as quickly as it came.

"I'd like to think your uncle knew he could count on me."

Liberty drew her gloves from her pocket and began pulling them on, giving herself time to control her anger. She wanted to scream at him that she knew he was responsible for Harland Swanson's death. She wanted to snatch Hank's gun from its holster and shoot Randall from the saddle. But she had no proof that Randall had had anything to do with her uncle's death. Nothing but instinct. And instinct wasn't reason enough to kill a man.

She finished smoothing her gloves into place, and sure that she had her expression under control, she lifted her head to look at Randall.

"Was there anything else?"

Randall cleared his throat. "We still haven't resolved the question of this man who was claiming to be your husband."

"Perhaps I can resolve that for you."

Liberty turned as Matt pushed open the screened door and stepped onto the porch. He moved to stand beside Liberty so that he and Hank were flanking her.

"I'm Matt Prescott."

"That's the man I saw, Pa." Curly Randall spoke for the first time. "That's the one that said he was married to her."

From the expression on John Randall's face, he'd sooner have seen a grizzly bear come out of the ranch house than Matt. Remembering what Hank had told him about Randall's apparent plans to marry Liberty, Matt could understand the other man's annoyance. A husband was an awkward complication to his plans. Plans he'd probably thought all but in the bag, from the way his son had announced his father's engagement.

"You and Liberty are married?" Randall got out, his voice strained.

"That's right. Is there any reason for that to be a concern of yours?" Matt's tone fell something short of cordial.

"As I just said, I thought Liberty was a widow. Naturally, when I heard that there was a stranger claiming to be her husband, I wanted to be sure she was all right."

"As you can see, she's fine."

"Glad to see it," Randall said heartily. "And I'm glad to meet you, Matt." He moved as if to swing down from his horse and approach Matt for a handshake. Perhaps it was the proximity of Hank's hand to his gun or the chill in Matt's eyes, but he appeared to think better of the notion and settled back into the saddle.

"I imagine you'll be taking Liberty back to your own place. When you go to sell the Rocking S, be sure and contact me. I'll give you a good price."

"The Rocking S isn't for sale," Liberty snapped, her face warm with anger at the way Randall was bypassing her to talk to Matt.

"Well, now, your husband may think differently on that subject," Randall said, giving Matt a man-to-man look.

"It's *my* ranch and it's not for sale." Liberty jerked loose from the restraining hand Matt had put on her arm. "Not to you, Randall. Not now. Not ever."

She stepped forward. Her hands gripped the porch railing, the leather of her gloves stretched taut over her knuckles.

"Get off my ranch, Randall. You're not welcome here."

"Now, really. There's no cause to throw a fit," Randall said. "I understand that you're fond of the place but I'll offer you a good price. Your uncle was on the verge of selling to me before his unfortunate accident."

"Accident!" Liberty felt the last shred of control desert her. "My uncle was murdered. Shot in the back by a sniveling, yellow-bellied coward who didn't have the guts to face an old man head-on." She fixed Curly Randall with blazing eyes. "Someone who's good with a rifle and who's a spineless skunk."

"Why, you little…" Curly's hand moved toward his gun. Before he could draw, both Matt and Hank had him covered. His fingers froze on the butt of his gun, his eyes blazing, not with fear but with frustration.

"Get your hand away from your gun, Curly," his father snapped.

"We gonna let her get away with that?" Curly's hand lifted away from his holster.

"Get away with what?" Randall's smile was tight and hard, his eyes as cold as marble. "Naturally, all of us were very upset by what happened to Harland. Even more upset that the killer is unknown."

"Oh, he's known, all right," Liberty said.

"That's enough, Liberty." That was Matt, his low voice holding a warning.

"No, it's not. It's not nearly enough." She broke off when he reached forward and caught hold of her upper arm, drawing her back from the railing. She turned to snap at him to get his hands off her, but the warning in his eyes stopped her.

She'd let her temper override her common sense. She'd all but come out and accused Curly Randall of killing her uncle. Not to mention telling them both to get off the ranch. But she wasn't going to take it back, not a word of it.

"My wife asked you to leave," Matt said pleasantly. He slipped his gun back in the holster, aware that Hank's was still drawn.

John Randall looked from one man to the other and saw no give in either. His mouth tightened into a thin, hard line, his eyes going cold as ice. He was smart enough to know that the time for friendly talk was at an end. Without another word, he tightened his big hands on the reins, the bit sawing at the horse's mouth as he turned the animal.

Curly Randall waited a moment, his eyes going from Matt to Hank and finally settling on Liberty. The cold threat in that look sent a shiver down her spine. They both knew he was the one who'd killed her uncle. His stare told her that he wouldn't forget the names she'd called him.

Stiffening her back, she tilted her chin upward and returned look for look. Not for the world would she let him see that she was afraid of him. The feel of Matt's hand resting on her shoulder made the facade easier to maintain.

It wasn't until Curly reined his horse around and followed his father that she allowed herself to draw a breath. She felt almost light-headed now that the confrontation was over.

"Always nice to see neighbors," Hank murmured. He slid his gun back into its holster and glanced at Liberty. "He'll make a bad enemy, ma'am."

"He was an enemy before this," she said. "It's just out in the open now."

"True enough." Hank nodded. He looked after the two men with narrowed eyes. "That Curly, now, he's a killer. Had a man like that in my regiment. He enjoyed the killin' a mite too much for my comfort. Young Randall's like that. He'd as soon kill you as look at you."

"Sooner," Matt said, thinking of the look in the younger man's eyes. Like Hank, he'd known men who enjoyed killing.

"You still want to go out today?" Hank asked Liberty.

She hesitated a moment, remembering her argument with Matt; remembering, too, just how that argument had ended. He wanted her to stay at the ranch house. After the confrontation with Randall, she wouldn't have minded staying close to home. But if she did that, Matt was going to think it was because he'd told her to.

"Yes." She flicked a quick sideways glance at Matt but could read nothing from his expression. "I'll just get my hat," she told the foreman.

"I'll meet you down at the barn."

Liberty turned and went back into the house, aware of Matt following her. Her hat was in the kitchen. As she stepped into the room, she was vividly aware of the kiss that had taken place there only a short time ago.

She didn't have to look at Matt to know that he remembered it, too.

For those few moments, she'd forgotten the years he'd been gone, forgotten all the reasons she had to be angry with him and her determination to hold on to that anger, to use it as a shield between them. When she was in Matt's arms, all she'd thought of was how right it felt to be there.

But she wasn't in his arms now and she had no intention of being there again. At least, not until a few things had been resolved between them.

She lifted her hat from the back of the chair on which she'd hung it and turned to look at Matt, her chin raised in unconscious challenge.

Matt looked at her, wondering if she had any idea just how beautiful she was. He wanted to pull her into his arms and kiss her until he saw that slumberous look return to her eyes. He wanted to feel her melting, soft and sweet against him, her arms twining around his neck to draw him close until not even a shadow could slip between them.

But the wary look in her eyes made it clear that she wasn't interested in picking up where they'd left off. The interruption had given her plenty of time to remember all the reasons she had to keep him at arm's length. Equally clear was the fact that she expected him to mention the embrace.

"You may have started something by challenging Randall so openly," he said, his tone neutral.

Liberty blinked, trying to shift her thinking. "I know he killed Uncle Harland. Or at least that son of his did. I've put up with his visits this past year be-

cause I had no proof. But when he actually said that
Uncle Harland had known he could depend on him, I
couldn't bear to look at him another moment.

"I suppose you think I shouldn't have told him to
get off the ranch."

"No. You've a right to throw anyone off your
property you see fit." He shrugged. "I just think you
should warn the men to expect trouble. If Randall did
kill your uncle, there's no saying that he'll stop at one
murder. Especially now that you've made it plain that
he won't get his hands on the ranch by marrying you."

"Marrying me!" Liberty's eyes flashed at the
thought. "I'd sooner marry a rabid wolf. Probably be
safer, too. I've given him no reason to think I'd marry
him," she added, wanting him to have no doubt about
that.

"When I asked after you at the fort, Curly was
there. He told me quite plainly that I shouldn't bother
to look you up. Said you were to wed John Randall."

"And you believed him?" she asked indignantly.
"You thought I'd marry another man, even though I
had a husband?"

"You had no reason to think I was still alive," Matt
said with a shrug. He was careful to keep his satisfaction from showing in his face. So she'd continued to
think of herself as married. She hadn't forgotten him
any more than he had her.

"Well, I certainly wouldn't have married him,"
Liberty said again. She turned her hat between her
fingers. "Did it bother you? To think that I might
have been planning to marry another man?" Her tone

was casual, but the look she gave him from under her lashes told him that his answer was important.

Matt covered the distance between them in two long strides. Before she had a chance to do more than draw in a startled breath, his long fingers caught her chin, tilting her face up to his until their eyes met.

"I wanted to tear him apart with my bare hands," he said huskily.

"Oh." Under that fierce golden-brown gaze, Liberty couldn't manage anything more than that soft exclamation.

Matt held her a moment longer, his fingers lying on her skin like a warm brand. Just when she was sure he was going to kiss her again and equally sure that she'd melt at his touch, he released her. His hand dropped away and he stepped back.

"I want you to be a little more cautious from now on," he said.

"Cautious?" She drew a shallow breath, forcing herself to remember what they'd been discussing. "Because Randall may try something?" she asked.

"Yes."

"Surely he wouldn't dare harm a woman."

"That all depends on how badly he wants the Rocking S. If he wanted it badly enough to kill your uncle..." He finished the sentence with a shrug. "If something happened to you, your aunt would probably sell to him, wouldn't she?"

"Yes." Liberty's hand crept to her throat as she tried to absorb the idea that Randall might want the ranch enough to kill her. "I never said anything to Aunt Marybelle about my suspicions. She was so upset over Uncle Harland's death, there didn't seem any point in upsetting her more."

Seeing her white face, Matt felt something tighten in his chest. He wanted to put his arms around her and tell her that she didn't have to be frightened—he'd never let anything happen to her. But he couldn't be with her every minute and she'd be safer if she was on guard.

"I just can't believe he'd risk killing a woman," she said slowly. "If anyone found out, he'd be facing a lynch mob."

"You're probably right."

Matt had his doubts, but there was nothing to be gained by frightening her any more than he already had. Seeing the uneasiness that lingered in her eyes, he reached up to catch the thick plait of hair that lay over her shoulder.

"Chances are, Randall will turn his sights elsewhere after the way you sent him off," he said.

"Yes." Liberty wished his eyes were as sure as his words.

They stood together, linked by Matt's hold on her braid. His eyes skimmed her face, lingering on the softness of her mouth. For the space of a heartbeat, Liberty thought he was going to kiss her. Not that she wanted him to, of course. She'd already decided that the earlier kiss had been a mistake—one she was not going to repeat. Any second now, she'd turn away.

But it was Matt who drew away. Just when she was sure that he was going to bend down to kiss her, he blinked and seemed to shake himself. Dropping her braid, he took a step back.

"If we're going to take a look at the north pasture, we ought to get started."

"The north pasture?" So much had happened in the past hour that she had a hard time remembering that she'd started the morning with specific plans. It seemed as if half the day must have passed since she and Matt were sitting together at breakfast.

"I'd guess Hank has the horses saddled by now," Matt said, turning to lift his hat from a hook near the back door.

"Yes, of course." Liberty settled her own hat on her head and tried to look as if being kissed had been the last thought on her mind.

She strode briskly from the kitchen, aware in every fiber that Matt was only a step behind her. Somehow, at the moment, the Randalls didn't offer as much threat to her peace of mind as Matt's immediate and rather large presence in her life.

For the next few days, Liberty and Matt were careful to circle the issue of their marriage and its future. It wasn't as difficult as it might have been. Spring was a busy time on the ranch, with calving to tend to, as well as moving the cattle onto the summer range. There was more than enough work to occupy the daylight hours.

By the time the sun went down, Liberty was tired enough that it was possible to keep her thoughts from dwelling on Matt. Well, at least, she managed not to think about him all the time.

Before he'd kissed her, she'd been able to tell herself that any feelings she'd had for Matt were dead.

Certainly, they were still tied together by the vows they'd exchanged. And it was only for the sake of those vows that she was willing to entertain the thought of making their marriage a reality.

But the moment she'd felt Matt's arms around her, she'd been forced to admit that she'd been lying to herself. She'd melted like butter left in the sun as soon as he kissed her.

The years that he'd been gone had been nothing more than mist, dissolving under the heat of his mouth. She'd forgotten her hurt and her anger. Forgotten everything but how right it felt to be in Matt's arms, to feel the hard strength of his body against hers.

She wanted to believe that she'd felt that way because he was her husband. After all, it was natural— proper even—that she should respond to the man she'd married.

But she hadn't been thinking about her marital obligations when she'd been clinging to him.

Sighing, Liberty turned away from the window and reached down to pick up her gloves from the dressing table. She'd been standing there staring aimlessly out the window for more time than she cared to admit. Lately, it was hard to keep her mind focused on anything other than Matt's reappearance in her life.

During the day, she avoided Matt. At night, she tried to avoid thinking about him. The more she tried not to think about him, the more she couldn't get him out of her mind.

Maybe, instead of avoiding him, she needed to spend time with him. He'd asked her if it would be impossible for her to be his wife. Before she could answer that question, she had to get to know him. Not the Matt Prescott she'd known six years ago, but the man he was now.

Liberty pulled her gloves restlessly through her fingers, staring unseeingly at her reflection in the mirror over the dressing table. She was his wife in the eyes of the law. And though she'd tried to pretend otherwise, in her heart she'd never stopped thinking of herself as a married woman, not even when she'd half believed he must be dead.

Her chin firmed. She'd buried her head in the sand long enough. It was time to take the bull by the horns and stop pretending that Matt's arrival hadn't changed her entire life.

"I'll ride up the creek and see what the problem is," Matt said. He tightened the cinch on the roan's saddle and then straightened to look at Hank over the animal's back. "Any sign of trouble from Randall?"

"Nope. Sal's been keepin' an eye on his place and he says there's nothin' out of the usual run goin' on."

Matt frowned at the barn beyond Hank's shoulder. "Randall's not going to hire an army. If he does try something, he'll likely go for another ambush. It worked the last time—or would have if Liberty hadn't talked her aunt out of selling. He obviously didn't count on that."

"Well, he knows better now," Hank drawled. "She sent him off with quite a flea in his ear." He gave a slow grin. "That's a woman with a fine spirit."

"That she is." Matt's grin was reminiscent. "If I were Randall, I'd keep a considerable distance from her."

"I doubt he'll do that." Hank's grin faded. "The man's as much a killer as his son, he's just had more practice hidin' it. He prefers fists to guns. I've heard him boast that he's killed two men with his bare hands and crippled more than that."

Remembering the man, Matt found the boast an easy one to believe. Though he'd only seen him on horseback, he'd seen enough to know Randall was a big man, stocky but with not an ounce of fat on him. And he had solid, beefy hands that could probably break a man in two if given the chance.

Shaking his head, Matt reached out to gather up the reins. "I've no intention of brawling with the man. I just want to be sure he's no danger to Liberty."

"Reckon you might have to kill him to be sure of that," Hank said.

Matt had been about to mount but he paused, his eyes hard and cold as they met the other man's. "If that's how it has to be . . ." He didn't bother to finish the thought. He didn't have to.

"You decide to start a war, you can count me in," Hank said coolly.

"Count you in for what?" Liberty's voice preceded her.

Matt swung toward her, feeling her beauty catch at his throat. All the years she'd haunted his dreams, he'd told himself that time had gilded her image, that she couldn't possibly be as beautiful as he remembered. He'd been wrong, and it hit him every time he saw her.

"Poker in the bunkhouse," he heard Hank say, answering Liberty's question.

"Be careful playing poker with Hank," Liberty warned Matt lightly. "I've heard the hands complain that he's got the devil's luck."

"I'll keep that in mind," Matt murmured. It was as much conversation as they'd exchanged in several days. Since the day the Randalls showed up—the day he'd kissed her—she'd shown a definite tendency to avoid his company.

"Dave told me you were going to ride up the creek and see what's happened to cut the flow," she said.

"I was."

She drew a quick breath as if she needed it to get the next words out. "I'd like to go with you."

Matt stared at her, wondering if he'd heard her right. Surely, there was something he'd misunderstood. But she was standing there staring at him, waiting for his response. As the silence stretched, her chin lifted slightly, contrasting with the uncertainty that flickered in her eyes.

"Unless you'd rather go alone, of course," she said sharply.

"No." Matt shook his head. "No, of course not. I'd thought of asking you," he lied. "But I didn't think you'd want to go."

"Well, I do want to go," she said with a just a touch of belligerence, as if daring him to think it strange that she was suddenly seeking out his company.

"I'll saddle the pinto for you, Liberty." That was Hank, breaking the tension that had suddenly sprung up between the other two.

By the time the pinto was saddled, Liberty had had plenty of time to decide that the whole idea of riding out alone with Matt was a bad one. There was no telling how far they'd have to ride before finding whatever it was that was obstructing the little stream's normally dependable flow.

As she swung into the saddle, it occurred to her that they might even be forced to spend the night out on the range. The thought made her fingers tighten on the reins, causing the little pinto to toss her head nervously. Liberty automatically calmed the animal, wishing her own uneasiness could be as easily soothed.

Chapter Fifteen

Spring seemed to have finally managed to elbow winter aside. The sun shone down from the clear blue arc of sky. The land was awash with the fragile green of new grass. By the middle of summer, everything would be an overall tan, showing green only where there was year-round water.

Harland Swanson had chosen the site of his ranch with considerable care, locating it where water and grass were plentiful. Liberty thought there could be no place more beautiful on earth, especially in the spring when the whole world was fresh and new.

Pennsylvania's rolling green fields might be prettier, but they seemed cramped and stingy in comparison to the vast sweep of land ahead of her. If her parents hadn't died when they did, she'd probably have lived out her life without traveling more than a hundred miles from her birthplace. No doubt, she'd have been content with that.

But once she'd seen the magnificent emptiness of the west, she'd never have been able to go back. She'd always have been haunted by memories of jagged purple mountains that cupped lush green valleys, of the vastness of the prairie.

"During the war, I'd sometimes think about this kind of country," Matt said quietly. "Sometimes, I half believed I'd imagined it. It didn't seem like anything could be so wide open and peaceful."

His words so closely matched her own thinking that Liberty shot him a quick look, wondering if it was possible that he'd read her thoughts. But Matt's eyes were skimming the land before them, a sort of hunger in their depths that told her how much he'd meant his words.

He'd said little about the years he'd been gone, nothing about the things he'd seen and done. She'd thought about him more than she liked to admit, wondering where he was, what he might be doing. She'd devoured every tidbit of news that filtered to them, trying not to think that he might have been killed in one of the battles she was reading about.

"We got reports, of course," she said. "It didn't seem possible that so many men could be dying. Was it as bad as it sounded?"

"Worse." The flat word and his bleak expression conveyed as much about what he'd gone through as any long speech could have done.

Liberty would have liked to ask him more, to know more about what had happened to him during the years he'd been away. But something in his face told her that it was a wound that had yet to heal—perhaps never would heal completely.

They spoke little after that but the silence was not an uncomfortable one. Liberty had decided to try to get to know the man who was her husband, but for the moment, it was enough to simply ride next to him and enjoy the warm spring air.

She felt a subtle easing of the tension that usually lay between them. It had been foolish to pretend that avoiding Matt was going to solve any problems.

They'd gotten a late start and it was midafternoon when they reached the source of the blockage. In a place where the stream had cut through the side of a small hill, the bank had caved in, tumbling a mound of rocks and soil into the stream. The cave-in was no more than a couple of days old, but a shallow pond had already formed behind it.

"If the flow were a bit stronger, it would probably have already worked its way through this," Matt said.

"In the middle of summer, it's little more than a trickle, but there's always some water. The cattle depend on it."

"Well, it's going to take more than one man with a pry bar to break that loose." Matt reached into his pocket for the makings of a smoke and studied the problem.

"We can come back with the men tomorrow and break it loose. I've some beef and bread in my saddlebags. It seems a long time since breakfast." Liberty looked around for a good place to spread the blanket she'd brought.

Perhaps the informality of a simple picnic would give them a chance to talk. She still wasn't sure just what it was she hoped to gain from seeking out Matt's company. Maybe a little clarification of what he wanted from her. Perhaps, then, she'd understand what she wanted.

"Seems odd, the bank caving in like that." Matt narrowed his eyes at the mound of dirt and rocks, his tobacco pouch forgotten in his hand.

"What's odd about it? The water undercut the bank and it collapsed."

"That's the one place where a cave-in would be likely to collapse," he said. "And why would it collapse just now? There's been no rain to weaken the bank."

"What difference does it make?" she asked impatiently.

She wasn't interested in analyzing the reason for the bank's collapse. She was more concerned with getting at the real purpose of this expedition. Now that she knew what had stopped the water's flow and could see that it was an easily solved problem, she was more interested in the less simple problem of their marriage.

"I just don't like the look of it," Matt said. He slipped the tobacco back into his pocket and looked around uneasily.

They were in hilly country and there were too many places where a man with a rifle could lie low and have a pretty good shot at anyone near the dam. The cave-in would have been easy enough to cause. And it was obvious that someone from the Rocking S was bound to check on the stream's sudden reduction.

There would have been no way for Randall to know that Matt and Liberty would be the ones to come, but maybe he hadn't really cared. Maybe Liberty's death wasn't essential to his plans to gain title to the land. He didn't have to kill her if he could make it clear that the price for keeping the land would be a high one.

Liberty might be willing to risk her own life to keep the ranch, but Matt knew she wouldn't feel the same about risking the lives of her men. If Randall wanted to send a clear message to the Rocking S, all he'd have to do was position a man somewhere overlooking the area of the cave-in and then wait for one of the hands to show up.

Liberty's presence could turn out to be a real bonus.

"Head toward that brush over there," he said abruptly. He was already turning the roan.

"Why?" Matt's tone had Liberty obeying the order even as she questioned it.

Before he could answer, he caught a flash of light from the corner of his eye—the reflection of sunlight off a rifle barrel.

"Yhah!" Matt leaned out of the saddle to slap Liberty's mare on the rump. Startled by the blow as well as by his shout, the little pinto gave a leap that nearly unseated her rider. A bullet kicked dust just beyond where the mare had been, the report following a heartbeat later.

Hearing the rifle shot, Liberty realized instantly what had happened. The cave-in had been caused specifically to get someone to come look for it. And when they did, they'd be a sitting target. Matt had realized that, and that was why he'd questioned the timing and placement of the blockage. If he hadn't slapped the mare when he had, that bullet might have found its target.

Liberty crouched low over the pinto's neck, letting the little horse run all out. A glance over her shoulder showed her the roan keeping pace with her horse. The big gelding's longer strides could have taken him past the pinto easily. Matt must be holding him back, keeping between her and the ridge where the shooting seemed to be coming from.

There were more shots, and they seemed to be coming from more than one place, but it was impossible to be sure. Surely, she and Matt must be almost out of range, she thought.

As if to prove her wrong, she heard the whistle of a bullet and saw it kick up dirt only a few feet ahead of the pinto. Instinctively, she tightened her fingers on the reins, swerving the mare to one side, trying to make a more difficult target. Just a little farther.

The pinto's hoof came down in a shallow hole. Ordinarily, she could have adjusted her stride to compensate for the irregularity, but running flat out as she was, there was no time for adjustments. With a frightened whinny, she stumbled. Liberty felt her start to fall and kicked her feet loose from the stirrups.

Behind her, Matt saw the mare stumble and knew she was going down. The fall might not injure Liberty but she was certain to be momentarily stunned. The seconds it would take her to recover could cost her her life. As if to emphasize that point, he felt something tug at his sleeve and heard the ugly thwap of a bullet hitting a rock nearby.

He slammed his heels against the roan's sides, and the big horse responded with a burst of speed that brought him level with the pinto just as Liberty kicked her feet out of the stirrups. Leaning out of the saddle, Matt caught Liberty's waist in one arm, sweeping her off the mare just as she tumbled to the ground.

The breath knocked from her, Liberty threw her arms around Matt's neck and clung for dear life. Behind them, she saw the pinto scramble to her feet and trot a little ways before stopping, seeming unharmed by her fall.

"Try to get your foot in the stirrup," Matt said. His arm was like an iron band at her waist, but it was obvious he couldn't hold her like that for very long.

Liberty moved her foot, seeking the stirrup. She found it without too much trouble. Matt had pulled his foot out of it and Liberty slid her boot into place. His arm eased around her waist as he felt her take some of her own weight.

There'd been no more shots since the pinto's fall, but Matt kept the roan at a fast trot, not slowing until they'd put several miles between them and the site of the cave-in. When he finally stopped, Liberty's leg was trembling with the effort of balancing herself against the horse's side.

"Swing up behind me," Matt said as he lowered her to the ground. What she really wanted to do was collapse on the ground, but she drew a deep breath and took the hand he held down to her.

With her seated behind him, her arms circling his waist, Matt nudged the roan into a quick walk. The ambushers had been between them and the ranch house, forcing them to run away from the safety it could offer. On the other hand, the broken, hilly

country they were in now offered them more conceal-
ment than the flat prairie nearer the ranch.

"Do you think it was Randall?" Liberty asked.

"Unless you've got enemies you haven't mentioned."

"No. No other enemies."

She still found it hard to believe that Randall would
try to kill her. Even after what had just happened, it
didn't seem possible.

"How could they have known I'd come out to check
the cave-in?" she asked suddenly.

"They couldn't. They probably had orders to shoot
whoever showed up. Randall probably thinks that
killing one or two of the hands might persuade you to
change your mind about selling to him."

The way Liberty's arms tightened around Matt's
waist told him that Randall was probably right.

"When we showed up, maybe they just considered
it a bonus," he said.

"There was more than one, wasn't there?"

"Two. Both pretty good."

"They missed us."

"It was a difficult shot. Besides, they didn't miss
entirely," Matt said ruefully.

"What do you mean they didn't miss entirely? Are
you hurt? Where?"

"My arm. And it's just a crease."

"Let me take a look at it," she demanded, trying to
get a look at the injury.

"When we stop."

"You can't just let it bleed." She'd managed to
catch a glimpse of his blood-soaked sleeve.

"It's almost quit by now. I don't want to stop yet. We need a place we can defend."

"You think they'll come after us?" The thought was enough to momentarily sidetrack her from his injury.

"Maybe. They know we're on one horse. They may not have orders to kill you specifically, but they may just decide it's an opportunity they shouldn't miss."

"I hadn't thought of that. So what are we going to do?"

"We're going to try to keep from getting killed. If we're not back by morning, Hank will come looking."

"And after the trouble we had with Randall, he'll come loaded for bear." She laughed suddenly.

"Being shot at amuses you?" Matt's voice showed he questioned her sanity.

"I was just thinking that we've been here before. Six years ago. The two of us, looking for a place to hole up. Only one horse between us. It was even the same horse."

Matt chuckled. "He must be getting a little tired of this."

"I can't say I blame him."

Liberty could have added that there were other similarities between the two times. Just as she had six years ago, she felt safe with Matt. Though she was older now and well able to take care of herself, there was something about his presence that made it easier to believe they'd come through this intact, just as they'd beaten much greater odds six years ago.

There was purpose in the way Matt guided the roan. It was obvious that he had a specific destination in mind, so Liberty allowed her head to rest against his back and closed her eyes. Sleep was impossible, but she could almost pretend that there was nothing to worry about beyond the fact that they'd missed supper.

"We'll stay here tonight."

She must, in fact, have dozed off, because she came awake with a start when Matt spoke. Peering around his shoulder, she felt her heart give a startled bump. Was it possible that time really had spun backward?

Sitting in front of them, as solid and plain as it had been then, was the little stone cabin where they'd taken shelter from the snow six years ago. Liberty closed her eyes, feeling almost dizzy. But when she opened them again, it was still there, gray and squat, the windows covered over. She couldn't remember when she'd ever seen anything that looked half so wonderful.

"Give me your hand and I'll help you down." Matt's voice was calm, reflecting none of the shock she felt. Of course, he'd obviously known they were coming here. Was it possible that he didn't remember what had happened here?

But when he dropped to the ground beside her, his eyes met hers and she knew his memories were as vivid as hers.

"Looks like we've come full circle," he said, one side of his mouth kicking up in a half smile.

"Looks like." She turned to look at the cabin. "I didn't realize this was where it was."

"It seemed like a good place to spend the night," he said. She could feel his eyes on her profile, trying to gauge her reaction.

"Yes," she said slowly. "It seems like a good place." She shook herself and forced a smile. "I'll go see what shape it's in. Do you think it will be safe to start a fire?"

"If the wood's dry enough." Matt cast a considering look at the sky. Following his gaze, Liberty was surprised to realize that it was nearly dusk. "It will be dark before long. If they followed us, they'll have to make camp."

"Do you think they'll follow us this far?" Liberty glanced over her shoulder, as if half expecting to see gunmen ride into sight.

"I don't know. Depends on how well paid they are."

"Randall wouldn't have to pay his son. He'd come after us just for the pleasure of it." Her shoulders twitched in a convulsive shiver.

"Well, unless he's part wolf, he can't track us after dark," Matt said.

"True." Liberty glanced down at his arm, her dark brows drawing together at the sight of his blood-stained sleeve. "That needs to be tended to," she said, touching him with gentle fingers.

"After I've seen to the horse. I think he's earned a rest." He gave her a quick smile and brushed his fingers over her cheek before leading the roan past her. Liberty stared after him, her heart beating faster than it had any business doing.

While Matt saw to the roan, Liberty gathered a few armfuls of dry wood and then coaxed a fire to life. With that done, she swept the worst of the cobwebs from the corners, using a pine bough as a broom. At least she didn't have to worry about sweeping the dirt floor, she thought with wry humor.

By the time Matt strode into the cabin, she'd about run out of tasks with which to occupy her time.

"I brought water from the well. The bucket leaks a bit," he said, setting it down near the door. He reached up to lift his saddlebags from where they'd been draped across his shoulder. He gave the table a dubious look and then wisely chose to set the bags on the floor.

"There's some jerky in there," he said, nodding to them. "You must be hungry."

"I had beef and some fresh bread in my saddle-bags," Liberty said. She made no move to get the jerky. She should be hungry but she wasn't.

"I didn't come so well prepared." He moved forward into the firelight.

"You've broken the wound open again," she exclaimed, seeing dampness on his sleeve.

"Yes." He glanced at the injury without much interest.

"Here. Sit down and let me take a look at it." She hurried forward and took hold of his good arm to lead him closer to the fire.

It occurred to Matt that it was the first time she'd touched him voluntarily since his return. He could hardly count the way she'd clung to him on horse-back—that had been a matter of survival.

If he'd been alone, he probably wouldn't have paid much attention to the injury. It was little more than a shallow burn, hardly worth the effort of looking at it. But Liberty obviously didn't feel the same. And he wasn't going to protest if she wanted to fuss over him. If nothing else, it would give her something to think about besides the attack this afternoon.

He obligingly handed her his knife when she asked for it and then watched with unconcealed interest as she used it to tear several strips off the bottom of her petticoat. He'd wondered if she was wearing anything beneath that split skirt.

"It seems as if every time we're together, you end up losing a petticoat," he commented.

Liberty looked up, half-smiling as she remembered the way he'd ruthlessly cut up her second-best petticoat all those years ago.

"They're easily replaced."

She went to the water bucket and dipped one of her new rags into it. Funny how she didn't feel any tension at all. A few hours ago, if asked, she'd have said that she'd rather walk barefoot across a cactus patch than be in such an intimate situation with Matt. She'd expected to be alone with him. She *hadn't* expected to be alone with him in the cabin where they'd first made love.

Yet now that they were here, it felt almost inevitable that they should be here. Full circle, Matt had said. Maybe that was just what had to happen. Somehow, here, she found herself remembering all the good things about their time together—the way he'd protected her, kept her safe. He'd made her laugh when it seemed as if there couldn't possibly by anything to laugh about. And he'd never treated her like a child.

The anger she'd held for him all these years didn't seem quite so strong suddenly. Perhaps it was because they'd both come close to death today, but it was easier to remember the good times than it was to remember the hurt and anger. It was easier to remember how much she'd loved him than how close she'd come to hating him.

She shook her head and wrung the excess water out of the cloth. Maybe she should have taken time to eat, after all. She was starting to have the strangest thoughts.

Liberty turned away from the bucket and then stopped, feeling her breath catch in her throat. Matt had taken off his shirt—a perfectly reasonable thing to do. What wasn't reasonable was her own reaction. It had been six years since she'd seen him without a shirt. She'd almost managed to forget the tanned width of his shoulders and the broad muscles of his chest. The sight of them now made her feel unexpectedly light-headed.

She drew in a slow breath and told herself not to be foolish. It was lack of food that was making her feel dizzy, not the way the muscles shifted beneath Matt's skin or the mat of hair on his chest that tapered to such an intriguing line across his stomach before disappearing beneath his belt. She swallowed hard, trying not to let her memories take her any further.

"I wish the light was a little better," she said, as she sank to her knees beside him.

"Here." Matt shifted his torso, angling his injured arm toward the fireplace. "Does that help?"

"Yes." If what he'd been trying to do was increase her pulse, it helped a lot.

She cleared her throat and forced her attention to his injury. Once the dried blood was washed away, it was easy to see that the bullet had done nothing more than carve a nasty gouge in the flesh of his upper arm. The wound was not deep nor was it long.

Living on a ranch, Liberty had learned to deal with minor injuries. She'd even been known to stitch up a cut a time or two. She'd certainly seen injuries a great deal worse than the one in Matt's arm. But none of them had affected her the way this one did. This wasn't one of the hands. This was Matt.

As she wound a strip of petticoat around his arm, she tried not to think of the fact that, if the bullet had hit just a few inches farther in, it would have gone through his shoulder. He could have bled to death long before they'd reached safety. She could have lost him again, this time forever.

She hadn't realized until now that she'd never really believed he was dead. She'd told herself she did, but deep inside, she hadn't accepted it. She couldn't. She'd needed to believe that he was in the world somewhere. Because if he wasn't, the world was an empty place.

She still loved him. She'd always loved him, even when she almost hated him.

"There. I think that should hold it," she said, trying to keep the turmoil she felt from showing in her voice. Obviously, she was not completely successful.

"Don't look so worried. I've had cuts worse than that on my eyeball," Matt said, intending to make her smile.

But Liberty remembered him saying the same thing when she'd cared for the cut on his stomach—the cut he'd gotten while saving her life. And now, six years later, he'd been hurt again while protecting her.

Maybe it was the stress of running for her life. Or the tension she'd felt ever since Matt's return, a tension caused as much by her own stubborn denial of her feelings as by anything else. Or perhaps it was the sudden realization of those feelings. Whatever it was, Liberty felt something crumple inside.

"Hey, that was a joke," Matt said, startled to see tears well up in her eyes.

"You could have been killed," she said, her voice trembling.

"Not by that wound. It's hardly more than a scrape."

"But what if their aim had been a little better?"

"It wasn't." He reached up to brush a solitary tear from her cheek, feeling the softness of her skin under his fingers. "Don't cry, honey. I'm not worth it, even if I'd died."

"Don't say that!"

That first tear was followed by a second and a third, each one burning into Matt's heart. He cupped her face between his palms.

"Don't cry," he whispered. "It breaks my heart to see."

When the tears didn't stop, he lowered his head to kiss them from her cheeks. At the soft brush of his mustache against her face, Liberty gasped softly. She closed her eyes and tilted her face upward, her mouth brushing his. She heard Matt's indrawn breath and felt him still.

"Liberty?" The husky question shivered over her. Slowly, she forced her eyes open and looked up at him.

"Kiss me, Matt. Make love to me. I need to feel us both alive." The look in her eyes was an invitation to heaven on earth.

"Are you sure?" The blood was pounding in his head, making it difficult to think. He wanted her desperately. He'd spent years wanting her.

"I'm sure." There was no doubt in her eyes, only a need that echoed his own.

He should draw back. Their brush with death had left her feeling vulnerable. He shouldn't take advantage of that vulnerability. But only a saint could turn away from the need in those green eyes. And he'd been called many things over the years but never a saint.

Liberty's eyelids drifted shut as Matt's mouth closed over hers. She'd been waiting for this, aching for it ever since he came back. The one kiss they'd shared had only deepened the hunger she'd refused to admit she felt.

She opened her mouth to him, just as she'd opened her heart years ago. His tongue traced her lower lip before delving inward to taste the honeyed sweetness of her mouth. Her tongue came up to fence with his, touching and withdrawing in an ancient competition.

Matt felt her response run over him like the sweetest of fires. All the sleepless nights that he'd lain awake aching with need for her had honed his hunger to a razor edge.

His hands dropped away from her face, one flattening against her back to draw her closer, the other boldly cupping her breast through the soft fabric of her blouse. Liberty shuddered and pulled her mouth away from his to stare up at him. Cursing the need that had made him move too quickly, Matt started to lower his hand but Liberty caught his wrist and drew him to her again.

Watching her face, Matt dragged his thumb over her nipple. Her eyes were half-closed, her lips parted, her cheeks flushed with desire. He caught the taut peak between thumb and forefinger, plucking gently, and she shuddered again, her breath leaving her on a soft whimper.

She reached for the buckle of his belt at the same moment he reached for the buttons on her blouse. He'd intended to take it slow and easy, to drag the moment out. But with the blood pounding wildly in his veins and her trembling with a hunger as deep as his own, he was incapable of slowing the pace.

Clothing disappeared as if by magic, leaving them bathed in firelight. Liberty lay back on a bed made of their discarded clothing and lifted her arms to him. With a groan, Matt came to her, his hips cradled by her soft thighs. He had just enough control left to slow the headlong pace, entering her body slowly, giving her time to adjust.

It was as if it were the first time again. Liberty groaned, arching her hips to take him deeper. He filled the emptiness in her body, as well as the emptiness in her soul. She'd never known true completion except in Matt's arms.

Her hands lifted to cling to his shoulders as he began to move within her. The slick friction generated a pleasure that filled her to the very depths of her soul.

It was too powerful to last as long as they both wanted. There'd been too many years alone, too many nights of dreaming for the pleasure to be long denied. Liberty shuddered beneath him as she was spun headlong into fulfillment. Matt's climax came only a heartbeat later, driving her higher still.

I love you.

Liberty heard the words, but she couldn't have said whether they were his or hers or only in her mind. For the moment, it didn't matter. All that mattered was that they were together and she was whole at last.

Chapter Sixteen

It was a long time before either of them had the strength to move. Matt shifted at last, lifting his weight from her and rolling to the side. Liberty had to swallow a moan of protest at his leaving. She didn't want to be left alone again. But Matt's arm was already sliding beneath her, drawing her close against his side.

The firelight flickered over their entwined bodies, painting them in patterns of shadow and light. Matt brought up his hand to sift his fingers through her moonlight-pale hair.

"I used to dream about your hair," he said huskily.

"Did you?" Liberty curled her fingers into the mat of hair on his chest.

"God, I was such a fool to stay away." The whispered words were nearly a groan as he thought of all the time he'd thrown away.

For the first time, Liberty felt no anger at the reminder of the years they'd been apart. With her head pillowed on his shoulder and her body flushed and warm from his loving, nothing could completely shake the feeling that her world was in order.

"Why did you stay away?" she asked softly. For the first time since he'd returned, she was really ready to listen to his answer, to try to understand. Perhaps to forgive.

"I asked myself that a thousand times." Matt rolled onto his back and set his forearm over his eyes. "Everything seemed right at the time. It was only later that it began to seem like a mistake."

"Was it because of what I said—about hating you? About not wanting your child?" She could hear her hurtful words echoing down through the years.

"That was part of it," Matt admitted. He slid his arm from beneath her and leaned on his elbow, looking down at her. The fire cast light over one side of his face and left the other side in shadow, making him look mysterious.

"I was angry when I left," he said slowly. "Furious. I'd done the right thing and married you and you'd turned me out, said you never wanted to see me again."

"I didn't want you to marry me because it was 'the right thing.'"

"You made that quite clear," he reminded her without rancor.

"I wouldn't really have done anything to hurt your child, if I'd been pregnant." She wasn't quite ready to tell him how she'd cried when she found out there was no baby.

"I think I knew that, even then."

"Then why did you leave and why didn't you come back?"

"Because I was a fool." He reached up to brush the hair from her forehead, his mouth twisted in a rueful smile. "I left because I thought spending the winter apart would give you a chance to cool off. I *thought* you'd be grateful to see me come back. I was a jackass."

Liberty lowered her eyes, afraid he might be able to read just how right his guess had been. By spring, her anger and hurt had been replaced by a determination to make him love her. Only he hadn't returned.

"As for staying away..." Matt sighed and shifted his gaze to the fire. "When war broke out, I felt it was only right to enlist. I believed in the Union, in keeping the country together. It all seemed very simple at the time. There'd be a few months of fighting and then it would be over and everyone would go home again. Only it didn't work out that way."

Watching his face, Liberty wondered what images he saw in the flames. Nothing pleasant if his bleak expression was anything to go by. Wanting to erase the pain from his eyes, she reached up to touch his cheek.

Matt blinked and looked down at her. Seeing the concern in her eyes, he felt the memories fade. For a moment, he'd almost been able to smell the blood and despair that had filled so many years.

"The longer I stayed away, the harder it seemed to come back," he said slowly. "You'd been so young when I left and you were pretty convincing when you told me not to come back. I told myself you were better off without me. You'd give me up for dead and marry someone who could offer you something more than I ever could.''

''Then why did you come back?'' she asked. Her eyes searched his face, trying to read what it was he felt for her.

''I kept thinking about you.'' He lifted one shoulder in a half shrug. ''I finally decided to come and see you. I figured once I'd done that, I'd be able to get you out of my mind.''

''And now?'' She held her breath, waiting for his answer. After what they'd just shared, he couldn't possibly be thinking of leaving. And if he was, she'd just have to change his mind.

If there was one thing she'd finally realized, it was that her heart had never let go of him. If he didn't love her now, she could change his mind. Love could grow, if given a little care.

When he hesitated over his answer, she smiled at him from under her lashes and stretched slowly, her breasts brushing against his chest, her thigh rubbing over his.

''Do you think you can get me out of your mind now?'' she asked him. She lowered her head and let her fingers dance boldly along the hardening length of him.

Matt's thoughts scattered in a hundred directions. He wasn't sure what he'd intended to say next. Had he been going to tell her that he'd stopped fighting the hold she had over him? Or had he been going to say that he loved her—had probably loved her six years ago and had simply been too blind to see it? He couldn't quite grab hold of either thought.

"I think you're a witch," he said thickly. His hand came up to cover her breast and he lowered his head to kiss the smile from her mouth.

Tomorrow would be soon enough to tell her how he felt. At the moment, there were more urgent matters to attend to.

When Liberty woke, she could see the sun coming in through the crude boards that covered the windows. The wood was nearly rotted through, allowing the sun to slant through onto the dirt floor.

Who had built this cabin and why had they abandoned it? she wondered lazily. But she didn't really want to know the answers. If she knew too much, it would spoil some of the fantasy. She had the fanciful thought that perhaps the cabin wasn't really there at all. That maybe it only appeared for her and Matt and vanished as soon as they were out of sight.

The thought made her smile. But really, was it any more fantastic than the fact that she was lying here in Matt's arms, in the very place where they'd first made love?

Liberty tilted her head until she could see Matt's face. He was still sleeping, giving her the freedom to let the love shine in her eyes. Last night had been the fulfillment of a dream. Or nearly so. The dream wouldn't be completely fulfilled until she was sure that he loved her. But that would come with time.

Matt might not love her but he wanted her, and she was old enough to know that wanting could turn to love. He'd come back because he couldn't forget her.

And he'd made it clear that he was interested in making their marriage a real one.

Would it be so impossible to be my wife?

The remembered question made her smile. What was impossible was for her to be anything else. It had been foolish of her not to recognize that her hurt and anger toward Matt had lasted so long and run so deep because her love for him was just as strong and deep.

Moving carefully, she eased out from under the arm that lay across her stomach. Matt stirred but didn't wake. Liberty rose to her feet and, moving quietly, she dressed, blushing when she found her chemise in the far corner of the cabin. Matt had not been patient in removing her clothes. But his impatience had been no greater than hers.

She combed her hair with her fingers but didn't bother trying to find any of her pins. Matt had scattered them over the floor in his eagerness to see her hair tumbling into his hands.

She glanced at Matt's still form one last time before easing open the door. The contents of the water bucket had leaked out overnight, creating a muddy patch near the door, which Liberty avoided as she lifted the bucket and took it out with her.

The weather reflected her optimistic mood. The sun was shining. The sky was blue. And Liberty was sure she'd never seen a more beautiful day. Yesterday's danger seemed a long way away. The gunshots, the wild flight to safety—it didn't seem real anymore. It was almost as if it had all been staged just to give her and Matt an opportunity to patch up their differences.

The fanciful thought made her smile as she approached the old well. The Randalls still had to be dealt with, she reminded herself. But not right now. She knotted the length of rope around the bucket's handle and then lowered it into the well. Right now, she didn't want to think about anything but Matt.

But it seemed that wasn't meant to be. She lifted the half-full bucket and untied the rope before turning away from the well.

Standing not fifteen feet away, with a pistol pointed straight at her heart, was Curly Randall. There was another man with him but Liberty was only peripherally aware of him. All her attention was for Curly— the gun he held and the evil grin that lit his features. The bucket dropped from her suddenly nerveless fingers.

Matt awoke suddenly, reaching for his gun even as his eyes opened. He was aware of several things at once. He'd slept more deeply than he had in years. Liberty was not in the cabin. And something was very wrong.

He rolled to his feet and reached for his pants, jerking them on and then stamping his feet into his boots. There was no sound out of the ordinary, nothing to explain the feeling of trouble. He didn't know what had awakened him. A sound, perhaps? Had Liberty cried out?

Gun in hand, Matt approached the door as carefully as if it had been mined with dynamite.

"Where's Prescott?" Curly asked.

"He's dead." Liberty's answer was instinctive. As far as she knew, Matt was still asleep. If they burst into the cabin, he'd be vulnerable.

"Dead? You hear that, Joe? She says he's dead."

"Didn't see no body," Joe grunted.

"Perhaps you didn't look in the right place," Liberty suggested haughtily, fixing Joe with a contemptuous look.

"I don't think she likes you, Joe." Curly grinned, his pale eyes glittering with amusement.

"I could teach the hoity-toity little bitch some manners." Joe leered at her, making his meaning clear.

Liberty tilted her chin, refusing to give in to the nervous quaking that was threatening to take hold of her knees. She had to stay calm and think of a way to warn Matt. She could raise her voice but Curly was no fool. If she suddenly began shouting, he was going to know exactly why she was doing it. The important thing was to warn Matt in some way that wouldn't be obvious.

"I'd hate to call a lady a liar," Curly said conversationally. "But I'm just not at all sure I believe you. Prescott doesn't strike me as the sort to die easy."

"I don't care if you believe me." Liberty allowed a note of hysteria to creep into her voice—not a difficult task under the circumstances. "He's dead. There was so much blood," she moaned. "Blood everywhere. I tried to stop it but I couldn't. I couldn't.

"I rolled his body into a wash and then came here. I thought I'd be safe here. But now the two of you are going to kill me." Her voice had been slowly rising, the control disappearing from it as she spoke. "Go ahead," she shrieked. "Kill me! Get it over with!"

She hoped Curly wouldn't be prompt in taking her up on her invitation. He was watching her with narrowed eyes, as if not quite convinced of the authenticity of her performance.

"Prescott?" He raised his voice, dividing his attention between Liberty and the cabin. "You in there, Prescott?"

"He's dead. I told you he was dead." Liberty sank to her knees, lowering her face as her shoulders shook with sobs. Shielded by the folds of her skirt, her fingers groped on the ground for a weapon of some sort. Anything at all that might give her an advantage.

Matt was surely awake now and knew the situation. He knew there were two of them, even if he couldn't know their exact position.

"Prescott? If you're in there, you'd better come out, else I'll have to shoot your wife. Nothing fatal," Curly promised conversationally. "Busted kneecap, maybe. Mighty painful but not likely to kill her."

"I don't know why you won't believe me," Liberty sobbed. "I told you he was dead."

"For your sake, I hope you're lying. I'd hate to bust your kneecap for nothing." He grinned at Liberty. "Stand up."

"No! No, I won't." The fear in her voice was effortless. "Just kill me. You're going to do it, anyway. Get it over with!"

"I don't like to rush things. I like to take things slow and easy. A man makes fewer mistakes that way. Get her on her feet," he said to his companion.

"Seems a waste to shoot her," Joe grumbled as he approached.

"You're not going to need her kneecap," Curly said. "Prescott! You've got till the count of three."

Joe dragged the sobbing Liberty to her feet. Neither man noticed that her right hand was clenched into a fist.

"One."

There was no response from the cabin. If Liberty hadn't known better, she would have believed it empty.

"Two."

Curly cocked the gun and aimed for her knee. She appeared to be near to fainting, forcing Joe to support most of her weight.

"Three!" Curly Randall grinned demonically and started to tighten his finger on the trigger.

And the clearing exploded with action. With a shriek, Liberty came to life. Her hand came up, hurling dirt in Joe's eyes at the same moment that she threw herself away from him. The bullet that would have shattered her knee hit the stone wall that surrounded the well and ricocheted off with a vicious whine.

At the same moment, the cabin door exploded outward with force enough to tear it from its hinges. Matt left the cabin in a rolling dive, hitting the ground shoulder first.

Curly reacted with the speed of a wild animal, spinning toward Matt and triggering his gun as fast as he could. Bullets kicked up dust around Matt, but he came to his feet unharmed.

His first bullet caught Curly in the shoulder, the second slammed into his throat. Curly's finger was still twitching on the trigger as he fell, but he was dead by the time he hit the ground.

"Matt! Look out." He spun at Liberty's warning to see Joe drawing his gun, his eyes still red and watery from the dirt she'd hurled. Liberty didn't wait for his reaction. The heavy wooden bucket, swung with all the force she could muster, thunked against the back of Joe's skull. His eyes rolled back in his head and he collapsed like a felled ox.

It had all taken place in the space of less than a heartbeat. An instant before, the clearing had been filled with the sound of gunfire. Now the silence was thick.

Liberty stared down at Joe's unconscious form as if uncertain of how he'd come to be there. Her fingers loosened on the bucket, which slid to the ground with a thud, rolling onto its side.

"Are you all right?" Matt's voice was low and urgent; the hands that caught her shoulders gripped painfully tight.

"Yes." Slowly, she lifted her gaze to his face, feeling the tears she'd only pretended to burn at the backs of her eyes. She looked past Matt to where Curly Randall's body lay sprawled in the dirt. "I didn't hear them come up."

"They must have left their horses somewhere and come up on foot." Matt drew her to him, his arms circling her back, holding her so tightly, the breath was almost crushed from her.

"I tried to warn you," she said.

"I know. I already knew something was wrong. I woke up and you were gone and I knew you were in trouble. When I heard Curly—" He broke off.

"We can use this one to put Randall out of commission," he said, nudging Joe's limp body with the toe of his boot. "I know his type. He'll be happy to talk. Once it gets out that he tried to have you killed, Randall will have to move on."

"So it's all over," she said slowly.

"The trouble with Randall should be. The man's smart enough to know when he's beaten."

He eased her just far enough away from him to put his hand under her chin, tilting her face up to his. Golden-brown eyes examined every inch of her, as if that was the only way he could be sure she was safe.

"If I'd come out sooner, he'd just have killed us both," he said.

"I know. I was so afraid he'd kill you." She rubbed her cheek against his hand.

"As long as he didn't hurt you." Matt bent to kiss a single tear from her cheek. "I couldn't go on without you."

"You couldn't?" Liberty looked up at him, her breath catching at the expression in his eyes.

"I'd only be half-alive."

"Matt. Do you…are you saying that…you care?" She stumbled over the question, feeling as if her whole life depended on his answer.

"I'm saying that I love you," he said softly.

"Oh, Matt." She didn't have to say the words. He could read them in her eyes. "I love you, too. I never stopped loving you."

The last word was smothered by the pressure of his mouth on hers. She rose on tiptoe and threw her arms around his neck, giving herself wholeheartedly to the kiss.

Out of near tragedy had come joy. She had the ranch. She had her life. And she had Matt. She could never ask for more.

* * * * *